Blood Legacy

Every legacy has a bloodline...

By

Amber Anthony

Paperback ISBN 978-1-7343822-3-5
eBook ISBN 979-8-2016708-8-7

Credits

Edited by Michelle's Edits
Cover Artist: Kelly Ann Martin, kam.design
Photography by konradbak (DepositPhotos), cokacoka (DepositPhotos), heckmannoleg (DepositPhotos)
Published by Amber Anthony
Printed in the United States of America
June 25, 2021

Blood Legacy, Tales from the Gaoler, Book Two

Isla Cathcart is a good Scottish woman.

Gerry McIntosh is a good Scottish vampire. *Ssh, don't tell Isla he's a vampire.*

Isla's extended family has a true claim to an ancient Scottish castle given to her twelve times grandmother by Henry VIII. How can she prove that ownership when it was stolen by royal bureaucracy and misogyny?

Enamored with bonnie Isla, Gerry recruits his vampire friends to help her. *Ssh, don't talk about those vampires either,* or the fact that they own the international resorts that want to partner with the Cathcarts.

When Isla discovers Gerry is *'undead'* all bets are off. Will their differences be the stake through their relationship?

Isla discovers there are good and bad vampires in the world. Can Gerry prove to Isla that while many vampires are crazy dangerous, he's only crazy in love with her?

Dedication

We dedicate this book to our loyal family of readers and peers who encouraged our return to the paranormal realm.

Thank you, Elaine, and Sharon for the Scottish perspectives!

Thank you, Michelle for your third set of eyes.

Note: Whiskey vs. Whisky. Irish Whiskey and Scotch have different production processes and are spelled differently. So if you are reading the word spelled two ways, yes... *it will happen in this book..*

Brenner's Edicts for the Undead

- Vampires are the ultimate Doms.
- Stay out of mortal's relationships, *no good comes from intervening.*
- Never get involved with mortal females, *they break too easily.*
- Emotional relationships with mortals are difficult, *they can't detach.*
- Immortality is an illusion; *vampires can be killed.*
- The number one mannerism for appearing human: *inhale/exhale, repeat.*
- To be irresistible to donors, *hang out with your fangs out.*
- The first bite is the sweetest.
- Pale is the new tan.

The Vampire's Golden Rule
It's not the bite you get, *it's the bite you give.*

Prologue

Saturday, 2nd January 1971 was like so many other mid-winter's days in Scotland, damp, grey, and cold. Gerard McIntosh, his girlfriend, Fiona Duncan, and a new chum from the university, Conall MacCalla shuffled through the tight rows of seats at Ibrox Stadium. Today they were going to watch Rangers play Celtic in an Old Firm football game.

A grimy shroud of cigarette fog hung closely over almost eight thousand fans. Gerard chuckled, "I don't know how they're going to breathe down there on the pitch. What a dreich day!"

Conall, ever-ready with historical insight, scoffed, "Years ago coal soot and wood smoke would have been added to the tobacco fog. The air is practically pristine now."

Fiona shot an accusatory glance at the college history professor. "So, we buck up and quit our bitchin'?"

Gerard wrapped an arm around his girlfriend and gazed longingly at her cameo-like profile. "Fi, when are you going to make me an honest man?"

Conall began reading the program. He sniffed at Gerard, "And a damn fine place to ask for her hand, don't you think?"

Gerry grimaced. "I asked for that a week ago. Now I'm asking for an answer." Gerry noticed the couple sitting in the row before them, shoulder-to-shoulder, holding hands and tilting their heads romantically close. During his chat about marriage, the teenage couple grinned and exchanged playful kisses. The girl, just a wisp of a thing, shivered under her Rangers jacket.

Conall sat with a heavy Rangers blanket folded on his lap. Gerry reached around Fi and tapped Conall. "How about you let the young lovers cuddle under your blanket?"

Conall and Gerry unfurled the colorful wool and leaned forward. "Would you two want to borrow my friend's blanket?"

The girl blushed furiously. "I didn't realize how brisk the wind would be. Even my Kyle here can't keep me warm."

The boyfriend turned to Gerry. "I can't keep her warm like I usually do... here in a stadium." The young lass playfully swatted her boyfriend with mittened hands.

Gerry and Conall spread out the blanket behind them. They stood and cocooned themselves, waiting for the game to begin.

While the tension played out on the football pitch, Gerry was distracted by everything around him. Fiona wasn't returning his affectionate cuddles. Lost in conversation, she hung on Conall's descriptions of a class he'd be teaching in the second term at the University of Glasgow.

Clearly Gerry was the odd man out, the only one watching the game. The young couple huddled in Ranger colors, made out between playful whispers. When Gerry turned to his friends for conversation, he couldn't get in a word. Fiona and Conall heatedly debated Scottish radicalism. *Why am I even here?*

At halftime, Gerard shamelessly eavesdropped on Kyle and Lyra's hopefully devoted conversation. "You know it's the only place in three countries where I can polish my skills. The family distillery needs that level of expertise. I need the education to keep the business alive. It's our future."

Lyra sagged closer to Kyle, nodding. "I know. And I want you to be the best master distiller in our land. It just seems you'll be at the ends of the earth."

"Oh, come on, girl. I'll be home once a month and on breaks. You could travel to see me."

Gerry grinned at the thought of a Scottish father letting such a bonnie lass leave for an unsupervised weekend visit with a boyfriend.

Kyle continued, "You have to work with my mum and dad on the new images for packaging. We talked about this; we each have a part to play. While I'm away, graphics school should be your greatest focus." He kissed her lightly. "Just think, in a few years, we'll be married and taking over the business."

The young couple's sweet regard and easy body language melted Gerry's heart. Meanwhile, in his row, Conall stopped yammering about the politicization of Scottish nationalism and the professor's eyes danced at the radical feminist next to him.

Hands deep in his coat pockets, Gerry shivered. "Fi, give the man a break. Have either of you even watched the game?"

Fiona turned to Gerry. "I have no love for the sport. I came to enjoy the two of you and the pub dinner afterward." She looked at the scoreboard and back at the crowd. "See, people are leaving already. We can catch the final score at the pub. You know Celtic will win."

Ranger fan Gerry's enthusiasm flagged. He recognized Conall was the target of Fiona's flirtatious body language. *Well, I've got my answer about a future union.*

When the three stood up, the couple in front of them turned. Kyle offered the blanket. "Let us give you back your blanket."

Conall waved him off. "Naw, it's yours. You'll enjoy it more than I." The young couple looked between the game and the throngs of people pushing up stairway thirteen.

Lyra's teeth chattered, and Kyle wrapped his arms around her. "Let's go. You're frozen and we're losing. We'll get something to warm you up."

Amber Anthony's Blood Legacy

Chapter One

Isla Cathcart looked out the wall of glass at José Martí International Airport in Havana, Cuba. As she held her phone to her ear and listened to the dial tone, she watched the heat shimmer off the pavement outside. February surely was different here. Back home, Scotland was brittle, cold, and damp. When the family wanted to get away it wasn't hard to choose the sunniest and least expensive destination their travel agent recommended.

The other members of her family collected the luggage, leaving her to make the last entreaty to the Crown Estate Scotland office before their holiday began. Isla dreaded the price of the international call, but it had to be made.

"Crown Estate Scotland, International Desk." A deep voice answered. It was an unfamiliar voice, which was unusual since she called daily.

Isla paused. "Excuse me, I may have dialed the wrong number. Is this the Crown Estate in Scotland?"

His baritone rumbled. "Aye, this is the Crown Estate, you've reached the international desk. We come in at five. May I help you?"

Isla chuffed out a breath at having to repeat her monologue to this stranger. "They're all gone?"

"Who might *they* be?" His voice was slightly amused. "You realize it's after-hours here?"

Isla checked her watch and shook her head. "I forgot the time difference." With an exasperated sigh, she began. "Well, maybe you could help me. What did you say your name was?"

"Gerard McIntosh, madam."

She turned away from the warm glass and began her speech. "This is Isla Cathcart..." she heard his intake of breath and ground her teeth, *Of course, he's heard of me*, "...of the Cathcart Estate claim."

"Aye, madam. However, your agent is out of the office. Were you looking to drop your claim? I can pass that along."

Is he dismissive or what? I'd like to grind his bones for bread. "No, I'm pressing our claim. I've heard there's a new bidder."

The man's tone was evasive. "I've not heard about that, madam. A local claim is not in my purview. I'm sure if you'd care to call back tomorrow, your agent would be available."

Why don't I believe him? Those words rolled off his tongue reflexively. "So, there is a new interested party."

"I didn't say that."

"You didn't have to." She could sense his irritation. "I'll make that call as you suggested, and I'll tell them Mr. McIntosh was of no help."

"And they will believe you as once again, I'm not privy to your claim."

She clicked off the call as her family approached with full luggage trollies.

★★★★

On their second day, the family discovered the beauty of their five-star hotel in Havana, posed in stark contrast to the local neighborhoods. The warm breezes became stifling when Isla and her younger brother Bram, interested in the lives of the locals, left the resort.

The real Cuban island was comprised of a colorful melding of paved streets giving way to cobblestone side streets. Clowders of stray cats meowed pitifully for handouts. Women sat, some with pushcarts, some with boxes selling fruit, and woven straw souvenirs. The more industrious families offered home-cooked meals in their front yard. The fragrant food drew the adventurous for a meal cooked on hotplates in a living room.

Bram looked at his watch and then at the cleanest of these home restaurants. "Shall we give it a go?"

Isla narrowed her eyes and pulled her brother to a wall of woven palm fans. Hiding behind a colorful fan, she made a face. "You're off your head if you think I'm eating street food." She purchased the fan and walked off from her brother. He trotted behind and pulled her a couple of blocks to a real restaurant on the fringe of the neighborhood. "This is my style, mojitos, and tapas."

The brother and sister ordered, and while their drinks were mixed at the colorfully lit bar, the couple next to them smiled and leaned in their direction. The debonair man spoke first. "I can tell by your accent you're Scottish. We're on our honeymoon from Toronto. We're thinking of heading to Scotland next."

Bram extended his hand. "Hope you don't mind the cold this time of year. We've escaped with our family for a week. Where are you lodging?"

The honeymooners smiled expansively. "We've rented a villa for the month. It's absolutely royal. It's been just us for two weeks. You should drop in."

Isla watched without comment and thought, *that doesn't bode well for the marriage.*

Drinks and food came and went, and still, the honeymooners talked. She felt like she couldn't look away from the Canadian's eyes. She'd only had one drink, but she was mesmerized. She stole a glance at Bram. Their holiday unhinged her usually buttoned-up brother. His posture in the chair was ultra-relaxed, and his gaze dreamy. Truth be told, she felt the same, and then she felt nothing at all.

Sometime before the stroke of midnight, she swatted at a buzzing mosquito and realized she was lying on a poolside lounge chair at her resort. Snoring loudly, Bram laid on the chair to her right. *How much did I drink?*

****

Gerard McIntosh, unbeknownst to his employer, the Crown Estate, was a tall strapping vampire of eighty years. He stared at his reflection as he poured his evening's breakfast. *The hair's getting a little long, Gerry.* He ruffled the coarse waves of auburn hair off his forehead as he grinned his swoon-inducing smile. Perpetually thirty, he felt at the top of his game.

His game was about managing the international desk of the Crown Estate of Scotland. It was a vast collection of lands and holdings across the country, the proceeds of which were sent to the Treasury.

As he tied his necktie, he thought about the negotiations with an Australian group angling for wind farm property to test an innovative design. His vampire's gift of discernment allowed him to scent such things as fear, confusion, and bravado. This was how he closed the contract when the Aussie group held their meeting in Glasgow. With vampire skill, he closed a fifty-year lease at a hefty profit.

When he pulled his liquid breakfast from the fridge, he noticed he was running low. After work, before he went to ground tomorrow morning, he would need to contact Fluid Mart, which was one step below mortals buying groceries from Asda. He sighed. How he missed the Gaoler in Edinburgh. There he could tap a living pint and stay for the night.

Consort Group International, that owned Gaoler clubs all over the world, knew how to roll out the reddest of red carpets for the undead. Mortals sought escape from daily drudgery through fantasy flings feeding vampires. *Oh, those were the nights.* He could visit Fluid Mart for a fresh feed, but students looking to earn a little mad money weren't the tastiest. *Too many boxed dinners and fast food.* Gerry sighed again. He had a few more months to wait for his holiday at Erne Castle, the CGI resort.

He was delighted when Adam Lachlan, the Erne Castle Resort Manager, dropped by the office to inquire about Cathcart Castle in Girvan. Of course, it would be more than a year before the vamp-friendly resort would be up and running. Perhaps his friend would include him in the screenings for the donor pool.

Gerry's trousers stirred at the thought. *Down, boy.* It had been months since his most recent mortal girlfriend stomped off in a fury. She wanted a taste of forever in the worst way. With her? Forever would have been in the worst way. He wished her luck across the pond.

****

Last night Isla was shocked to awaken poolside next to her brother. This evening, thanks to her headache and the spell of amnesia, she drank sparingly. Whatever she had at the neighborhood bar left her feeling weak, and dizzy, with a pounding heart and terrible thirst. She was not ready for another go-around tonight. Nor was she ready for a tipsy dunk in the pool with her sisters.

The rest of her family, especially her brothers, seemed to have no such hesitation. The two tables to their left were guzzling tall fruity drinks and, judging by their drunken songs, they sounded like fellow Scotsmen. Bram jokingly referred to them as fellow liquor warriors and raised his glass to toast the fifty-something man. "To our wives and girlfriends—may they never meet."

The man grinned lasciviously and nodded, swallowing down his red drink. Drew, Bram, and Ian tossed back shots of Cuban rum.

Ian shook his head and stuck out his tongue. "This is rubbish." He spat out to the side. "Drew, your family makes fine whisky. What are we doin' drinking this shite?"

Drew nodded emphatically. "More's the pity. We couldn't bring our own into the resort. How else do they sell this?"

The sultry woman with the man at the next table cocked a head their way. "What's this I hear about some nectar of the gods? Did you say you own a distillery? Where is it?"

Drew smiled drunkenly. "Only the most beautiful castle on the water. Cathcart Castle in Girvan."

"Sure, and we're from Glasgow." The man chuckled. "What's the name of your drink?"

Ian fumbled for a business card. "You should be talking to me. I'm in charge of distribution. We service all the pubs. Our brand is Cathcart Royal Wildcat."

The man smacked the table. "I've had your Sherry Oak 12 Year." The man waved a hand at the pool bar's server. "Server, bring us Scotch Whisky." He turned to Drew. "Cathcart? Why is that name familiar?"

Isla rolled her eyes. *Here we go.* Bram fisted the table, and the umbrella shook. "It should be familiar, Cathcart Castle, and we are the Cathcarts, though the bloody crown won't acknowledge us. Without our own Isla Cathcart and her service to Henry VIII, there would be no Cathcart Castle."

Ian nodded. "Aye, they make us beg and lease back our own property. At least the bloody crown doesn't charge us for the spring in the cellar." He put a finger to his lips. "Shh, that's what makes our scotch so bloody good."

Drew took away Ian's shot glass. "That's enough for you, lad. You're giving away company secrets."

Isla's gaze caught the stranger's steelier gaze, and he glanced away from the only sober eyes in the Cathcart family. "We don't want company secrets. Let me ask you, have you been on a night fishing trip here?"

Maisie's husband, Ian, shook his head brightly. "Yeah, I love night fishing. My family are professional anglers."

The woman at the other table batted her eyes at him. "There's no time like the present. We can have fishing rods in our hands in thirty minutes."

Isla thought it quite remarkable that the ship's crew danced around their newfound friends as if they were benefactors. She was the only family member sober enough to wonder why something bordering on a yacht was a charter fishing boat. The boat was exquisitely set, with three teak fighting chairs along the stern. Isla consistently refused drinks from the waitstaff as she watched them dance and laugh with the crowd. She did finally accept a flute of champagne as the boat headed out to sea with her brothers belted into the chairs.

The captain raised his flute in the air. "To Hemingway!" Isla toasted with the crowd and finished her flute.

****

Sun filtered directly into Isla's grey eyes, and she blinked them open only to find herself in a bed, groaning. She turned her face into the pillow and realized it was a hospital bed. *How did I get here?*

Her younger sister, Caitrin, moaned in the next bed over. "I'm feeling slaughtered. What did we do last night?"

Isla held onto her aching head, just the movement of her shoulder-length auburn curls hurt. "I only drank one glass of champagne. What is it about this island?"

Caitrin shook a finger at her older sister. "Here we think we're self-respecting Scots and we can't stand up to fizzy juice."

Isla sat up and realized she was in a hospital ward entirely populated by her family. "Drew! Wake up." Her eldest brother Drew moaned and turned over. "Hello, anyone?"

****

Dr. Ramon Ortega adjusted the lens on his microscope. "That explains it. These people have elements in their blood we can see rebuilding your cells. That's causing the rejuvenation."

The geriatric voice barked. "Why, what is it about their blood that differs from all the others?"

Ortega looked through his microscope again and rubbed at his forehead as he spoke. "I'm hazarding a guess that something they ingest in their home environment supplements your healing. The longer they've been here, the less potent the response."

Samuel's voice through the phone was typically demanding. "Then if you've gained all the data you need, Doctor, we must return them to their home environment. I plan to look thirty by summer."

Ortega frowned, understanding his discovery meant he was heading for damp Scotland. He sighed. "If that's your wish, you need to come up with a plan."

Samuel tsked harshly. "Doctor, *you* need to come up with a plausible explanation why they need daily blood draws. I'm not a physician." His ironic laughter left Dr. Ortega cold.

****

A petite nurse dressed in white slacks and a top with a nurse's cap trotted into view. In accented English, she soothed. "Please don't excite yourself, miss. Dr. Ortega will be in to see you soon. All the members of your family are recovering well."

Isla stared. "Recovering from what? Where are we?"

"You are in Clínica Central in Havana. You've been here a week and the doctor will tell you more."

Within two hours, the family was awake and ate a hearty breakfast. Drew paced the room in seersucker slippers and a robe. "Where are my clothes? Why am I here?"

A doctor wearing sharply creased linen slacks and a pristine lab coat walked to the center of the room. "Good morning, I am Dr. Ortega. You are all members of the Cathcart family, am I correct?"

"Aye." Drew watched him suspiciously.

"You were brought in suffering from abdominal pain and weakness. Our initial assessment was food poisoning, but that proved to be an incorrect diagnosis." The doctor walked up to Drew. "Will you be the family spokesperson?"

"Aye, I will."

"Are you aware you and the members of your family are suffering from a condition called hemochromatosis?"

Drew looked baffled. "Hemo—what?"

12

"It's a disorder of the blood. Your body stores too much iron and this can lead to liver failure, cancer, and heart disease."

The family members gawked at each other. Drew barked back, "We've heard no such thing."

Maisie, the eldest sister, cried. "The only complaints any of us have ever had is a touch of arthritis here and there. Drew, here, has a fluttery heart."

Dr. Ortega nodded wisely. "Both symptoms of this disease."

Always the drama queen, Caitrin yodeled. "What do we do now, are we bound to die?"

The unflappable Dr. Ortega smiled benignly. "We've already begun your treatment. We drew therapeutic amounts of blood from each of you daily. You see, the treatment for hemochromatosis is frequent blood draws to rid your body of excess iron. Other than that, no treatment is necessary."

Drew frowned. "But for how long?"

"For the rest of your lives. Do you have resources in Scotland to do daily blood draws?"

The family looked at each other in confusion. "I have no idea." Drew began.

Isla cut him off. "We have a national health service, surely they can help us."

Dr. Ortega pursed his lips. "Ah, yes, the UK's health system. I'm afraid their financial limitations may be a problem. From what I've heard, they don't approve daily draws. Especially for a family of your size." He sighed and turned to leave. "Well, that's a shame. I'll arrange for your discharge in the next hour."

Drew burst out with what everyone else was thinking. "Wait, you can't send us out of here without a plan."

Ortega looked sympathetic but indifferent. "I'm not sure what you think the people of Cuba can do to help you. You need to return to Scotland and find your own answers."

"What if this happens again?" Maisie demanded. "We all blacked out. On a boat. In a strange country. You must help us explain this to our doctors at home. They've all missed something!"

Dr. Ortega hesitated. "Well, there might be help from one sector. I don't know if they would be willing. They run a private research institute now."

"In Scotland? Isla questioned.

"In Ayr. They retired there. They are quite elderly."

Bram threw up his hands. "There are six of us, one of us can't learn to draw blood? Ridiculous. Let's get out of here." He threw off his covers and began searching through drawers. "I want my clothes."

Isla shook her head. "But we're not trained for that, it's dangerous. Who are these retired men, do they have traveling nurses? All of us can cover the costs."

The doctor shook his head solemnly. "Your blood will require monitoring, not just drawing." He thought for a moment. "Allow me to contact the doctors. I should have an answer, eventually. I can mail you the information."

Isla raised a halting hand. "Doctor, I don't believe you understand our situation. We live in a small village with one health clinic. Sometimes it takes weeks to earn an appointment…"

Ortega raised a patient brow. "If you insist. Let me make an urgent call. For a case such as yours, I would make myself available to the doctors. We may publish a study together."

Drew dug his hands into his robe pockets and looked at the small man sternly. "Get us out of this hell." His family cast judgmental looks his way. "Please."

Chapter Two

February 10th, Gerry closed the top of his BMW convertible and made his way to the office. The day was overcast, and he'd fed well that afternoon. It was a great day to ride with the top down. *What could go wrong?* He expected CGI's earnest money to be waiting for him when he arrived. It was a Friday, and he thought he'd make an impromptu trip to Erne Castle for a bit of a bite this weekend. Shooting his cuffs as he exited the carpark, he turned up the brick walk to the office door.

With some concern, he heard nearly running footfalls and panting breath headed in the same direction. Gerry opened the door and held it for whoever was behind him.

That turned out to be a lass in a flurry of tartan from her pencil skirt to her shawl flying behind her. Standing statuesque, her lovely face framed by the softest shade of an ivory angora cowl sweater, she was a 'force.' Chestnut spiral curls had not yet settled from the speed of her movement. In certain lights, the grey in her eyes was dense enough to appear reflective. The effect was startling in a mortal, but a vampire could never miss the blush of emotion in her cheeks and lips. As the woman propelled into him, her urgency was a cloud surrounding her.

"Allow me." He bowed his head slightly.

"Thank you." She raced past him. She halted at the receptionist desk, and at finding it unmanned, she turned to Gerry, fists on her hips. "Oh, bloody hell." She looked at her watch and her entreaty rose to the angels. "I cannot bloody believe I didn't reset my watch after I came off holiday."

Gerry's grin spread as her curls settled to frame her rosy cheeks. "Who are you looking for?" Gerry scanned the empty office.

"I was looking for Ms. Browne at the Southern Scotland desk."

Gerry gestured at the room of vacant chairs. "She would have to be a wee one to be here. I'm afraid you've missed her. My co-worker and I are the only agents after five o'clock."

She looked so distressed; he was prompted to offer. "Is there anything I can do to help?"

"I wanted to drop off our earnest money cheque for Cathcart Estate. Can you accept it?"

"I'm afraid I don't have access to the vault. Are you from CGI?"

Isla drew herself up to her full five-foot-eight height and narrowed her grey gaze at the stranger. "Perish that thought. I am a true descendant. Isla Cathcart was my twelve times great grandmother."

Gerry moved within the office, going to his desk, powering up his computer, and dropping his keys in a drawer. Sliding out of his wool jacket, he hung it and then turned to her, straightening his waistcoat. "And of course, you have proof?"

"I would have proof, that is, I *could* have proof if the Queen would release Henry's letters patent."

Gerry tilted his head at her. "Have you applied to the Palace?"

She snorted and refolded her shawl over her shoulders. "Yes, of course. The Palace ignores us."

Gerry strolled toward the front door. "Oh, my, what a shame, but I'm afraid you will have to come back Monday during normal business hours to drop off the cheque."

Isla gave him side-eyes. "Your voice is familiar. I think it's the condescension. What's your name?"

Gerry's brow rose as he bit his lower lip. "Gerard McIntosh." He stood stiffly, his thumbs in his trouser pockets.

Her finger shot at him. "You're the one." Isla narrowed her eyes ominously. "I rang here from Cuba and got *you*. What a waste of an international call."

Gerry raised an index finger to her. "Once again, a problem with time zones. You know, phones do not take the place of a quality time piece." He tapped his antique Rolex Oyster watch. *Isn't she fiery? Look how red her cheeks get. What do I have to do tonight other than sit around and wait for the phone to ring?*

The front door opened and his co-worker, another member of the undead, twenty going on ninety-three, strolled in with two travel mugs, talking on his Bluetooth. Seeing a mortal with Gerry, Randall stopped short. "Oh, we have a guest, I'll ring you later." He nodded to Gerry and Isla. "I do beg your pardon."

She waved a hand at the young, blond man. "He has manners."

"Let me redeem myself and take you for a glass of wine or a brandy?" Gerry reached for his jacket.

Isla spoke to the stranger and waved a hand at Gerry. "Can you believe him?"

Randall looked between the two of them and his brows v'd. There was an edge to his voice. "On so many levels, I find him unbelievable." His light tone returned. "But the bistro across the street does a very pleasant tea. They have a nice sherry."

Gerry felt her scrutiny as she hefted her purse on her shoulder and combed back a few stray curls. "Oh, why not?"

"Really? Suddenly I'm no longer the spawn of Satan?"

As the two of them walked out the front door, Isla mumbled. "No, I've dated him."

Gerry halted at the door as Isla's foot hit the walk and he spoke in subtones to Randall. "If anyone calls, take a message."

Randall, still holding both travel mugs of A positive, narrowed his eyes as the door closed.

****

The warmth of the bistro greeted them first through the glow of the mullioned windows. Gerry swung open the door and ushered Isla inside. He led them around the crowd and into a corner table. Isla looked longingly at the burning hearth half a room away. She removed her gloves and briskly rubbed her hands. He didn't seem to feel the cold.

The older woman server cocked a hip tableside and smiled at Isla "Welcome to The Kind House, I don't believe I've served you before." The grey-haired lady pulled a pen out of her pocket and waited. With a grin, she turned to Gerry. "Mr. Mac, good to see you with a friend." Her head bobbled in Isla's direction. "Your usual for two?"

Isla's jaw dropped. "Do you usually order for the table?" Her words stopped the server in her tracks.

"Miss Isla has not had time to peruse the menu, but you may bring the sherry." The woman nodded with a chuckle.

Isla studied the man, not the menu. His posture at the table was virile, with one hand resting on his thigh, the other over his unused menu. The size of his fist gave her a shiver. With his rugged good looks, he resembled a warrior capable of wielding the two-handed Claymore with grace and speed. The thought of seeing him on a battlefield with no shield made her quiver. She wondered if those full lips ever said anything other than 'no.'

When she delayed paying attention to the menu he prompted. "See anything you like?" His long finger tapped the plastic menu between them. "It's all hearty."

"I've eaten, the sherry will be fine."

He nodded. "My thought exactly."

When the sherry arrived, they touched glasses in a silent toast and sipped. Gerry put down his glass and leaned his chin on his palm.

Why does he have to be so dreamy? Is that his sensitive pose?"

"Alright. Tell me honestly now," he tapped his finger on the table and his brows v'd. "Why do you want that broken-down wreck of a castle? Three-quarters of it aren't livable. You couldn't borrow enough to make it so. What's the point?" His finger drilled the table.

I'm going to grab that finger and snap it off. Isla held the glass to her lips as annoyance gripped her. "It's my family's land. It belongs to us."

"I understand clan pride. But pride doesn't pay the bills. Erne Castle in Kildare was in ruins and my client not only renovated the estate but now the entire county is thriving. He never could have done that if CGI weren't behind him."

"CGI, so you are in cahoots with them."

"Hardly. I told you before, I'm not involved. My point is Richard Hiatt, who is a billionaire in his own right, would not have had the money to turn that property if the assets of CGI were not behind him."

"I should have seen how you'd be involved with those perverts."

"Perverts?" Gerry inserted a finger into his starched shirt collar and crooked his neck. "Have you frequented Erne Castle?"

"See there, you admit it." She pointed a finger at him, raised her hand to the server, and held up her empty glass.

Gerry grinned as he nodded for a second round. "You're listening to rumors. Who would say such a thing, except competitors?"

Their sherry arrived and this time, Gerry reached into his breast pocket, removed a small dropper vial, and added four drops of a red liquid to his drink. "Vitamins."

Holding her new glass in both hands, she leaned into him and whispered. "Well, I heard they have some kind of orgy room in the cellar."

Gerry held his glass by the stem and swirled his 'vitamins' in his sherry. "I visit a few times a year. Would you like to go with me?" He held up a halting hand. "Not that *we* would have sex."

Her gaze was stony while she thought, *Why not? Am I so forbidding, so unappealing?* When he did not speak, she sipped silently. Moments ticked by. "The audacity of a place where people meet and then go directly to have sex." When she shook her head, she felt the top would blow off. He had the gall to smirk at her and his tongue swept his bottom lip as if he were about to speak. "You approve?"

Gerry shrugged. "Aye, in the old days, one had to take one's chances at a pub and go on to find a room. Seems tidier this way. Much more discreet."

The thought of falling into this kind of tryst and having it come off seamlessly boggled her mind. A smile came to her lips as she imagined walking into such a room on the arm of the man across the table.

Gerry raised his glass to drink, and her smile caused him to point "You're thinking about it aren't ya?"

Primly she squared her shoulders. "I believe your point was the enterprise was backed by significant capital we don't have."

Gerry nodded. "That was my point. But it doesn't have to be if your claim holds up, maybe you'd partner with an organization like CGI?"

She negated that with a shake of her head. "I believe your imagination is running away with you." She gave a little snort. "As if I would go to a sex club." He took out his phone and scrolled. "What are you doing?"

"I'm marking the date when I learned you were a prig."

"Ach!" She vibrated outrage.

Gerry raised a brow. "I'll count the days until that ice begins to thaw."

Isla stood and looked down her nose at him. "Don't hold your breath." Walking away, she didn't understand the odd smile on his face.

****

The private jet arrived under a full moon at Glasgow Prestwick Airport. The ground crew pushed the air steps up to the door as the taller man argued with his companion in a sing-song patois. "I will walk down these stairs if I have to crawl. I'm done, I tell you."

The more infirm of the two men sat fidgeting with the blanket over his knees in his wheelchair. "Go ahead, waste that energy. When will you feed like that again?"

The jet's crew worked, eyes down to the brother's arguing. "We have enough from the blood draws in Cuba to sustain me. Now, we need to know why you're still in that chair."

The other sniffed. "Fine. I can't tell you anything."

Walking haltingly to the Range Rover, leaning on an ebony cane, the man waited for the attendants to carry his younger, but older-looking, brother Jonas down the stairs and place him into the SUV.

One dusky hand covered his face as they buckled him in. "It's too much. Too much pain from the plane down the stairs and into this car. I need to feed." As an attendant arrived with a travel mug, he gratefully accepted it. "I curse our headstrong sister."

Samuel settled himself next to Jonas. With a smirk and raised brow, he shook his head. "She is no longer headstrong." His laugh was demonic and cut off by a coughing jag.

Jonas chuckled. "You're right there, brother. She no longer has a head."

Samuel grunted. "Her final concoction of Humanité was nothing like what we used. Where did we go wrong?" He looked to their companion physician.

Dr. Ortega raised a brow. "Gentlemen, the last quantity of Humanité was five years dormant when you sent it to be analyzed and reproduced. Your Poppa had all research destroyed and let me remind you, I did not recommend using what was recreated from the simplistic report you received from that cockamamie lab."

Jonas tapped a bony finger on his knee. "That cockamamie lab was the only resource we had, and we needed the revenue."

Ortega shook his head. "Your revenue must have dwindled significantly when your buyers began decaying to the point of decrepitude."

Samuel waved a dismissive hand. "Luckily, we have mortals who desire their party drugs. Those are far simpler to deliver with far better revenue."

Jonas threw back his head and growled. "How could we know one use could have such debilitating effects?"

Ortega shook his head. "The formula you've recreated is pernicious."

Samuel narrowed his faded eyes. "Now at last there is hope. Look at me. A week ago, I could barely feed. I looked like Methuselah. Now, I could pass for ninety and it's all because of this family and their healing blood. My question is, do we need their blood until we return to our former splendor, or will we need to propagate this family for the use of their blood?"

Ortega shook his head. "This is uncertain. Don't celebrate by draining your golden geese."

****

When Adam Lachlan insisted on taking Gerard to dinner, he was not used to eating like this. The men walked down the Glasgow pavement past a number of noisy bistros and pubs.

Gerry halted outside the most peculiar-looking shop. "I'm afraid we only have one vamp-friendly bistro that also serves mortals."

When they walked into the brick front shop the girl behind the counter fluttered her extra-long black lashes at the two men. Her voice was monotone and throaty. "Welcome to the Arcane Veil, how may I help you?"

Adam stopped in his tracks, gawking at the pound-shop goth boutique. Black-velvet walls held cards of costume jewelry, fashion accessories, and smart-ass greeting cards. "What in Odin's name is this place?" he asked Gerard under his breath.

Gerry nodded to the goth. "One undead, one mundane for dinner."

The goth wiggled out from behind the counter on her five-inch platform, patent-leather boots and waved a hand of dagger-length black nails at them to follow her. "Walk this way."

Adam shook his head, his blond hair falling over his ears. "That would be impossible, you don't have those boots in my size."

Gerry shook his head. "Hold your horses, mate. You're about to see more of the impossible. I'll warrant CGI has nothing like this."

Adam's head pivoted as they left the shop through a curtain of ebony beads. The scent of deep fat fryers permeated the atmosphere. *Deep-fried blood? No way.*

The goth led them to a circular booth in a corner where Adam could watch the circus. They evidently had a couple of themes going here. One was fast food served quickly in a goth décor; the other was cut-rate skull tchotchkes.

The tile floor was a tad sticky as Adam slid into the black-leatherette booth abutting the flat, shadowy wall. The table wobbled on four uneven legs as Gerry sat beside him. "You eat here a lot?"

Gerry blinked hard. "Why do you think I want to land this deal with CGI? This is the only game in town. There's a place the next town over but it's vamp exclusive, and their cover charge is ridiculous."

Adam nodded as Gerry picked up the table tablet to place an order. He handed it to Adam. "My order's fairly simple, what are you having?"

Adam scrolled down the mundane menu. "Fried fish, fried chicken, fried clams, fried pork chops. Hmm. What is this fried pizza?"

Gerry shrugged. "You've had pizza?" Adam nodded. "Imagine it fried."

"Not easy to do, but I'll try it." Adam scratched at his neck the longer he sat there. "Buddy, we have got to rescue you from this."

Their orders took about five minutes before a tall tumbler of blood and a steaming basket of fried meat-lover's pizza was brought to the table.

"Hi, my name is Drucilla. Tonight, your blood is from a Glasgow College of Art and Design student who majors in intaglio. The pizza is

23

a heart-busting thick crust covered with five high-fat meats dipped in beer-batter and deep-fried. Enjoy."

Adam stared at the crunchy fried triangle. Gerry toasted him. "Eat up."

He nodded to the basket as Gerry began sipping his meal. "I think I'll let the steaming stop before I take a bite." He slid sideways to watch Gerry's expression change as he sipped. "I can't taste that, but I get an overwhelming sense of ink and solvents."

Gerry licked his bottom lip and put down the glass. "Aye, that and Ramen. Tell me something good and take my mind off this travesty of a meal. How's your gorgeous wife?"

"If we get Cathcart Castle, you'll see for yourself. She's excited about bringing some of her clan over. You'll have flying horses abounding."

Gerry smiled kindly. "If there are flying horses, you'll be glad the Scots are in their cups."

Adam laughed. "They're a little more discreet than that. Her dream has always been to have a horse rescue. Erne Castle was fortunate enough to buy an entire teaching stable when the owners got out of the business. Willow doesn't think so, but I think she'll miss her students. When can we close?"

Gerry nodded at the black plastic basket. "You gonna eat that?"

Adam picked up the fried triangle and took a bite. "This is actually pretty good, terrible for me, but good. I'll lose my six-pack on one dinner, but hey, it's a business meal." He winked at Gerry. "Did I tell you, I've convinced my childhood pal Kieran, a five-star chef, to come aboard when we get Cathcart? What do we need to make sure this deal goes through?"

Gerry sat down his glass and ran his tongue over his fangs. "Honestly, you have a lock on this, Adam, unless someone comes forward with a prior claim to the land. I will tell you, there's a family by the name of Cathcart who have been leasing some of the property.

They claim they have rights to the estate from Henry VIII. They have the name alright, but no documentation. The only thing I can see that would stop you is if Henry rose from the grave and wrote them out a deed." Gerry shook his head and picked up his glass. "Trust me, after having limited dining choices since I moved into the area, I want to see the resort blossom more than anyone."

****

The day after they returned from Cuba and every day thereafter a variety of pleasant university students drew blood on the Cathcart family each afternoon at tea-time. There had also been a small army of student scientists taking collections of soil, water, indigenous plants, and even samples of the air.

Today, the Cathcarts were surprised to see a shiny black Land Rover arrive behind the student who drove a demolition derby car. Isla stood at the door watching them approach, remembering university days with a similar vehicle. They stopped and the student reacted with near reverence toward the two gentlemen who alighted behind her.

Isla had been asked to gather the family for a discussion at teatime. As the student finished her tasks, the two gentlemen in dove-grey suits introduced themselves to Isla as Doctors Samuel and Jonas Moreau. They were nothing if not charming. "But please, call us Dr. Sam and Dr. Joe. Your contributions are helping our research program enormously.

Isla led them to the conservatory. "You'll have had your tea?"

Both doctors waved off her offer. Dr. Sam's eyes twinkled, "I was hoping to taste a wee dram of your whisky."

One-by-one the other members of the family filtered into the room and were introduced. As soon as Drew's blood was drawn, he went to fetch their finest 18-year scotch.

Drew proudly poured glasses of scotch for everyone in the room. Dr. Sam stood and raised his glass. "To a healthy future together."

Drew clinked glasses and the group sipped consideringly. Isla surveyed their guests. *Well-dressed, polished, but from Ortega's description, she expected absent-minded professors.* Not the urbane men she saw before her.

Dr. Joe peered at the amber liquid and remarked. "You've made an unrivaled commitment to the sense of wood and spirit since 1958, but why have you only marketed your spirits throughout the UK since 2000?"

Drew held on to his glass and Isla felt his suspicion. *These men are keeping us alive; he should be charitable in his assessments.* Her chin jutted upward as she spoke. "You've got to have money to make money. Since 1958 our family has fought to reclaim the estate our ancestor was awarded for service to Henry VIII."

Isla watched the brothers exchange looks from behind their glasses. Dr. Sam smiled pleasantly. "Fought with whom to reclaim it?"

Drew huffed a breath. "Nowadays it's the bloody Crown Estate Scotland. They have the property for sale, and we could lose it forever if our claim is ignored."

Dr. Sam tilted his head to Drew. "Do they have a buyer in mind?"

Isla shook her head in irritation. "Including us? There are twelve bidders, but the only serious competition is from Consort Group International, some sort of sex club from what I heard in Ireland."

Her brother Bram chuckled. "Isla, that's the closest you've been to sex in years..."

She shot him a deprecating look. "That corporation has money to burn."

Dr. Sam sniffed. "Joe and I have heard of this group. It's disgraceful, they go into moral communities and bring their debauchery."

Bram crossed his arms over his chest. "A curse on them. They'll not have our legacy."

Dr. Sam narrowed his hypnotic gaze. "But if they have these resources, how do you attempt to beat them in the market?"

The entire family assembled hung their heads. Isla's cheeks burned. "They say if we can prove our claim, they'll have to give it to us."

Dr. Sam thought a beat. "Wouldn't it improve your lot if you had more resources?"

Drew ran a hand through his thick hair and laughed. "We're waiting for the money tree to sprout."

Dr. Joe made a soft gesture to his brother. "Brother, we should broach this question."

The two brothers took a considering beat while Isla crossed and uncrossed her legs. "What are you driving at?"

Dr. Joe smiled widely. "Consider this... Due to your health situation, we have assumed a great deal of financial responsibility. We propose that we enter a further partnership that can be lucrative for all of us."

His words dropped on Isla with a hammer. She stood shaking her head until her brothers stared her down. Bram gestured from Isla to their guests. "You've got to give the men a chance to talk."

Isla poured water into her glass and swished it with the remnants of her liquor. "Great partnerships thrive because the partners need each other. Why do you need us? At this point, we owe you and will continue to owe you as long as you give us medical treatment."

Ian shook his head at Isla. "Hear the man out..."

Dr. Sam nodded. "Thank you, Mr. Bruce. What we propose is seeding you with the capital to take your liquor worldwide, as well as develop a business of Cathcart collateral. Don't you envision bars and taverns with your signs and glasses?"

Dr. Joe nodded. "You can't go into a bar without seeing a big-name scotch, *be* the big name."

Isla winced. "That costs millions. We don't have millions."

Dr. Sam smiled benignly. "We do and all we ask in return is we receive twenty-five percent of your international business. We would engage an advertising program and every bartender would wear your shirts, etc. The glasses would bear *your* name. People would crave your products."

Isla flushed and couldn't speak. Maisie almost cried. "You're our guardian angels and now this?" She grabbed Isla's hand. "This could be our ticket."

Isla frowned heavily. "Not unless we keep our land and the spring." She looked at the Doctors Moreau. "I make it my commitment to haunt the Crown Estate Scotland office until someone listens to us."

Dr. Sam stood. "It would protect our interest to protect yours. If we have your agreement, I'll send out a solicitor by tomorrow with papers." He kissed Isla's hand. "You're such a winning personality, you go and charm this estate away from the crown."

****

In the back in their Range Rover, Samuel and Jonas drew the privacy panel to discuss their next steps. Jonas complained. "You know if we try to buy the estate, the Crown will investigate us thoroughly. That feels like too much scrutiny to me."

Samuel nodded. "Exactly why my plan has always been to help the Cathcarts gain title to their estate and then take it for ourselves."

Jonas gaped at his more astute brother. "But how do we ensure they get the title?"

Samuel shook his head dismissively. "The way we always do."

Jonas returned a blank look.

****

Early March 1st, Dr. Willow Lachlan flipped on the lights in the carriage room and poked around until she found the antique trotter sulky carefully covered with a tarp. The 1850 engraved plate on the back of the padded seat hung by just one tiny screw. The wooden poles were dry and cracked. The seat padding was a lacework of leather left by rodents. In the six years Erne Castle was a Consort Group

International resort, this sulky sat undiscovered. Now uncovered by a stable expansion, it was worthy of restoration.

Willow was the Erne Castle Stable Manager, due to her telepathic abilities with animals. Of course, being a Pegasus shifter gave her a natural inclination to work with the resort's creatures. She fingered the brittle leather of the harness and tsked. This entire rig would have to be sent to restoration specialists in Belgium. But when it came back, wouldn't it be a perfect museum specimen to donate to Racehorse Rescue, her Pegasus clan charity in Kentucky?

CGI would donate the cost of restoration, of course, and it would buy them a world of goodwill from the horse community. Their equine work had opened an unexpected revenue stream for the resort. Horse lovers from all over the world came to ride at Erne Castle and Willow became something of a celebrity teaching animal communication. Adam teased her that using her telepathy was cheating. Her students had to communicate the hard way.

She pulled out her phone and dialed her mate. "Hey, Sparky... how's the weather in Girvan? Rainy?" Adam's chuckle turned her on. *That will have to wait.* "Have they buckled on the purchase price? Are you coming home, or do I have to fly over and drag you back by your terrible horns?"

"I might enjoy flying back with you dragging me by my horns. But good news, Cathcart Castle will be the crowning achievement of my hundred and fifty years of land development. Now that we're partners in CGI, Rick, Matt and Venus have given us free rein on this property."

Willow smiled. "We're still feeding vampires, right? We can't turn that money down."

"Well, yes we are. Just with less leather and whips. Our appeal is to those who wish to *feed* the vampires. I snagged a couple of gourmet chefs and donors are going to deliver some top-rate vamp dining."

Willow grinned. "Back here, where the draw is vampires looking for yummy sub/donors, you will never believe what we found walled up in the barn."

Adam hesitated. "Did I know them?"

Willow tittered. "No, it's a thing, not a person."

"Oh, go ahead, tell me."

After Willow described every aspect of the timeworn sulky, they agreed to send it off for the two-month restoration before she donated it in the name of CGI.

Adam's voice warmed with pride when he told her. "You supported me with moving dragon-folk to Chile. When we get the estate, we'll have two hundred acres here, are you ready to branch out? We can start a horse sanctuary if you want staffed by Pegasus folk."

Willow gasped. "That's a wonderful idea. I would love that. No wonder I married you."

****

Three weeks later, at the end of March, Isla arrived in Brussels midmorning and went straight to the leather worker's shop. The door opened and the scent of leather was as rich as Cognac. A man behind the counter sat tooling a magnificently tanned hide.

Isla unbuttoned her coat and smiled as the man raised his head from his work. "Liam Peeters? I'm Isla Cathcart."

"Mevrouw Cathcart, how wonderful to meet you. I was finishing the prototype for the limited-edition presentation box." He stood and wiped his hands as he approached the counter.

"Oh, I adored the pattern you sent me. You've represented the clan crest so nicely. Is it ready for me to approve?"

"I'm finishing the tooling, but there are several more steps before I'm done. You can see it now if you wish." He led her back to his worktable. They passed a woman sewing a small and oddly shaped item.

Isla smiled and nodded. "That's an odd cat bed."

Liam chuckled. "Ah, that's a story in itself."

"For the cat?"

"Oh, no. The carriage restoration shop across the alley is having us recreate this sulky seat. You know for harness racing."

"Interesting." She smiled as Liam held up the tooled leather for her approval. "That's exquisite. You're a true craftsman."

****

Crossing over to Scottish air from northern Europe, the plane got bumpy. Isla set her watch an hour from Belgium time and then a thought occurred to her. Gerard had not called her after their tea. *Not that I would have given him the time of day...*Their drinks were pleasant, but the conversation disturbing. How could an old-world charmer, be devastatingly handsome and naughty to boot? She squirmed under the seatbelt just thinking about him in that impeccable suit and tweed waistcoat.

What's under all that? Did he ever wear a kilt to work? Stop it, he's the enemy. I walked in there on behalf of my family, and he brought up CGI. I fancy the devil.

If he were really interested in her, he could stroll over to Ms. Browne and get her home and cell number... unless Ms. Browne had scruples about that sort of thing.

The trouble was, he came in after hours, so there was no 'accidentally' running into him. *What if there was some confusion about* time? A plan began to form in her mind...

****

Gerry leaned back in his desk chair; his feet propped on the open bottom desk drawer. Randall left for the express office with a stack of outgoing documents. Because he was alone, Gerry slipped off his monks and admired his new argyle socks as he chatted with Adam. "Yes, the earnest money is in for the Cathcart Estate. I understand they're considering a contract, but you know there are two other bidders. One is extremely insistent."

"But we're a foot up on this, aren't we?"

"Yes, of course... but there's this woman. She's part of the Cathcart clan trying to claim the estate. Her insistence is mindboggling. She calls daily. Her last pronouncement was if the family lost the property, their distillery would be out of business."

Adam was silent a beat. "Distillery? That could be an interesting revenue source. Would they be open to a business merger?"

Gerry chuckled. "She's rather prickly about that and has no time for CGI. The word over here is you run sex clubs." Gerry pulled the phone away from his ear at Adam's laugh.

"Oh, Gerry, you should have seen Willow's face when she discovered what we do here." The men laughed together for a beat. "Perhaps she needs a weekend trip to see the good we do?"

Gerry winced. "I don't see that happening. I said, she was prickly and from her remarks about CGI, I'd say she is a prim, fussy one. She's consumed by this claim. I doubt she has any social life at all. It's very sad. When Henry gifted her ancestor the estate, women were not allowed to own property. I imagine that's how the estate was lost."

Adam paused. "How many mornings have you gone to ground thinking of her?"

Gerry bolted upright, his feet firmly on the floor. He stood and carried his phone as he paced. "Stop that. Get out of my head you flaming dragon."

Adam pressed. "How has she gotten under your skin?"

Gerry stared out at the dark street. Cones of light fell under the streetlamps as people made their way home for dinner. "It's her passion." Gerry's words softened as he recognized Isla a block away.

Adam barked. "Well, you know what Rick says about a woman's angry passion? He learned it from Anna."

Gerry slid back into his shoes as Isla turned up the brick walk. "If it's Rick, I'm afraid." As Isla's hand hit the doorknob, Gerry signed off. "I've got to run, old man."

Gerry turned to the foyer and watched Isla shake out of her cape and look around. Her crystalline, grey eyes met his and she shook her head, wild curls dancing. "I've done it again."

"Pardon me?" Gerry met her at the receptionist's desk as embarrassment flowed from her.

Isla looked down as if contrite. "I was in Belgium today to approve the leatherwork for a limited edition. I thought they were two hours ahead of us. It must be just one."

What a cunning display of duplicity! "Do tell." Gerry tapped his finger on his generous bottom lip. "But you are here just in time for tea. And look, here comes Randall now."

Isla jumped as Randall's silent steps came up behind her. "Oh, but I couldn't pull you away, not again."

Sure, you could, anticipation is coming off you in waves. Gerry slid his hands into his trouser pockets. "You get two more teas before it's a date."

Randall smirked at Gerry as he slid behind his desk. They exchanged what Isla perceived as a silent nod and Gerry gestured her towards the door.

"How do you know I'm not in a relationship?" She bordered on curt.

Gerry's palm fell to the small of her back and he looked down into her challenging eyes. "I just know."

"That's not very flattering. You assume I can't attract a man?" She stopped short under the streetlamp.

Gerry melted at the sight of her, illuminated like an angel. He shook his head and drew back curls from her face. "It's the kind of man you attract."

She drew back from him and caught his hand in both of hers. "And you're going to tell me?" She dropped his hand and curled her fingers around his lapels. Looking up at him her eyes sparkled.

"Aye. You attract the kind of man who doesn't know what to do with you. And then he leaves you unsatisfied."

Isla sputtered. "But of course, you could satisfy me." She shook his lapels and he swept her against him. As his lips descended on hers, Gerry snagged her around her waist. Without a breath between them, they were consumed by each other.

Gerry felt her swoon into his arms, and he knew as she shivered into the embrace, it was a foot-popping kiss. *You bet that fine ass you'd be satisfied. If you only knew.*

Gerry finally surrendered her lips when he knew she had to breathe. She fell away with a gasp and Gerry's hands retreated into his trouser pockets as a private part of him stirred. He nodded. "I'm not sure you're ready for a guy... like me. But I persist."

Chapter Three

Isla, her mind still on Gerry's kiss, entered the rambling farmhouse where her family grew up. She unwrapped her scarf, removed her hat, stuffed her gloves in her pockets, and sat on the bench to remove her boots to dry in the tray. The last bit of outerwear to come off was her heavy wool coat. She rubbed her hands together, feeling the chill of March's lion weather. Hearing someone in the kitchen, she followed the sound of the tea kettle to the warmest room in the house.

Maisie methodically set out her favorite mug and tea. She looked up when Isla entered and flounced into a chair. "What would you say if a fella said you weren't ready for a man like him?"

Maisie tossed back her head and laughed. "He doesn't think much of himself, does he?"

Isla deadpanned. "Well, you haven't seen him, and he hasn't kissed you."

Maisie leaned against the kitchen counter. "But from the look on your face, *you* know what he looks like and how he kisses."

Isla's posture melted into the chair. With a sigh, she grinned. "Does it show?"

"Aye, a wee bit."

"What do I do with an arrogant man like that?"

Maisie joined her at the table and sat. She rested her chin on her hand and her other hand fell over her belly. "You marry him the way I married Ian. Then you make a beautiful baby, due in October."

Isla turned. "You what?"

Maisie and Isla danced together around the large farmhouse kitchen. "Ian is at the pub buying rounds for everyone. He's on cloud nine. Typical of that kind of man, *he* did all the work."

Isla shrugged. "Well, I don't see my situation going that way."

"And why not?" The tea kettle called, and Maisie pulled down a second mug for Isla. "Ian was a rounder when I met him. Being married three years has grounded him. When are you seeing your man again?"

Isla bit her lip. "We're talking about going to the symphony next week in Glasgow."

Maisie winked and shimmied her shoulders. "The symphony? Fancy, are we?"

Isla was already daydreaming about their next kiss.

****

Gerry grew restless with the inactivity in the office. Truth be told, he was bored with this job, talking on the phone with people thousands of miles away was interesting only if a big deal was being made. The rest of the time, answering the same questions endlessly became unfulfilling in a hurry. He needed contact with real people.

He'd heard the commotion outside for nearly two hours. The enormous lighting ballasts turned night into day. Gerry slipped to a side window of his office and saw the Star Wagons lined up on the side street. The entire neighborhood had been alerted to the filming of a paranormal action film about a daring immortal. Gerry laughed. *Aren't we all?*

Gerry stood on the office stoop and sucked in the scents of excitement. That got his blood rising. Groups of women huddled together behind the barriers waited girlishly for the leading man. Men casually exhibited interest by staring at their phones and emitting high amounts of testosterone.

It was a controlled circus as people who looked important grumbled at people with less than confident body language. Mixed among the scents of the crowd was a familiar fragrance Gerry would never forget. He raised his head and searched the faces in the crowd for Isla. There she stood, like a stargazer lily in a bouquet of carnations. Her raucous head of auburn hair was somewhat controlled by the gaudy plastic tiara that said 'bridesmaid'. It didn't take more than a second or two for Gerry to catch the fruity fragrance of rum punches that lit the bridal party's cheeks with fire and raised the volume of their laughter.

The film's leading lady and man walked into the center of the street along with their stunt doubles. Some other worker bees measured the marks. The leading lady grinned and waved to the crowd. She was handed a megaphone by an assistant's assistant. "Thank you all for coming out tonight! I know it's late and chilly. We will be right here tomorrow morning to kick off the Arts in Ayr festival. Check out my sister's stained-glass booth, okay?"

People applauded and phone cameras flashed. The leading man walked up behind his co-star and Gerry immediately scented their familiarity. He chuckled. *You dog.*

"They never told me how beautiful Scottish women are." The crowd went wild. Gerry watched Isla's cohorts quivering in their knickers for this guy. Yeah, he was tall, v-backed, and packed into a pair of cargo pants that left no imagination as to his gifts, which seemed impressive. His feet were. Gerry crossed his arms over his chest and buried a laugh. "We have to ask you to remain perfectly silent when they call 'action'." The star grinned and gazed out from under impossibly long eyelashes. "Every one of you that is silent, gets a photo with me tomorrow at the festival."

The wedding bunch shimmied like one huge amoeba of lust. *Oh, Isla, he's wearing a cup.* Before the film crew moved to their marks, Gerry slipped through the crowd to arrive behind Isla in the wedding bunch. "Big night tonight?" He gestured to her tiara.

At the sound of his velvet baritone, the bouncy blonde in front of Isla turned and squeaked. "Ooh, are you in the movie?" Gerry shook his head no. "That's too bad, you should be."

Gerry's teal eyes shifted left and right at Isla. "Do you think I'd make a good immortal, or would it typecast me?"

Isla gave him a deprecating smirk. "Max Older is a photojournalist, he's sensitive but tough. Don't you read?" The group of women turned to him at that question.

"I read." He took a step back in defense.

Isla gestured to him. "Gerry McIntosh, of the Crown Estate, these are my friends. Friends, this is Gerry."

"Hello, friends. When is the wedding?"

The brunette giggled under a cloud of tulle. "This weekend. Is Isla bringing you?"

Isla's expression blossomed as she stared at Gerry her eyes slightly unfocused but faded as she turned to her friend. She hooked a thumb at Gerry. "Apparently, I'm not ready for this one."

One of the previously silent gals stifled her tipsy laughter. "But I could be. Hello, Gerry."

"I couldn't refuse an invitation from the bride." Gerry humbly nodded.

Isla's three drinks showed when she waved gayly. "Oh, I give up. Be my plus one."

Gerry's eyes twinkled. "Can I convince you to come into the office to give me the particulars? I want to dress appropriately."

The gals oohed as Gerry led Isla around the back of the crowd and up the steps of the mansion office. As Gerry opened the front door, Isla leaned and missed the pillar. Gerry caught and steadied her. "Would you like a glass of water? Tea, perhaps?"

They got inside the building and Gerry led her to his desk in the corner. "Look out my window, you can see the Star Wagons down the side. I've got a ringside seat."

Isla plopped into the chair opposite him and grabbed a pen and sticky note. "You talked your way into this." She bit her bottom lip as she wrote an address, scratched it out, and then crumbled the paper. "I don't remember the address. It's the Ayrshire Manor... Do you have a kilt?" She rested her forehead on her arms.

"I do. Unfortunately, I'll be in Ireland this weekend."

Isla's next words blew out on an air of inebriated fatigue. "The men are supposed to wear kilts if they have them..." She lifted her head in surprise. "What? You can't come?" She let her head drift down again. "I'm sleepy."

Gerry came around the desk by her side. He brushed the unruly curls behind her ear. "You remind me so much of your mother."

Her head came up again. "My mother? She and my dad both died years ago in a motor accident."

His fingers stroked through her hair. *How easy would it be to spend hours with her in my arms?* "Your parents were so much in love. It's only fitting they went together."

Isla's head bobbled with a quizzical expression on her flushed face. "What?"

"They did everything together..."

"You couldn't have been more than twenty when they died. How did you know my parents?" Her question sobered her.

Gerry gave the room an assessing gaze and then folded his arms across his chest and tucked his chin. "It's a wonderful story, but tonight is not the right time." He felt her smile widen as his grin grew across his face.

Her tipsy expression returned as she gazed into his eyes. Isla propped her elbow on the desk and rested her chin on her hand. Her eyelashes fluttered in fatigue. "You're very handsome. Do you think I might be ready for another kiss?"

Gerry leaned down to her, tilted her chin a little higher, and touched his lips to hers. Gradually the kiss gained heat. He found himself standing and pulling her into his arms without ever breaking contact. His tongue split the seam of his lips to taste hers. Her sigh gave way to his plunder and heat exploded between them. Her arms wrapped around his torso, and he thought about hefting her up on the desk to move between her legs. As he turned and caught her around the waist there was a clatter at the window.

That broke the moment. Five flushed faces pressed against the glass as they knocked and goaded them on. Gerry ended the kiss and stepped away from Isla. With a courtly bow to their audience, he quipped. "Looks like we were the stars of their show."

Isla fought to straighten her clothing. "Oh, I'll never hear the end of this. You're probably lucky you are unavailable Saturday night."

"Let me make it up to you. I have tickets for Spartacus, the ballet. Be my plus one. We can meet at the pub by the theatre, and I'll drive us home."

****

On the day of the ballet, Isla stared into her closet. Looking over her shoulder at Caitrin, her younger sister, she begged. "Look at these clothes, it's all wool and I'm covered from neck to toes. Don't you have something that looks a little less... forbidding?"

Caitrin filed her manicure. "You know a Scottish woman begins her seduction when the coat comes off."

"At least I can wear soft fabrics, you know something a man wants to pet."

Caitrin's hand landed over her lap. "We all know what they want to pet."

Isla wrapped the sleeves of a light angora sweater around her shoulders. "I know what I want to pet."

Caitrin's brow disappeared almost into her hairline. "I believe you're smitten, my dear, but is it the man, or are you hunting the elusive moose?

Isla burst out a laugh. "Moose?"

Caitrin waved her hand. "If he's a player, you might just tag your first moose of the season."

Isla threw her fluffy bedroom slipper at her sister. "You're a foul one to talk."

****

Gerry hated lying to his dates about meals and daylight activities. If there were any fascinating undead women in all of southern Scotland he wouldn't have to deal with these contrivances. For this reason, Gerry rarely had more than three dates with the same woman.

By the fourth date, they would find out his apartment had no food and was the temperature of a walk-in freezer. On the other hand, where could he take a mortal woman for dinner without eating? You could claim medical testing the following day just so often.

Mortals who were into vampires tended to be quirky. He wasn't looking for Ms. Forever and Ms. Right Now, was getting trickier by the moment.

About that kiss, the foot-popping, trouser-snake rousing kiss on a street corner. He had to admit he'd not been this fascinated with a woman since... well, he'd never been this fascinated by a woman.

Gerry parked his car in the nearby carpark, pocketed his ticket stub, and hurried across the street to the pub. When he entered, he saw slightly weaving junior-executive types attempting to engage his lady in conversation. He could hear her politely say, "I'm actually waiting for someone."

****

After watching Isla experience his favorite ballet, Gerry keyed the ignition and braced himself for the first test of their relationship. It would be an hour-plus ride through the dark countryside after what turned out to be an emotionally upsetting ballet. Who knew Isla would weep at Spartacus being sent into the gladiatorial ring and forced to kill a close friend? And damned if it didn't start Isla's tears.

Gerry nodded in her general direction as they drove out of the carpark. "It seems that parts of the ballet disturbed you." She was silent as she dug for more tissues. "That particular piece of music, the Adagio when Spartacus is reunited with his love, his wife Phrygia, always stirs me." Gerry patted over his heart.

Isla shook her head and threw up a gloved hand. "But their captors made her a concubine, a whore." She sniffed into the tissue from the bottom of her purse.

He nodded into the darkness and drew a deep breath. "And Spartacus rescued her... along with the other slave women." He closed his eyes briefly. "Think of the romantic triumph of that moment."

Isla sniffed back. "But he dies, and she's left to mourn him...It's the saddest ballet I've ever seen."

Gerry slanted her a look. "Aside from that, Mrs. Wallace, how did you enjoy Braveheart? *Most new couples talk about food.* The buzzer went off in his undead brain, *nope.* The next subject, family. He needed to get off the subject of the tragic ballet, the music he loved, and the exquisitely sensual adagio. He should have chosen the Sleeping Beauty ballet with true love's kiss. *Who am I kidding?*

Out of the corner of his eye, he saw Isla fidgeting with her purse. The scent of peppermint filled the BMW. "Care for gum? I get carsick sometimes."

Wonderful, only an hour and a half ride home. "No thank you. It interferes with my dental work."

She began tightening her scarf and jacket. With a heady sigh, she placed her gloved hand on his forearm. "Is there any way you could turn up the heat?"

His crooked grin slipped. "Heat? Turn it up?" His gaze traveled the mountain of wool in the passenger seat. *Only if I could unwrap every part of you.* "Certainly." *Trapped in an overheated closed car with a woman percolating her desire for the next kiss. What could go wrong?* "Is your castle haunted?"

Isla slapped her lap and chuckled. "Oh, don't tell me you believe in the paranormal?"

Gerry tucked his chin and focused on the road. "You don't?"

"I'm not very fanciful. Are you?"

Gerry clicked his teeth and raised his brow. "How do you know I'm not a werewolf from the moors?"

Isla shot back. "I think you're a wolf of some variety. Not the kind of guy I'm ready for, remember?"

"What if you found out I was a werewolf, would you be ready for that?"

Isla ducked to look out of the car window. "It's a waning moon, I have some time to think about it."

"Ah, then you do like me."

"Don't get a big head. One kiss isn't a romance." The lights of an oncoming auto illuminated her wistful expression.

"Aye, romance is more than one kiss." Gerry sensed she'd let slip more of her feelings than she wanted. "Maybe, you need another..." He made his voice casual. "You know for comparison."

Isla's voice rose an octave. "Is your house haunted?"

Gerry chuckled. "By the ghosts of former relationships."

"Oh, yeah, well, that must be disturbing."

They rode in tenuous silence for a kilometer marker. "I'm sorry if I've made you uncomfortable, We should have discussed the ballet before I bought the tickets."

****

With its white limestone trim, Cathcart Castle shone in what little moonlight broke through the clouds. Solar garden lights lined the drive from the Tudor castle to the nineteenth-century farmhouse.

As the car approached the formidable but uninhabited castle Gerry grinned as clouds moved away from the moon and the estate took on a spooky vibe. "It looks like it *could* be haunted." He caught

Isla's skeptical glance. "Or maybe Catherine should be chasing through the moors for Heathcliff."

Isla laughed. "We do occasionally see Catherine and Heathcliff."

Gerry frowned. "Oh, really? I never thought they were very romantic. He was a sociopath, and she was co-dependent."

"Alright, then. Who would be your ideal lovers from literature?" Her voice was flippant.

Gerry tapped on the steering wheel as the car rolled to a stop. His hands were steepled as he thought. With a nod, he spoke. "Tristan and Isolde, is love greater than death?"

Isla cocked her head at Gerry with an almost automatic response. "Love is greater than anything."

He gave her a measuring look. "Is that a church-school response?"

Isla was indignant. "No, it's my philosophical response."

Gerry turned in his seat to face her. "Why haven't you been snapped up?"

"You're talking apples and oysters. I've certainly been infatuated. Even perhaps loved, but marriage is not only love. Marriage is about... Oh, If I had to tell you, you wouldn't understand."

Gerry rethought going in for a kiss. *This is no superficial lass.* "Has anyone ever told you how fiercely beautiful you are?"

Isla flattened herself against the car door and looked up at him through her lashes. "Everyone likes to hear they're pretty or handsome. I'm sure lots of people have told you you're handsome. But we were talking about something deeper."

Gerry rested his arm on the steering wheel and for a beat buried his face in his elbow. "Will I ever get you right?" He shook his head and when he lifted it and turned, her lips were there. *How did I not hear her movements?* Ready to speak, her soft lips landed on his full bottom lip. Her weight teetered over the console and collided with his. His arms flew around her to deepen the kiss. *Don't screw this up.*

Gerry leaned back and gloried in her soft weight over him. With a deft hand, he reclined his seat and she clamored over the gear shift onto him. *It's a shame she is layered in wool.* Her hands framed his face as her tongue split the seam of her lips. *Who is moaning?*

Gerry sighed at the loss of her soft hands in his hair when she sat up, ripped open her unbuttoned coat and the unrelenting heat of her covered breasts fell on him. *How did this turn from philosophy to first base in an instant?* Not that he was complaining.

Her fingertip trailed across his cheek and landed in the divot of his chin, as her lips traveled up his neck. First, she bit his earlobe, and then her hot breath inhaled over his ear.

That was it. Gerry was up with her in his lap. He couldn't move the car seat back any further. His voice was a throaty rumble. "Roll back onto your seat and kindly recline it."

Her impish smile told him she understood. Gerry was out of his jacket and over her in a heartbeat. To his surprise, her hands did not make it around his back.

"Isla, where is your hand?" He felt her caress him through his trousers.

"That's not the gear shift?"

Up on his elbows over her, his gaze narrowed. "Are you checking my tweed for its tensile strength?" He nuzzled her earlobe as she kept her hand right there.

"I feel lots of something there..."

"Shh, no more talking." He flipped himself under her and was rewarded with her warmth straddling him. *Thank Eros for full skirts.* Their tongues danced a lively rhythm as he felt her heart nearly beating out of her lovely chest. His hands caressed the angora surrounding two of the most heavenly breasts he ever found in the dark. "Oh, God, this sweater... it's so soft. Does it feel this good on your side too?"

She whispered. "With your hands on the outside? Yes."

Their hips began a deadly rocking as his hands traveled under her skirt to cup the silk of her panties. He was millimeters away from his dream as her heat bore down on his tweed. "Is anyone likely to come upon us here?"

Isla's hands flew to his broad shoulders as she ducked and spied the farmhouse in the distance. "I think they're in for the night. But if anyone is working late at the distillery they'll walk past here to get to the house." Gerry groaned under her heavenly weight. "Are you feeling brave?"

"Brave? Bravery has nothing to do with it."

"It does when you're with a woman with large, strong brothers."

His hands skated to her waist as he tried like hell to move her off his throbbing and contained flesh. "If I had been brave, I would have stopped for a room at the inn."

"I can't say yes if you don't ask." She began a painful retreat to reality. Now she sat in the driver's seat and Gerry was a notch away from exasperation. "We could go back to my place if I can shift gears."

"Oh, dear. I'm sorry, you best let me off at home."

"It'll be a minute before I can walk." Gerry moved the mirror to check for lipstick and finger comb his hair back into place.

****

Maisie was asleep on the sofa with Dr. Who on the tellie. As the front door closed, she was up like a shot. "You're finally home? What time is it?"

Isla blushed as she slipped out of her coat. She smiled sweetly and played a yawn. "I need to get some sleep." Isla turned and Maisie roared with laughter. It stopped Isla in her tracks.

Maisie pointed. "Of course, you're tired, it takes a lot of energy to tuck the back of your skirt into your panties in a car."

Isla's eyes grew round as plates. She pulled her circular skirt out of her hot pink panties. "Very true." She held her head high as she ascended the staircase. *Oh, my God, that's the last sight Gerry saw of me?*

****

April 18th was a beautiful sunny day without rain. Perfect to load the sulky and Willow's luggage into Consort Group International's 737. Rick Hiatt and his mate, Anna, were on hand with their Rottweiler, Player, to say goodbye. Animals didn't usually do well with vampires, but Player was no average Rottie.

Within a year of being comfortable with Rick and Anna, he presented himself as a cursed canine shifter unable to hold a mortal form for more than eight hours at a time. All inquiries into reversing this curse were met with dead ends. Player was around more than his dark-skinned alter ego, Trevor Nagel.

Rick, five hundred years of vampire perfection, was the former Duke of Erne, Earl of Mayo. Erne Castle his place of birth and where he was eventually turned into a vampire. Years ago, when his Cupcake, Anna, requested the ultimate bite, it pleased him to turn her in the same room where he'd been made. Since that night six years ago, they'd gone to ground every morning together, and never regretted a moment.

Anna stood with her hand in the crook of Rick's arm. She bumped shoulders with him. "I don't want to jinx anything, but we're going to have the castle's residence entirely to ourselves for a month." She wagged her brows at her mate.

"Jinx something?" Rick looked down at his ravishing redhead. "I dare anything to go wrong. It's top-shelf B Negative, Japanese whiskey, and hot sex for us every night."

"Ooh, promise?"

"If we run out of Japanese whiskey, there's always scotch."

Willow blushed and shook her head. "It's nice to see the honeymoon isn't over."

Rick looked smug. "Oh, but you haven't seen anything yet."

Anna's fangs dropped as she placed a gentle hand over Rick's smile. "Fitz, button-up."

Chapter Four

Willow watched from her window seat as the plane taxied to the private gate at JFK International Airport in New York. A hubbub of swirling blue lights illuminated the morning sky. The flight attendant passed to make ready the door and Willow caught her arm. "What's the emergency out there?"

The attendant stooped to look out the window. "It's not us, we came in smooth as usual." They dismissed the law enforcement presence and Willow gathered her purse and unbuckled her seat belt.

Deplaning, she grew disturbed as the horde of law enforcement officers moved toward her. An official held up his credentials. "US Customs, ma'am. I'm Agent Dulaney. We have a warrant to search your plane." He held up papers. "Please follow my team." A taller more imposing man stepped into her space and led Willow to a small office in the hanger.

Within minutes, the entire plane's crew sat with her watching as a swarm of agents opened every hatch and began unloading the plane. The K-9 handler was too far away for Willow to 'talk' with the animal. Nose down, the bloodhound went directly to the sulky as it rolled out of the hold.

Willow's eyes widened when an agent brazenly sliced along the edge piping of the fine leather on the newly restored seat. The bloodhound yodeled wildly and was rewarded with a treat. At this moment Willow felt the dog's triumph. *I found it, it's there. Love me, there it is.*

Willow's eyes narrowed as she projected to the dog. *It? What is it?*

It's what they want. It's what I was trained for. Job done; the dog was led off.

Willow frowned as the initial agent advanced purposefully. With a stern expression, he nodded to the agent guarding her. "Your passport, please." Willow produced the document and he looked repeatedly at the photo and then at her. "You're Willow Greer Lachlan?"

"Yes."

"Still a citizen of the United States although you live in Ireland?"

"I work in Ireland. What is this about? You just destroyed the seat of a two-hundred-year-old sulky meant for a charity auction. It just came back from two months of restoration in Belgium."

"Ma'am, did you accompany this sulky to Belgium?"

"No, it was shipped. What is going on?"

Agent Dulaney recorded notes on a tablet. "Mrs. Lachlan, the seat of your newly restored sulky is filled with an illegal substance."

"I surmise from your being here as we landed, that we've been framed." She turned and gestured to the crew. "We're not part of this smuggling. Earlier this week, the crew brought the sulky back from the restoration company and we left Dublin last night. None of us have anything to do with this. I want to see my lawyer."

The agent gave her a skeptical look. "Interesting that you would want to see your lawyer so early in the inquiry."

"Unless you're going to release me to go about my business, yes, I do want to see a lawyer."

"I'm afraid you'll have to come with us."

****

The brothers Moreau now did business with the Cathcarts by phone. They were too dashing and young to pass for the distinguished geriatric gentlemen they initially portrayed. A nightly tincture of Cathcart blood had restored them to their usual vigor. When they got cocky and missed a night, the next evening they knew it. The decision was made without much regret to abandon their former globetrotting with a commitment to remain in Scotland.

Samuel picked up the phone on its second ring. "Sir, this is Agent Bob Dulaney. I'm calling to confirm we picked up Willow Lachlan at

JFK this morning. As you predicted, the package arrived. She's currently in custody."

"I'm glad to hear our tip thwarted her crimes. It was kind of you to follow up with us. Where do we send the donation?"

Jonas smirked at his brother. "So, they have her?"

Samuel's lips twisted. "Yes. I think Adam Lachlan and the rest of them will be appropriately distracted from the purchase of the Cathcart Estate. Our unknowing donors should be pleased."

****

Willow sat in a standard utilitarian holding room. Grateful that they didn't handcuff her to the loop in the table, she drummed her fingers, waiting for the attorney CGI sent.

The door opened and a sharp-suited woman stood one foot in the room, one foot out. "I want all surveillance off while I speak with my client." Willow heard a begrudging grumble, and the woman stood her ground until she was given the signal it was turned off.

The stranger clipped decisively toward Willow, her hand out in greeting. "Dr. Lachlan, I'm Pamela Ferris, your attorney. Before we start, do you need anything? Food? Water? A bathroom break?"

"No, I'm just so glad you're here. Matt contacted you?"

The dark-skinned woman sat. "Yes. I've been associated with CGI for several years." She unconsciously ran two fingers over the pulse at her wrist.

Ahh, a donor. Willow's brows v'd "Did they tell you what's going on here?"

Pamela placed her legal pad on the table and leaned toward Willow. "They gave me the picture. Apparently, they got an anonymous tip that someone in a CGI plane was smuggling drugs into the country. I think they're inclined to believe your story about the restoration on the sulky. Of course, they'll require documents to verify that..."

Willow interrupted. "I had them with me until they seized everything. Why are they holding me?"

Pamela sighed. "They're holding you because you refused to take a blood test."

Willow ran a hand down her forearm and smoothed her sleeve. She leaned across the table. "I won't allow them to draw my blood."

Pamela met her lean. "Why not? Do you have illegal substances in your system?"

The shifter flopped back in the metal chair. "Of course not." She leaned closer and spoke barely moving her lips. "My blood... it's not normal."

Pamela waved her fountain pen with a comforting smile. "Are you...?"

Willow shook her head and her brown eyes glittered. "I'm a Pegasus shifter."

Pamela's hands flattened on the table. "You're the one? I've heard about you. I'm going to demand your blood draw be in my presence and I'll make sure it gets to the right technician."

Willow winced. "How?"

The attorney dismissed her frown. "I have a way, don't worry. We'll be out of here by lunch. I hear the CGI apartment is pleasant. Matt and his mate will be waiting for you there. You'll have a lovely view of the park."

Willow thought the least she could do was work up a smile for the well-meaning attorney. "I hope they have a restaurant, I'm ravenous."

****

It was well past noon by the time Willow's blood was drawn, she was seen in court and released. She had her very own ankle monitor and they had her passport. Her stomach rumbled audibly, and she rubbed at a developing headache in her temple.

Pamela had the car service out front and fortunately, Willow was not a celebrity worthy of cameras and a news crew. Pamela joined her for the ride up to 15 Central Park West.

Matt rose early to greet them. Had it been a year since she last saw the matinee-idol handsome Matt Brenner? Being a vampire of one hundred and twenty-plus years, he looked exactly the way he did the last time she saw him. He extended his arms out and crushed her to his chest. "I'm mad as hell, what did they do to you?" After a good hug, he released her and led her to the kitchen. "Has Cat ever told you, I'm a good cook?"

Cast from private jet to jail and now this elegant Central Park apartment, Willow wandered the kitchen staring at upscale groceries. "I think I remember her telling me that. But, Matt, I'm so damn numb and hungry. I'd eat wood."

Matt nodded to Pamela and began gathering ingredients. As he moved gracefully around the kitchen, Willow helped herself to freshly brewed coffee to stem her headache.

Pamela sliced an apple and slid the plate to her. "After you've eaten, you can relax for a while. We have a secure video meeting with Rick and the others at five PM New York time."

Willow sighed. "That sounds like a good idea." She looked at Matt. "You know they've held that priceless sulky for evidence."

Matt gave her a wry grin over his shoulder. "We have bigger worries than that. How do you like your tofu?"

****

By late afternoon, Cat Temple Brenner joined her mate Matt for the video meeting. Willow took an hour to soak in a whirlpool and then change into the clothes Cat had sent up from the boutique downstairs.

Willow fluffed her long, sable hair as she settled into the hostess pajamas and robe. "The police have everything of mine. I don't have a phone or underwear."

Matt winked. "I don't think Adam will mind. We'll get you everything you need in the morning."

Matt cued up the call and the wall-sized television filled with the image of Rick, Anna, and Adam in the Erne Castle residence living room.

"I have info from Giles." Rick shuffled some papers. "Who wants to go first?" Everyone looked back at Rick. He nodded with a smirk. "Okay. As far as we can make out, an anonymous call was placed to the US Customs office by a man with an accent."

Matt's brow rose. "What kind of accent?"

"The clerk Giles spoke to described it as a musical accent."

Matt's head fell back. "Sonnofabitch."

Willow narrowed her gaze and she exchanged bewildered looks with Pamela. Cat sat shaking her head. "You would think by now those idiots would keep on walking."

Willow threw up her hands. "Who?" She ate up the comforting sight of her husband's golden hair and aqua eyes. His deep voice answered. "Samuel and Jonas Moreau."

"Who are they? Moreau, that name sounds vaguely familiar."

Cat shook her head, blonde hair loose around her shoulders. "If I didn't hear that name for the rest of eternity, it would be too soon. When did they get out?"

Rick consulted his tablet. "Those bad boy vamps were put into custody in 1922 for fifty years. Being Moreaus, they had fifteen years tacked on for poor behavior. They got out in 1987 and began their world cruise because they were forbidden in the United States. They've graduated from bootlegging to drug running and made business associations in China. They haven't been seen for the past five years, some vamps thought they were dead. It seems they're alive and they don't have to set foot on American soil to get back at us for terminating their Poppa and their sister."

Adam consulted a folder. "It looks like our sulky was packed at the restoration facility, which burned down two days ago."

Willow gasped. "They were nice people...They are the best restoration crafters in the world. They've been in business for decades..."

Adam closed the folder. "Those nice people luckily weren't there. But fire is the Moreau's preferred modus operandi." He slapped the folder on his knee. "The Moreau's suspected ringleader in this caper was a woman named Isla Cathcart. She's mortal, probably one of their Renfields."

Willow huffed. "Has anyone noticed, I'm wearing an ankle monitor and people want to send me to jail?"

Rick gestured to Pamela. "Ms. Ferris, you've been worth your weight in gold, but perhaps you should check back with your client in the morning. We'll let you go."

Adam folded his hands in his lap and grew serious. "Lolo, I'm headed to New York on a commercial flight tonight..."

Willow smirked. "What happened the last time you flew commercial alone?"

"I met you..."

"Right, so get here quickly and don't talk to strangers."

"I'll be there in the morning. Have coffee ready. Meanwhile, we're lucky to have the undead detectives on the Moreaus. Knowing they're involved we've got to get on this before you're painted with a criminal record. I'll be with you to make sure no one actually throws you in jail. And if worse comes to worst, we'll go up to the roof and fly away."

Willow nodded as Pamela shook her head and covered her ears. The lawyer left in a hurry. Willow held a secret smile knowing that she'd be in a thirty-six hundred square foot gilded cage with the love of her life. For two shifters with the gift of flight, staying thirty-two floors above Central Park was aces. She giggled. "They have catering, right?"

With a nod, Matt stood.

Willow waved a hand. "Which room is the playroom?"

Cat shook her head. "I'm afraid there is no playroom…"

Matt extended a hand to his mate. "Cat and I scheduled a private flight. I'll rent a car at the airport. We'll be at the Castle by dawn."

****

By the time Matt and Cat arrived at Erne Castle more information had been ferreted out by Giles Pacquet, CGI's head of security, and his team of vampire detectives from around the world.

Anna loped into the lobby. "Matt, watch out." Player bounded away from her and ran full bore with his front paws landing on Matt's shoulders. All one hundred and twenty pounds of happy Rottweiler greeted Matt. "He misses you when you're gone. He doesn't have enough people to play with."

Matt bore up manfully under the enormous dog's enthusiasm. Cat melted in delight. "Oh, there's my buddy. What a good guy you are." She vigorously rubbed the dog's jowls until Player dropped back on four feet and circled Cat, herding her to Matt.

Matt turned toward Anna. "I guess we're home."

Anna pressed the elevator button. "How was your latest art show?"

Cat giggled. "He has a new following in New York. They think he's extremely hip and aware."

Matt's chest inflated a tad and he smirked at the women. "Yeah, well, ever since you showed me Sky Kingston's work, I've had to up my game. I'm glad she's stayed in Hawaii."

The elevator carried them down to the basement tunnel connecting the shared residence to the castle. "Giles is here. He and Rick have been combing through things since midnight. We'll catch a quick report and then get some slab time."

They met around the kitchen table. Anna had glasses of O Positive thoughtfully waiting for everyone. Giles threw down some color photos. "This is Isla Cathcart, associated with the Moreaus in Scotland. She was seen at Belgium Leatherworks, a subcontractor to the carriage works. She was there at the right time, close to the sulky seat that was loaded with Fentanyl. We don't know why the Moreaus have allied with the Cathcarts."

Matt picked up the photo and studied the Scottish rose. "She doesn't look like a criminal mastermind to me."

Giles continued. "That's the puzzle. From everything I can glean this is a nice woman. She has no affiliation with any vampire-feeding organizations. She isn't a hematologist. There's no criminal record. She seems devoted to her family..."

Cat shook her head. "How does she live? She could have an online shopping addiction."

Giles shook his head. "She lives frugally."

Rick interrupted. "She lives frugally working for the Moreaus? Isn't that odd?" Rick tapped the photo of the thirty-year-old woman dressed in Wellies and countryside clothing. "Does she keep a farm?"

Anna smirked. "Excuse me, are you dissing farm women?"

Rick refuted. "Not at all, cupcake." He shook his head. "But the modus operandi for the Moreaus is super classy model types and they pay well. So, is she frugal by choice, in which case, what's she spending her money on?"

Giles pushed over a printout of her financials. "Not on rent, cars, food, or travel. She makes small incremental deposits to a savings account."

Anna studied the photo. "She looks very unhappy."

Giles consulted his notes. "She might be. She has no lover that I can find, male or female. When she's not working, she goes home. Lights out by ten and up at six. She and the family live in a farmhouse on the estate grounds where they run a distillery."

Matt put on his detective hat. "Distillery? Could it be Humanité?"

Giles blew through his lips. "No, it's just small batch scotch. Officially, Isla works with the family in marketing. As for Humanité, that dropped off the radar five years ago when the drug caused accelerated aging."

Rick folded his arms over his chest and shook his head at Matt. "That poison wiped out a slew of millennium vampires. Overnight they became dust."

Cat placed a gentle hand on Matt's forearm. "We're so glad we banned it from the Gaoler." Matt nodded with her.

Giles looked at his dossier again. "It looks as if the Moreaus abandoned vampire drugs for mortal drugs. They don't usually traffic in the US. This stunt with the sulky was obviously about CGI."

"Does this woman... Isla... does she use drugs?" Anna held her photo.

Giles shook his head. "No. Not so much as an aspirin."

Anna looked wondering. "If we'd had no previous interactions with her, why did she orchestrate such a waste of product to frame Willow?"

Rick arched a brow. "Hell hath no fury like a Moreau scorned. Was she under orders?"

Matt rubbed his forehead. "We need more info about the Cathcart Estate. Why are the Moreaus tied up with this little distillery? Something doesn't fit."

Chapter Five

Anna sat with her phone tuned to her navigation system. "Well, if we're close, we should see a castle."

Cat struggled to keep the Land Rover on the road. "If you ask me, it's the wind and the roiling low clouds that are obscuring it." She turned to Anna. "This is miserable. *Why* would mortals live here?"

Anna pointed. "There it is..." Her enthusiasm dropped. "*How* can mortals live here? The structure is only about twenty-five percent intact. Does Adam realize the extent of its deterioration?"

"Somehow they're bottling whisky here. The outbuildings are in far better shape."

Anna nodded. "Bottling whisky, they can stay inside."

They parked in what looked like a new gravel lot near a sign stating, "Home of Cathcart Royal Wildcat Scotch."

Both vampiresses wrinkled their noses and prepared to charm their way into the Cathcart secrets. Anna spoke in vampire subtone as she and Cat approached the outbuilding under the sign. "I hear Gerry says to only speak with Isla."

Cat shrugged and opened the door on a delightfully Scottish shop manned by a muscled clerk in an athletic shirt moving cases into stacks around the room. Earphones protruded from under his shaggy hair, and he hummed with the music. When Cat stepped in front of him and gave a smiling wave, he jumped back nearly dropping the wooden case. "Jeeze, you're gonna kill me. May I help you?" He combed thick waves off his sweaty forehead. As his gaze took in both Cat and Anna his smile grew wider.

Anna's green eyes swept the room and returned to him. "I'm Dr. Anna Hiatt. And this is my friend, Mrs. Brenner. I'm here searching for Isla Cathcart. Is she available?"

He looked disappointed. "I'm her single brother, Bram."

Cat gave him an appealing smile and both women held up their diamond-laden left hands. "Bram, I can't believe some lucky woman hasn't snapped you up."

"You're not Scottish, you're not even British." He ran a handkerchief over his face.

Anna nodded. "You're right. We just landed from the States and drove right out here."

"My sister is at home. I can call her."

Anna asked. "Is that far?" She craned her neck to see in the direction he pointed.

"Ah, no, but it could take a moment." He nodded and pulled his phone from his pocket. "Isla, two ladies are asking for you. Have you had your draw yet?" He turned from Anna and Cat and mumbled a discussion. Both Anna and Cat's vampire hearing caught every word. "Well, tell that bleedin' vampire to prick you next so you can get out here. They're dressed quite nicely."

Anna and Cat strolled around the large gift shop between racks of jackets, hats, and sweatshirts bearing the Cathcart crest. Cat winced at Anna as she spoke in subtones. "Bleeding vampire?"

Bram returned to the ladies. "It'll be a moment. May I pour you a sample of what's going to America this week?" They nodded and followed Bram to a beautifully decorated bar area with signs describing their different liquors.

The well-practiced young man gave his presentation with the aid of a printed placemat with written descriptions. "I'm going to wow you with the tasting flight." He set up three shot glasses each and raved about the peat, the smoke, and all of the things the two vampires could *not* taste without a few drops of blood in each glass.

Cat picked up the first shot glass and admired the color. "Lovely."

"It's past quittin' time, I believe I'll join you." Bram poured half a shot and raised his glass. "Slàinte mhath."

Cat and Anna raised their shots and downed them in one swallow. Bram blinked as he let the liquor roll down his throat. Before he could speak about the next shot, the 184 proof scotch, the ladies had their glasses aloft, repeating his toast, and bam, they swallowed more than a wee dram like water. He held out his glass. "Well, ladies I see you appreciate the family brew." He drank his and shook at the bite.

The door opened and a young woman mumbled as she slid up her sleeve, cursed, and ripped off a bandage. The breeze from the door swept the scent of healthy B Negative blood toward Cat and Anna. They abruptly turned and put down their shot glasses.

Bram wiped his hands on his apron. "Isla, these are the ladies expecting to speak with you."

Isla continued fussing with her sleeve until she stopped before the strangers. "I'm Isla, who might you be?"

"They're from America." He pointed to Anna. "She's a doctor."

Isla worriedly noticed a pinpoint of blood coming through her sleeve. She pulled back the white sleeve and extended her arm. "Well, I've never seen that before."

Cat was at her side a little too quickly and pressed her cool fingers firmly against the tiny bleed. "Oh, someone's given you a hematoma. You're bleeding under your skin. We need to hold pressure on this for a little bit. You're still going to have a nasty bruise."

Isla nodded gratefully. "You must be the doctor. Did the Moreaus call you?"

Cat stared wide-eyed, while Anna stood back. "I'm a medical journalist, not a physician. I'm not familiar with any doctor named Moreau. I'm on holiday with my friend, Dr. Hiatt. She has her doctorate in art history. Our friend said he thought she might be able to help you with a problem. Who are the Moreaus?"

Isla frowned at her arm. "Dr. Sam and Dr. Joe Moreau are treating our family for hemochromatosis."

Cat tried hard to look like she knew what the disease was. She broke down the word and knew it had something to do with blood. "Your entire family suffers from this?"

Isla nodded gravely. "We just found out. Thank heavens, the Doctors Moreau are helping us. Our parents died young, and we weren't aware of this ... disease."

Cat released the pressure on the tiny bleed and resisted the urge to lick her finger. "How wonderful for you that you have such fine physicians. Perhaps some time you can tell me more."

Isla looked to Anna "How can I help you? Someone sent you to us?"

Anna smiled sweetly and held on to her shoulder bag. "I completed my Doctorate in history with a concentration on the Tudor era. The person who contacted us said you need help with documents."

Isla tapped her foot. "So, the Queen sent you from the States to tell me our claim on this estate is worthless?"

Anna bit her bottom lip and let Isla complain. "Actually, it's quite the opposite. You have a benefactor who contacted us and said they thought you were getting a raw deal from the Palace. They thought I might be able to help with authentication."

Isla covered her gaping mouth with her hand. "Oh, I'm sorry. You have to understand I feel like I've been riding a grindstone since the estate went on the market. Who is the benefactor?"

Anna shook her head. "That person would not identify themselves. I was told in their position they can't. Do you have any paperwork, museum photos?"

Isla led them back to the barstools and took a seat. She gestured to a parchment poster telling the story.

"In 1544 Henry VIII rewarded a brave lass, named Isla Cathcart with an established estate in Ayeshire, now the town of Girvan. She carried a message to the Crown from Edward Seymour, the 1st Earl of Hertford. The message warned Henry that Scottish troops were planning an attack on English ships carrying the spoils of war meant for his treasury. The Cathcart family occupies the castle to this day. This is all I've got. Thirteen generations of verbal history."

Anna frowned. "There's no record of Henry's letters patent on this?"

Isla shrugged. "According to the Palace, they were lost in a fire."

Cat turned to Anna while pointing back to the poster. "I wonder what Rick would have to say about that?"

Anna shook her head and scowled. "He's a wonderful resource," she closed her eyes in thought, "but only until 1534."

Isla stood attempting to follow the conversation. "Is that the end of his years of specialty? Couldn't he expand a little?"

Anna smiled. "We're going to find out."

****

Anna yanked open the Land Rover passenger door and dug into the cooler for their travel mugs. "Good gawd, Cat, did you get a whiff of her blood?"

Cat buckled into the driver's seat and held out her hand for her mug. "I just about don't have a lip, I bit mine so hard. No wonder the Moreaus are bleeding them."

"It would be a lucky vampire who got her blood." Anna clinked mugs with Cat and they both took a swallow. They recoiled at the taste. "What the hell did Gerry give us?"

Cat winced. "This is the dregs of something deep-fried. What are the donors eating? The local vampires need us." As they fought the hefty winds all the way back to the Glasgow Airport, Anna fidgeted in her seat. "I just can't wait to tell Fitz this entire bizarre situation."

"If I know Matt, he'll cook up some scheme to trap the Moreaus." She frowned at the travel mug. "Let's drink enough of this swill to get us home." Cat shook her head.

****

Player watched Rick pace. The dog's large head moved back and forth like a metronome as Rick wore out the living room carpet. Matt stretched out on the sofa, one arm behind his head as he sipped his evening cocktail. "Rick, relax, you're going to give that poor dog a headache."

Rick leveled an exasperated look at his business partner of over one hundred years. "You know I hate when we're apart."

Matt looked at his watch. "They're due in five minutes. Just enough time to fix me another drink and get one for yourself. Be a gent, make a couple for the ladies."

"This must be juicy for them to turn around and come home in one day."

****

When Cat and Anna dashed into their shared residence, they babbled about bad blood.

Rick gestured to a tray of drinks. "I've made cocktails."

Matt piped up, "Because I told him to."

Anna held up a hand. "What I want right now more than drinks is something to eat. You know, perhaps a footballer or a body builder."

She caught Rick's hands on her shoulders as he came in for a hug. "Excuse me?"

Anna wiped at her lips. "I need a meal from someone who cares about their body."

Cat waved a hand at the cocktail. "What in the deep-fried hell do they feed the donors in Glasgow?"

Matt strolled to the kitchen and returned with their best AB Positive. "This donor is a vegetarian."

Cat grabbed for the glass. "Bingo."

Between sips, Anna waved everyone into a seat. "My head is going to explode. You won't believe me unless you see the words come out of my mouth."

Cat nodded. "It's true. There's more to framing Willow than we ever dreamed, and it could stem from the spring water at Cathcart Castle."

The men tilted their heads like curious dogs as Cat and Anna tag teamed telling the Cathcart story.

Anna swallowed and covered her lips for a delicate burp. "Excuse me."

Cat jumped in. "Can you imagine the Moreaus posing as doctors? And this is weird, the family perceived them as being in their sixties. How is that possible?"

Matt considered. "There have been those rumors of accelerated aging with that last batch of Humanité…"

Anna emptied her glass and looked for more. "The brothers suggested a novel way to finance their medical care. They offered to bankroll worldwide distribution of Cathcart liquor as well as marketing items." The four vampires pondered that statement a beat. "And Isla volunteered the leather craftsman in Belgium who was doing the Cathcart special edition case was also making what looked like a pet bed. But she laughed when he told her it was a harness racing seat."

Matt sat forward and slapped his knee. "That's how Isla got associated with the drugs. On the job we used to say, association does not always mean relationship. So, Isla's in the clear."

Rick leaned on the mantel as he combed back errant hairs off his forehead. "But the Moreaus are not."

Matt laughed. "Looks like it. No way."

Anna drew them back. "Now this is strange. They haven't seen the brothers since that first visit. Everything else has been done by surrogates and the Cathcarts think that's because the doctors are so dedicated to their hemochromatosis research."

Rick raised a brow. "No one is being drained, they draw small amounts daily. What is it about the Cathcart blood the Moreaus *need?*"

Anna shrugged. "You and Matt must rent us a house in Girvan, and we need to sniff this out." She narrowed her gaze. "Isla came in from her blood draw and she had a little hematoma going. It took all my restraint not to lick it closed. That was some damn fine blood."

Matt picked up his cocktail. "They do run a distillery that claims the secret is their spring water..." He negated that with a slice of his hand. "But if it were only about the taste the brothers would drain them and move on." He looked up from the thought. "What's this about the claim to the estate?"

Anna turned to Rick excitedly. "I think they have a genuine claim. They lack the letters patent ceding it to the original Isla. They've been lost or destroyed."

Rick cocked his head. "When did this happen?"

Anna checked her notes. "The award was granted by Henry VIII in 1543, the paperwork seems to have been lost by the Duke of Somerset in 1547 around the time of Henry's death."

Matt rubbed his forehead. "An estate with spring water. Taking blood from the family. A claim to the estate. There are no coincidences. How are these elements related?"

Rick looked up suddenly. "Henry ceded this property to a woman? Specifically, a woman?" Anna nodded. "Then I'm going to let Matt accompany you back to Girvan. I need to see a guy in Altomünster."

Matt looked amused. "Of course, you do. Why?"

Rick smirked. "I think I might know where the letters patent went."

Chapter Six

Isla dressed down in her waxed Barbour parka. Her hands in heavy gloves filled the large bellows pockets. The adjustable hood barely contained the woolen scarf wrapped around her head and neck. She tapped her booted heels as she sat impatiently waiting for Gerry to arrive Friday evening at work.

The singular sound of his convertible perked her up nicely. She was flummoxed as he pulled up grinning into the wind wearing his sport coat and aviator sunglasses. He waved, raised the top and strolled toward her. *Why isn't he freezing?* Her teeth chattered as she stood.

"Isn't it a lovely brisk evening?" His smile was contagious.

"Brisk? It's a polar vortex. There are cold warnings out." She playfully punched at his shoulder. "And look at you. You're not one of those Polar Bear swimmers, are you?"

Gerry drew out his office keys and gave her a sideways smirk. "I can assure you, madam, I am no polar bear." He opened the office door and waved her ahead of him.

She headed directly to the radiator and rubbed her hands together. "Sometimes I can't believe I came back from Cuba."

Gerry winced. "It's very bright there. Lots of heat. I don't like heat." He dropped his keys in the desk drawer and hung up his jacket. He sat in his chair and gestured Isla to one across the desk. "What is on your lovely mind?"

She leaned toward Gerry. "Are you the benefactor?"

The front door burst open with a gust of wind. Randall shouted his good evening and stopped dead when he saw Isla. His smirk dropped when she turned to greet him.

Gerry nodded to his co-worker. "Did you pick up those papers?"

Randall snapped his fingers. "They're on the northern desk." He headed across the room and began shuffling envelopes and files into a drawer. Sitting down with keen eyes slanted, he swung his monitor away from public view.

Isla turned away from watching Randall and insisted to Gerry. "Are *you* the benefactor?"

Gerry shuffled papers and did not look up. "I can't talk about that here."

She leaned further into him. "You are, aren't you?"

Gerry glanced up at Randall with a vague smile but cut his gaze towards her for a beat. "Not here." He shook his head decisively.

She kept quiet but her scrutiny held. Gerry swiveled in his chair toward his undead coworker. "You know I'm not up to snuff this evening. I believe I'll head home for some rest."

With a pinched expression, Randall stopped typing mid-sentence and nodded curtly.

Gerry glanced at Isla. "May I see you out?"

Out of the corner of his eye, Gerry was just in time to see Randall pick up the phone. "I told you I would call as..."

In the lobby Isla tightened up her scarf and dug into her gloves, she glanced at Gerry with concern. "You're not feeling well?"

Gerry shoved his hands into his trouser pockets and his crooked grin sparked in his eyes. "I feel fine. Let's get out of here. I know a place. It's close."

Isla caught one of his hands in both of hers. "You are, aren't you?"

"A benefactor? I'd like to say yes, but I can't." He walked her to his car and opened her door."

"Whether you can say it or not, I want you to know we're very grateful."

"There's no reason for gratitude." He drove a short distance and parked on Harbor Street. He aimed a long finger upward. "See the top floor, on the corner? That's me." They exited his auto, he caught her hand and trotted with a boyish grin.

As he keyed his code, she whispered. "Do you live alone?"

His brow rose. "I do." He flung open the door.

Isla gasped at the change from a modern apartment building to a Tudor bachelor pad with cherrywood paneling and a bow-bayed reading area at the other end of a sumptuous sitting room. Tall bookcases flanked the marble fireplace. With a flip of a switch, the gas logs ignited. Soft, indirect light fanned out behind the fronds of lush, tall, potted palms.

Gerry took her coat, scarf, and gloves. "Anything else you'd like to peel out of?" He nodded with a wink and then hung up his sports coat. "I could use a drink to warm up. How about you?"

"Is that how you do it? Antifreeze in place of blood?"

Gerry placed his hand over his undead heart and bowed his head. "I'll never tell. It's your job to get it out of me."

Isla trailed along the room spying the tiny details of his ornate living area. "All of this would fit in at Cathcart Castle..."

"After the renovation?" Gerry looked over his shoulder as he mixed drinks.

Isla shrugged. "Well, that could be a while." She stood before the fireplace and warmed her hands. "This marble is exquisite. It can't be original to the apartment."

Gerry walked toward her with a delightful Bramble in crystal old fashioned glasses. "It was a housewarming gift."

Isla gawked. "That's some friend and some gift."

Gerry's smile rose to his teal eyes as he raised his glass to toast. "Here's to th' smiles o' Lassies we love, here's to th' friends ever faithful. Drink to th' hearts so loving and true and never may we be ungrateful."

Isla hefted her glass; they clinked together and drank. Gerry led her to sit in the leather wingchair overlooking the River Ayr. He sat on the ottoman before her and enjoyed her expression as she relaxed with the drink in her hand. "Please tell me you've had tea."

"Oh, I see, you have nothing but leftover haggis. That kitchen looks far too clean. I'll dine on this blackberry." She grinned at the fruit decorating the glass."

"I confess, not even a wee bit of haggis. If you're hungry we'll have something delivered."

"I had you going there for a minute." She winked over her glass. "I ate before I came. I stopped in to thank you."

Gerry leaned back on his elbow and stretched out his legs. "Thank me?"

She got comfortable in the chair and smirked. "Are we doing this again? I know you sent Dr. Hiatt and her friend."

"I do know the Hiatts." He nodded toward the marble fireplace. "Good friends of mine." He placed his drink on the floor and fiddled with his phone until soft music played from behind the palms around the room."

"How interesting. I didn't know palms could sing."

"It's my plan. Ply you with drink, lull you into a state of relaxation, and then..."

She softened into the wide wing chair. "And then?"

"Then tell you it's a two-drink minimum while I talk your ear off about why my clan's better than your clan."

She feigned haughtiness. "Is your clan royal?"

"Touch not the cat bot a glove. That's our motto. We're an ancient clan. But perhaps I'd rather prove the clan's greatest talent?" Leaning along the hassock, Gerry extended a long finger up the flat-felled seam of her jeans from her ankle to her knee. His hand landed there as if to claim it for the McIntoshes. He felt her gaze as he pressed higher. Isla downed the last of her drink, placed the glass to her side, and slid toward him.

"That's some talent." Her feet hit the floor and she melted toward him on the large hassock. With a blink of her eye, Gerry caught her and spun them both upright in the broad comfy chair. There she was sitting on his lap. "You work fast." She melted back against his broad chest and played with an errant curl on his forehead.

"Fast? It's been six weeks. If I didn't take a shining to you, I wouldn't be this persistent."

"If I didn't take a shining to you, you'd have a big red mark across your face."

Gerry bounced her on his lap. "What if our first tea was our first date?"

Isla narrowed her gaze at him. "Where are you going with this?"

"Ah, if it were, this would be our fourth date and we could get busy, and you would still respect me in the morning."

"Don't be silly. How do you know I respect you now?"

"Because my charms seem to disturb time and space for you. So, if you don't respect me now, you will soon. I told you about our McIntosh talents."

Isla arched into his embrace. "I'd like to see those talents." Before she could blink, his feet hit the floor and he swept her up in his arms bridal style. At what seemed the speed of light they were in his bedroom.

****

Within the night's glow, the room was dominated by an enormous canopy bed. Deep evergreen and navy draperies obscured her view of their destination. Gerry sat her sweetly on the bedside chair and made a trip around the mahogany behemoth, drawing back the curtains to reveal ivory linen sheets and a fluffy duvet. He leaned against the bedpost and extended his hand. "Will you join me, my lady?"

With her nod, he knelt before her and lovingly removed her boots. As he ministered to her, she collapsed against the barrel chair and bit her bottom lip. *You are about to get so lucky.* Her head fell back with a sigh as he hovered over her unbuckling her belt. "Just keep doing what you're doing." She felt his cool breath on her as his hands caught the hem of her sweater and she relinquished it to him. "Your talent is working." Their faces were separated by a breath as time stopped. Her hand rose to caress his face and a playful expression grew in his alluring eyes. "Oh, my, you are something."

She felt his hands around her waist and in a blink, he had her up with her legs around his hips. She yelped. "You gotta give a girl a clue. Damn, you're a fast mover."

Gerry carried her to the wall of windows overlooking Ayr South Pier and the Irish Sea. "Tonight, no matter how big the world is, you are the only important thing in it."

She caught her arms around his neck and shook her mane of curls around them. "If I live to be a hundred, I'll never meet another the likes of you." She brushed a soft kiss on his chin.

His palm swept wild hair off her cheek and his lips branded her with his first real kiss. She felt his tongue between the seam of his lips, and she returned the favor to taste him. "Aye, I could make that dream come true."

His previous speed was replaced with graceful smooth movement to lay her on the high bed. With a courtly smile, he pulled at the hems of her pants, and she fell back into the sumptuous covers while he made those jeans disappear.

She crawled into the middle of the wall of pillows and pointed to him. "I want to watch you undress."

"You vixen." His chuckle was deep and seductive as nimble fingers loosened his necktie. He grabbed each end. "Do you require a dance?" He slid the necktie back and forth as his hips swayed.

"Nice... Do go on."

He made it a game, shedding first the waistcoat, the belt, and his socks. With a bass rumble, his fists held his unbuttoned shirt closed.

"Which side is my good side?" He flashed one side of his sculpted chest and teased her by alternating her view of him.

"You move too fast; how can I tell?"

He flung back his arms and the dress shirt glided to the floor.

"Oh, my, that's some interesting Scottish topography." Her finger pretended to move over his lightly furred eight pack.

"I've been called a mountain of a man, I'm glad you appreciate geography." He moved out of his trousers and his keys and change sang as they hit the floor.

"Oh, I don't know, I have to see the southern regions. Have to check out the peninsula. It is rugged land or manscaped?"

Gerry sunk his thumbs into his boxer briefs that already danced on their own. "You do, do yah? Do you look with your eyes and your hands?"

"Well, I have to feel the lay of the land." She reached back to unhook her brassiere, but he was on the bed, naked in a second with his hand over hers.

"That's my job."

What is more seductive than this much man paying every bit of his attention to me? That 'peninsula' is prime land. She found a way to grasp him as he unclasped her bra. *It's every bit as broad and long as the Ayr South Pier.* She was swept away by his sultry amber aroma. The longer he hovered, blessing her neck and collarbone with wisps of kisses, the rising scent of musk and sandalwood wooed her.

She fell under his spell as his thumbs seized her panties at the hips and snapped them off. "All gone. They're mine now." Playfully, he brought them to his nose, and she felt his sex quiver when he inhaled her cassolette. "This will always be my first memory of us together." He tucked her panties under his pillow. "Every inch of you is delicious." She melted back into the soft bed as he rose over her on his knees. "Tonight, we'll have a banquet." She ran her hands down the fur of his chest and let her index fingers tease his treasure trail. He trembled like an eager stallion as his hands sought her bare breasts. "Your flesh is as soft as peaches... your breasts are as firm and sweet." Gerry moved over her, catching her hands in his. With reverent lips, he kissed the palm of each hand and place them on his hips.

"I see where this is going." Her tongue swept her bottom lip in unconscious invitation.

"Then it would be my joy to take you there." His body over hers obliqued the room's dim light. Within his arms her heart sang. His lips devoured her mouth working her into a primitive state of desire. He held her tightly against him and her hand trailed up the muscles of his broad v'd back as she surrendered. When his loving lips held her to the point of breathlessness, she broke away from him and taking his handsome face between her palms, peppered light, playful kisses over the contours of his smiling face.

"I see the games you like to play." Slipping out of her grasp he was down to the end of the bed with her foot in his hands. The sight of him, sitting back on his heels, his knees spread wide, his geography thick and lively caused her breath to hitch.

She posed her thumbs and fingers as if snapping a photo. "You couldn't be more perfect."

His grin grew as he laced his fingers and stretched his arms above his head. His muscular chest rippled with power. "Hold that thought." Gerry caught her right foot and caressed the high arch. "You're right-handed, and you lean on this foot far too much." One long finger rode the arch teasingly as she giggled. "I'm going to release all your tensions here."

His hands issued the exact strength to keep her from laughing. The sensations drove her deeper in the bed as she grabbed at the sheets and her lady bits cried out for that attention. He grinned at her with a naughty acknowledgment as if he knew exactly what she was thinking. Instinctively she knew when he got there, he would own that part of her. But from his leisurely pace, she feared she would have to wait and be driven wild within that time.

As he spoke, his devilish fingertips stroked her calf. "You know about chakras, the centers of spiritual power in our bodies?" She nodded, her eyes slightly unfocused as he kissed up her calves and licked behind her knees. "They say we also have chakras in our feet that relate to the second chakra of sexual energy and intimacy." He kissed the area on her foot and Isla shuddered with sensations.

I'm going to be a quivering puddle before he's done. "Gerry, you're killing me..."

His shaggy head rose from his oral travels. "Killing you? Well, that wouldn't be fun. I just like to think of this as bonding." With that insight, his face disappeared between her thighs and the gust of his breath caused her breath to hitch. He caught her thighs at his ear and mumbled into her flesh. "Take it easy, girl, I don't want to lose my head; the view down here is too good."

With that, he began the most sensuous assault Isla had ever experienced. While her body steamed and a thin sheen of perspiration glistened her, Gerry's delightfully full, cool lips stoked her fires as his tongue ignited them. Her hands released from the sheets and her fingers wove into his unruly curls.

The inevitable ended with Isla's thighs wrapped around his neck and her back bowed, delivering her into his lips. His boyish chuckle vibrated every bone in her body and her moans joined with his.

Receding from her grasp, Gerry knelt over her and collapsed back on his heels. Her eyes zoned right to the object of her desire. If his tongue was this deadly, what else did he have in his weapons of mass seduction?

He licked his lips and his head fell back in primal joy. "If you like that sort of thing, I'd like to do that again real soon." He ran his hand over his wet lips and then covered the crown of his glistening cock. Isla gathered whatever strength she still possessed and lunged toward him. He fell on his back, his legs out and as he grinned up at her she thought, *I'm going to ride him like the stallion he is.*

As her hips straddled him, she playfully pinned his arms out to the side where her fingers eventually laced with his. "Let's see if we can find a few other items to put on the list of things we'd like to do again."

His hands slipped her grip and he grasped her forcefully and lifted her onto him. The initial trip down his length initiated a deep moan of pleasure and as she found her rhythm their moans were indistinguishable.

Their give and take shook the massive mahogany bed, the curtains swaying with their tempo. When she thought his smile was calming, she deftly got her feet underneath her and began teasing him. Her light hand grasped his girth as she playfully dipped him in and out. It was his turn to strangle the sheets as she took him to the hilt and then pivoted so she could stroke his sack as her riding continued.

She arched her back and swept her long curls over his tight belly. "I could do this quite a while, how about you?" Her hand cupped him as she ground on his length. Out of the blue, Isla found herself on her knees, her face in the pillows. There was an animalistic growl from over her shoulder as Gerry thrust hilt deep into her.

"All night? We'll see about that..."

In some form, it *was* all night. They bandied back and forth dealing each other exhausting pleasure. Sometime just before dawn, Gerry dragged the heavy damask curtains closed around the bed and pulled her into his arms to rest.

****

Isla could guess it was around seven in the morning, which was the time her body always seemed to wake her. It was warm and dark in the bed with those heavy curtains closed. She pulled back one panel slightly to slide out for a morning bathroom run.

The apartment was cold, driving her back to bed. She slipped between the drawn panels and crawled in on her knees with the intention of waking Gerry with some morning delight.

Her hand touched frigid flesh. She recoiled and tore back the curtain next to him. His appearance was pallid, verging on blue. He wasn't breathing. She put her hand on his cold chest to be sure she wasn't imagining this. She covered her eyes with both hands and shrieked. "Oh, my God, I've killed him! Nooo!" Her screams were loud enough to wake the dead.

Gerry sat up straight with a start. "What's wrong?"

"What's wrong?" She cried, jumping out of bed. Pulling her curls over her shoulders guarding her breasts and covering her delta with both hands, she exclaimed. "You're dead! Or you were dead. Are you dead? Am I dreaming? In what private hell have I awakened?"

Gerry rolled to his side and leaned on his elbow. With one hand he patted the warm bed beside him. "Now, lassie, I'm not dead, exactly."

Gratified to see the color returning to his chest and face, she clutched at her heart. "Jesus, God!" She paced the room fanning her face and searched frantically for her clothes.

Gerry rose calmly and poured two fingers of brandy into a small glass from his bedside table. "Here, Isla." He walked it to her. "Isla, calm down, darlin'."

She clutched her clothes to her and in her panic found herself parroting him. "Calm down?"

His hand extended the glass to her, and he shrugged. "You can see for yourself, I'm not dead." She was beginning to shake with an overload of adrenalin as he wrapped both their hands around the glass. "Come back to bed now, you've had a fright."

In a tone of disbelief, she barked back. "'Come back to bed,' I've 'had a fright?'" The glass clicked against her teeth as she tried to drink.

He wrapped a chilly arm around her. "Come on now darlin'. You're alright. You gave yourself a fright, that's all." He cuddled her back to the bed.

"I gave *myself* a fright?" she whispered, outraged.

"I can't be dead. I'm talking to you." He held out his muscular arms and patted the pillow beside him.

She blinked up at him, draining the glass. He took it from her and placed it on the nightstand. "I saw what I saw. You weren't breathing, you had no heartbeat. You were…"

"About that." Gerry poured her another drink. "Let's talk."

"'Talk?' 'Talk!' Yeah, what about that?" Isla sat on her side of the bed; her knees drawn up with the covers to her chin.

He spoke with calm reasonableness. "I have a condition. I meant to tell you about it before we rested." She nodded at him warily. "After the kinds of calisthenics we did last night, all night, my pulse and blood pressure tend to drop. My respiration gets slow. It would be easy to think I was dead."

Her hand clutched over her thudding heart. "Oh, thank God. I've never had such a fright. I thought I'd killed you. I'll bet your neighbors have called the authorities."

"Well, that would be a complication nobody needs." As he worked his arm back around and she cuddled to him, he grew warmer. "I regret I didn't mention it. You did exhaust me." He laughed softly.

Her eyes were huge. "Will this happen again?"

"I hope so, and if it does, I hope you remember this conversation and give me a nudge instead of a shriek." The phone beside the bed rang. Gerry nodded and picked it up. "Oh, thank you for your inquiry. My friend thought her false eyelash was a spider. She's fine. Thank you for checking on me…"

Chapter Seven

Anna and Cat blew through the front doors of one of the finest fortified houses in the south of Scotland. Rick and Matt exchanged arched brows as the ladies crowed with delight.

Rick shook his head as he gave Matt two rings of keys. "They've been vampires for over six years, and they still act like kids in Disney World."

Matt pocketed the key rings as his brow rose. "Aren't they precious?" He raised his gaze to the eighteen-foot ceilings and gawked at the fifteenth-century artwork. "You've got to admit, this is impressive." He gestured to the angels in the ceiling frescos.

Rick patted his pockets and rocked on the balls of his feet. "What, Erne Castle isn't enough for you? This is just a rental while we take care of the Moreaus."

Cat slid up to Matt in her stocking feet. "This floor feels magnificent!"

Matt took her by the hands. "What's the matter, baby, have you spent too much time away from the Malibu Beach house?"

She looked at her watch. "Time, oh, Anna and I have to head over to the Cathcarts."

Matt looked at Rick. "What time is their blood draw?"

Anna tied back her long, red hair. "It was about sixish when Isla blew into the gift shop with that hematoma. It would make sense, if the Moreaus are in a compromised physical state, they wouldn't be up in daylight."

Matt palmed his car keys and nodded to Rick. "Why don't we take my car? It's rated for off-road."

Rick winced. "Off-road, you're going to drag me through the woods, aren't you?" He straightened his sport coat and headed to his boots lined up at the door.

"Oh, stop whining. I know the sixteenth century was no HBO special. Go back to your roots, you can rough it for a minute in a luxury SUV." Matt grabbed a dark cap and jacket as he looked Rick up and down. "For God's sake try to blend in."

Anna shouldered her purse and stage whispered. "Once a duke, always a duke." She pecked a kiss on Rick's cheek. "Don't worry, Fitz, you can play the duke tomorrow night when we have the Cathcarts over for drinks."

Rick sniffed. "I don't know why I allow this abuse."

****

Matt and Rick drove ahead of their mates. About half a mile away from the Cathcart Estate, they pulled off the road and set up road cones. The ladies waved to the men and continued past the Castle, up the gravel drive, and parked at the farmhouse.

They noticed the same beat-up Ford parked outside and knew they hadn't missed the phlebotomist. Anna typed off a text with a photo of the car. Cat turned to her friend. "Are you ready for this, Dr. Hiatt?"

Anna grinned. "I am if you are, Mrs. Brenner."

Cat shivered. "I hope they don't ask me to talk medicine."

Anna covered her face. "You really are a writer, aren't you?"

Isla answered Anna's brisk knock. "Dr. Hiatt, I was so pleased to get your call this afternoon. Welcome to our home." She stood back and gestured them in.

The scent of three or four different blood types filled the farmhouse. Both vampires took a halting step back as they saw the family gathered around the dinner table in stages of having their blood drawn. Cat patted Anna's shoulder and smiled graciously at Isla. "Poor Dr. Hiatt is squeamish around blood."

Anna's green eyes flamed as they narrowed at Cat. "That's why I went into history."

Ian's arm received the band aid, and the phlebotomist labeled the tube in preparation for leaving. Cat asked casually. "You're a Cathcart?" She gestured to the man's blond hair at a table of auburn-headed people.

He beamed proudly and gestured to Maisie. "I am by marriage. Funny that I should have the blood disease, too. But my family is from this area. Still, none of them have hemochromatosis."

Cat nodded wisely. "Fascinating."

Anna and Cat waited for the tech to gather her tote and bid good evening. They sat at the table and waved off Isla's offer of refreshments. When the family returned from the kitchen with their juice, Anna folded her graceful hands on the table and spoke. "I believe my husband has located your paperwork."

****

After pretending they were road crew, Rick heard the battered Ford heading toward them. They walked away from the cones and Matt pulled his black Range Rover behind the rusty Fiesta and followed at a conservative distance on the A77 toward Ayr.

Rick dialed Adam in New York. "Hey, Sparky, excuse the time difference. We didn't catch you two in flagrante, did we?" Rick winked at Matt.

Adam growled humorlessly. "Willow is in depositions, so it's just me hanging online waiting for you."

Rick picked up a small box from the back seat. "What is this domino you sent us?"

Adam sighed. "Once again, it's an extremely sensitive audio recorder that I synced with my computer. We'll get over two hundred hours of recorded conversation with time stamps."

"How close does Matt have to get it?" Matt scowled at Rick as he drove.

"Obviously, the closer the better. Under a table is very effective." Matt called out. "Yeah, I got it, Sparky."

Adam snorted. "You're the detective. By the way, use the flash drive to install the Trojan Horse."

Matt spat back. "In another life I was the detective. I'm an artist now."

Rick patted Matt on the shoulder. "Do you think the Moreaus are going to commission portraits the way they look now?" He turned his attention back to Adam. "We'll dial back once Matt has it installed."

Adam laughed. "'Cause I work for you. Later, gentlemen."

When the Ford signaled east, they turned onto the A70 and headed toward the outskirts of town. Rick nodded at a sign. "I guess the crematorium would be too on the nose. What's that ahead?"

Matt winced at the lack of trees. "That farm is in the middle of nothing, no cover."

Rick held out his hand for the keys. "I'll drop you off and ride back around in what, say twenty, thirty minutes?"

Matt shook his head and ordered, "You're coming with." The Fiesta turned onto the B744, and Matt pulled into a thicket of trees a good distance away as the Ford pulled up to an unassuming farmhouse.

Securing his gloves, Matt pocketed the keys and waved Rick out of the luxury SUV. "Showtime."

****

After a long haul through fields of potatoes, Matt and Rick scaled a stone barn's walls with graceful leaps. The two-story barn was converted to a medical lab down to a shining white-linoleum floor. In the darkest corner of the barn's rear roof, a mullioned window had a pane missing. It allowed the two vamps to eavesdrop on the conversation below.

These were not the young and fit Moreau brothers Matt and Rick remembered from 1922 Los Angeles. Samuel appeared more fortyish, but Jonas was an ill-appearing late fifties. Each of them lay on medical recliners as the tech set up IVs.

Even after decades, Matt could not forget the arrogant sound of Samuel's voice. "Dr. Ortega, why are our conditions backsliding? Each day, I rise a little older. The Cathcart blood is not working anymore."

A man in a white lab coat answered. "More precisely, the spring water augmenting the Cathcart blood is not working as effectively as it once did." The man dropped a dot of Samuel's blood on a slide and peered into the microscope. "Your mitochondria are no longer responding as efficiently. There has been no change in the donor blood. The change is in you." Samuel's wasted fist backhanded the unfortunate tech after he injected Cathcart blood into the IV line. "Please, Mr. Moreau, we can't keep hiring new techs. People will talk."

Samuel stretched out in the recliner and even from twenty feet up, Matt and Rick could see the rejuvenating effects of the Cathcart blood. Samuel's face plumped, wiping away deep marionette lines at his jaw and wrinkles across his forehead. Before their eyes, the man in the athletic tee shirt grew more robust and his complexion went from dusky to a rich brown.

There was no less a demanding tone of voice when he insisted, "You said, the miracle was in the spring water found on the Cathcart property. What are you doing to solve this problem? You're supposed to help us. If you don't help us. What use are you? You know what we do to useless servants."

Jonas worried his lined forehead. "What are you complaining about? I haven't achieved nearly the effects you have, but all I hear is your griping."

The doctor shuddered. "I can only surmise you have reached a plateau of tolerance. At this point, the youngest sister, Caitrin, has the most efficacious blood. A child would be even better. So far, there have been no offspring."

Matt and Rick exchanged horrified looks. Silently they shook their heads and waited until the Moreau brothers completed their transfusions. Samuel and Jonas rose, redressed, and returned to the large farmhouse. Rick skulked downwind as they returned to the electronic base of their drug-running operation.

Matt crouched against the roof and waited while the tech cleaned and put away the medical equipment. The doctor made notes in his lab book. Matt waited while the lights turned off; he heard the click of the door lock, and the two men exchanged goodnights.

With preternatural style, Matt scurried across the roof to a loose skylight. Seeing no security sensor on the window, he lifted it open and gracefully landed on the floor in a crouch. While the flash drive installed the program to connect Adam to the doctor's computer, Matt slid under the desk and attached the spyware and then shot images of the lab book on his phone. Glancing at his watch, he estimated Rick would be waiting for him at the car.

****

In the Cathcart dining room, Cat pulled out a notebook. "Can you share with me the story of how you came to know about your diagnosis?"

The family looked at each other with a combination of unease and confusion. Drew cleared his throat and spoke first. "Can you imagine going on a vacation fishing trip and waking up a week later in that country's hospital?"

Cat furrowed her brow. "All of you?"

"Yes, ma'am. All in the same ward." Drew ran an agitated hand through his hair and frowned at the bandage on his arm. "Then this doctor, he said he was a doctor, told us we needed daily blood draws..."

Half an hour later, when they finished relating the details of their experience, the Cathcarts looked to Cat as if expecting validation. She bit her bottom lip. "I'm not a hematologist, but even I know, it would be extremely doubtful that every member of a family would have hemochromatosis. By that, I mean even the members by marriage." She glanced around at the earnest faces looking gravely back at her. "It would be so rare that any reasonable scientist would suspect an environmental cause."

Isla raised a finger. "Oh, yeah, they did send a team of environmentalists to check out the water, soil, and air."

Cat nodded. "I'm sure others would like to examine the results of that testing; however, I'd recommend we get a second opinion. There is a very fine hematologist at the Queen Elizabeth University Hospital in Glasgow. I believe I could arrange for him to test all of you as soon as this week. If you agree, I can make a call."

Caitrin folded her arms over her chest and nodded. "I always thought it was a conflict of interest for Dr. Sam and Dr. Joe to sweep in and tell us we could finance our medical care by going into business with them."

Bram threw up his hand. "But we've never had cash like this before. The Moreaus have staked us."

I'd like to stake them. Cat nodded. "It's certainly irregular. If this were purely a study project, it would be underwritten by grants. Would you share a copy of the distillery contract? My husband might be able to help with that."

Drew looked at each member of the family. "What do you think?"

Ian frowned. "What if our questioning puts off the docs? What if they stop working with us?"

Anna's gaze swept the family. "What reputable medical group would object to a second opinion? On the other hand, I would ask each of you not to mention a second opinion until the tests are in. It's only a matter of forty-eight hours and then the discussion can begin."

****

Anna and Cat ran into the manor house when they saw Rick and Matt were already home. Cat threw open the door to the library where the men sat in front of the computer preparing to speak with Adam.

Cat turned to Anna. "Oh, let me be the one to drop this bomb."

Anna waved a hand. "You *are* the medical journalist, go ahead."

Anna sauntered to the bar and poured tall, cool beverages. "Gentleman, you may need a drink to hear this." They nodded and Anna brought a tray of A Positive to her friends.

Cat plopped in a chair and slid out of her sensible shoes. "Being 'medical' is boring."

Matt raised a brow. "It would probably be less so if you were a real doctor. Besides, I think you're still wearing your sexy underwear."

Cat withdrew a manila folder containing a copy of the distillery agreement between the Cathcarts and the Moreaus. Matt caught the weighty file and frowned. "Where's a Philadelphia lawyer when you need one?" He rifled through the inch of legalese.

Cat began the story. "Not only are the Moreaus robbing the Cathcarts of their blood, but my guess is, we won't know the half of it until we wade through this contract. To put them out for a week there had to be drugs. To convince an entire family of such an improbable diagnosis, they had to use thralling." While Cat spoke, Matt turned to the back half of the contract and at vamp speed scanned the agreement.

Rick sat back in the task chair and steepled his fingers. "Are there children in the home?"

Anna's gaze flashed. "Children? No, why?"

Rick nodded grimly. "Because we overheard their doctor suggest younger blood. Apparently, the treatment is losing steam. The brothers sat down looking forty and fiftyish and they left looking more robust, but not much younger. This mortal doctor will say or do whatever is needed to save his skin."

Matt shook his head at the contract. "I'm going have this scanned and emailed to Adam."

Rick looked at his watch. "Let's ring Sparky."

The image on the monitor was Willow's long thick hair down her back. Cat cried. "Hi, Willow, how are you holding up?"

There was a squeak of a chair and Adam's arms came out from under Willow's wealth of dark-chocolate waves. His flushed smile appeared over his mate's shoulder. "You're early." The chair spun to reveal Willow in Adam's lap.

Rick's expression was almost bored. "Hope we didn't interrupt you."

Adam grimaced. "Of course, you did. You have a sixth sense about that. What do *you* want?"

Rick smirked at Matt. "Make him a partner and he loses all respect."

Matt shrugged. Adam grit his teeth. "What do you want, old man?"

"What kind of old-world attorney are you that you haven't gotten Willow out of this jam yet?" Rick leaned into the camera.

"The case was dropped just this afternoon and they were thrilled to find the drugs bore markers that identified a trail. These stooges gave themselves away."

Rick nodded. "Excellent! Can you coitus interruptus long enough to get over here? We need an attorney. You're still licensed in the UK, correct?"

"Yes."

"Good." Rick nodded again. "This should be an easy matter to settle. How hard is it to solicit the Queen?"

Matt dropped the contract in his lap. "Have you begun reviewing the doctor's computer?"

Adam slid closer to the keyboard and looked at his second monitor. "He's got a terabyte of info I have to peruse. Lots of it is medical jargon."

Matt nodded. "That's okay, our resource will be meeting with us at six-thirty tomorrow. We can access it from the drive, right?" Matt looked at his watch. "Did they release the CGI jet?"

Rick shook his head. "I won't let that plane in the air until our mechanics have taken it apart and put it back together. Sorry, Sparky, you have to fly commercial. Tonight."

Willow walked behind Adam with a glass of wine. "Commercial? What?"

Adam looked up at her. "We're going home. The band is back together."

Chapter Eight

The following night, Dr. Aiden Clarke arrived at Ayrshire Manor an hour before the Cathcarts were expected for drinks. There was a heavy knock at the door and Adam made haste to answer it. With an enthusiastic embrace and several thumps on the back, he greeted the man who could have been his twin.

As Adam and Aiden strolled and caught up, their presence in the drawing room loomed large. In the middle of a general conversation, all three women halted and stared.

Willow coughed out words. "Adam, you never mentioned a twin."

Aiden smacked Adam on the back and Adam turned to his mate. "No way one clan could contain the two of us." The six-foot-six bookends wrestled and playfully threw punches. "Our fathers were brothers. We were hatched within the same season." Cat's jaw hung. "I'm Flight's End. This pollywog is the reprobate of Fisherfield."

Aiden feigned offense. "At least I wasn't run out."

"When was the last time you were in Chile? I believe I rehabilitated my image. Still practicing your quackery?" Adam offered his cousin a large, comfortable chair and joined Willow.

Aiden made the rounds of shaking hands and meeting the group before he sat down. He took obvious delight in needling his cousin. "Your Highness, we usually do business by phone, so this is a rare opportunity to get under your skin. Do you ever hear from that civil engineer your sister sicced on you?"

Adam shook a finger at his kinsman. "You're here on official business, Doctor, not monkey business. I burned her number."

Cat got out her notebook and related the Cathcart story to Dr. Clarke who shook his head in bewilderment when she was done.

"Impossible. I can't believe they had the gall to do this."

Rick barked out a laugh. "One thing the Moreaus never lack is gall."

Aiden nodded. "It will be simple to disprove to the family. But will that knowledge endanger them?"

Adam opened his tablet and flipped to a highlighted page. "I forwarded you the medical info from the doctor's computer. What do you think?"

Aiden took a moment. "Trying to evaluate vampire blood is tough enough. It seems when the Moreaus took this bastardized version of Humanité it started a degeneration of their mitochondria. The mitochondria are the energy plants of all cells. For some reason, this family's blood re-energized them, but not for long."

Rick nodded. "In your opinion, would younger blood from a Cathcart child, jumpstart the process?"

The hematologist rubbed between his brows. "Who knows? I study the biology of the vampire donors, not the undead."

Rick surveyed the group. "You see what I mean? I think this Dr. Ortega is throwing out a wild guess trying to save his hide. He's suggesting younger blood."

Dr. Clarke looked truly appalled. "He's suggesting children?"

Rick spread his hands. "Desperate people propose desperate solutions."

Matt stood and paced, rubbing the back of his neck. "We need to call Giles and get a team of responders here. The Cathcarts could be in serious trouble."

The doorbell gonged.

****

After Rick introduced himself and took her coat, Isla drew her shawl closer around herself. Her family followed the tall Irishman into a grand hall which was no warmer than the foyer. *What is wrong with these people? Doesn't anyone use heat?*

Anna saw her slight shiver and directed the family to the seats closest to the grand fireplace. "Please, everyone, introduce yourselves while I pour some of this remarkable Old Royal Wildcat." Anna regarded the label. "Twenty-one years old. Wow."

The family looked at Rick and Anna as they stood together. Bram pointed. "If I'd known you were serving us Cathcart liquor, I'd have brought it."

Rick waved a hand. "We love to support local businesses. I'm looking forward to tasting what the reviews call, 'a beautiful citrus palate'." He turned his back and spoke in subtones to Anna. "That satisfying butterscotch finish will be nothing without a drop of A Positive, cupcake. Got that?"

Anna pecked a kiss on his cheek and secretly placed three drops of blood in each of the vampire's glasses. Rick carried the undead's drinks on an ebony tray while Anna delivered glasses to the shifters and the mortals on a crystal tray.

Holding his glass of amber liquid up to the light, Rick nodded as the group joined him for a toast. "May you live as long as you want." He smiled at Anna, and she cozied to him. "And never want as long as you live."

Matt hoisted his glass higher. "Here, here!"

Isla, still chilled, walked to the hearth and rubbed her hands together. "So, which one of you located our letters? I have to be honest, while that technician was out bleedin' us today, all I could think of was the shite hitting the fan when they find out we've gone behind their backs."

Adam slid a hassock close to the hearth and carried a crocheted throw. "I can see this is at the top of your mind. Have a seat and warm up." She gazed up at the man with the aqua eyes and back at his doppelganger who said he was a doctor. "We're here to lighten your load, not complicate it." He turned to Rick. "Where are the letters now?"

Rick stepped forward with color photocopies of the letters patent and handed them to Isla who studied page by page and passed them on as she went. She blinked back tears and shook her head. "How did you find these?" Her gratitude shone with her blush.

Rick stood humbly; his hands folded before him. "It's all about knowing who to ask. It happens I worked on a project some years ago involving lost property rights among Tudor women. There is a monastery in Garmisch where, after Henry's death, his documents involving women and property were diverted there for safe keeping." The room sat silent. Rick prattled on about Tudor power plays and ended with, "...Seymour and Dudley, they all had dirty hands."

Isla's stared slack jawed. "You speak of them as if they're people from down the street."

Anna covered smoothly. "My husband lives his history." The magicals in the room stifled laughter while the mundane remained awed.

Isla grew animated. "There are no words, but what can we do to thank you? When will the originals arrive?"

Rick leaned on the mantle and steepled his fingers. "I'm having them certified by the National Archives. They should be here within ten days."

Isla's shoulders dropped. "That's so long."

Maisie drew herself up like a mother. "Hush, girl, we've been patient this long. We know we have them now."

Isla settled back down, drawing the lap robe close. "I cannot wait to wave it in the faces of that immoral CGI. I'll be damned if they get my castle."

Her family grimaced and Drew spoke up. "I'm sorry. I regret her display; she has been involved in a battle royal with a bloke at the Crown Estates and we just don't think a sex club would become our regal home."

Adam folded his arms over his chest as he got comfortable in the chair. "Sex club?"

Maisie caught Isla's hand before she could rev herself up again. "Did Mrs. Brenner say there would be a hematologist here tonight?"

Dr. Clarke nodded agreeably. "That would be I, dear lady." Caitrin flushed bright pink at the bass rumble of Dr. Clarke's voice. When he winked at her she giggled. "Mrs. Brenner," he cleared his throat, "filled me in on your very strange adventure. I believe it will be a simple matter to allay your fears. We will take a thorough history and draw your blood, looking for four key markers. If something untoward shows, there are more sophisticated tests. I'm curious, did they do liver biopsies? MRIs?"

The family looked askance at each other, and Drew answered. "Not that we know of. We were knocked out for days."

Dr. Clarke shook his head and blinked. "You were out for *days?* That is not something associated with hemochromatosis, certainly not involving an entire family."

Ian looked up alarmed. "Do tell. My Maisie's in the family way, I'm thinking she needs all her blood."

With that, Rick walked behind the family on the sofas and casually took a deep inhalation scenting for pregnancy hormones. His whiskey brown eyes went round as plates. He looked at Aiden and nodded.

Willow's eyes grew moist. "I agree with you, Ian, mothers-to-be need every protection."

Adam stepped into the conversation. "Speaking of protection. I'm an attorney, licensed in the UK. Matt shared some concerns he had about your contract with the Moreaus. I've skimmed it and I agree this is most irregular. It's heady stuff for them to have you sign a contract that awards them property when you currently do not have the title. I want to study the agreement completely before I say more."

The Cathcarts exchanged a variety of shocked expressions. Drew smacked at his forehead. "Give with one hand and take with the other? Is that what they did?"

****

Isla looked at the copies in her hand when coats were passed out in preparation for leaving. She looked up at Rick. "I hate to let them go."

Rick gallantly bowed and his well-warmed hand covered hers. "I would be a cad to take these from you. Keep them, the originals will arrive soon."

When the huge estate door closed behind them, Isla pulled out her car keys and suggested Bram ride with Maisie and Ian. "I have an errand. I have to drive into Ayr and serve up some crow."

Maisie nodded. "Sure and we'll have another wedding soon."

****

Gerry casually spun right and left in his desk chair as he listened to Adam's recounting of the evening with the Cathcarts. "Well, Gerry you called this one. She *is* as prickly as a cactus flower."

Gerry chuckled. "I know my way around her prickles."

"Oh, you do? Have you prickled her yourself?'"

Gerry barked a laugh. "I'm a gentleman, I'll never tell."

"So, yes, then." Gerry heard Adam slap the table.

The handsome vampire absent-mindedly capped and uncapped his fountain pen. "Did she leave in a good mood? I'm here at the office alone tonight. That prig, Randall, is off for a few days. All very mysterious." He sighed. "The last time I played hooky with Isla brightened my night."

"I thought you weren't going to tell." Adam's bass rumbled.

"Well, you got it out of me. But you knew that."

"I believe somehow, CGI is going to have to make nice with her."

Gerry chuckled. "She's not as buttoned-up as she would like you to think. There's leather along with that lace."

"Seriously, pal, there's a problem with the contract they signed with the Moreaus. Buried in gobbledygook is a clause awarding the Moreaus the entire estate in thirty-five years. Matt is sending for the responders. This grift is about to escalate."

Gerry stopped his chair's motion, both feet on the floor he rested his forehead in his hand. "How?" The bell over the door jingled and Isla's beguiling scent wafted Gerry's way. "Thank you so much for calling Ms. Windsor. I'll be back with you tomorrow."

Gerry's world glimmered as he watched Isla unloose her wild head of hair. The plush wool scarf settled around her shoulders and her complexion colored as she worked out of her coat. With supernatural agility, Gerry bounded over his desk and caught Isla before she turned to him. His kiss branded her forehead and she sighed as her hands dove under his sport coat to wrap her arms around his torso. "I missed you."

He nuzzled her cheek. "I missed you, too. What brings you to my lonely office in the dark of night?"

She wrestled out from his embrace and brandished the photocopies like a weapon. "It happens there *are* historians who believed me. Here's the proof."

"Someone believed you? Who would that be?" His hands capped her shoulders.

"You knew all along. You sent Dr. Hiatt to me."

Gerry's voice softened as his grin crooked. "Are you pleased with the results?"

Isla folded the papers in thirds and stuck them in her purse. With her fists on her hips, she posed, chin up. "Are you ready to deal with such a formidable woman?"

As Isla's gaze swept the empty office, Gerry moved from window to window drawing the louvered shutters together. "Ready?" Gerry returned to sit on the front edge of the reception desk. "I would be if I wasn't stuck here." He projected his best 'sad-sack' pout.

Using her teeth, Isla pulled each finger of her gloves off her hands. Gerry felt the tension in the room tighten to the point he almost heard a groan. *Fight it, see what she does.* While Gerry fought his baser urges he perched on the desk, hands folded in his lap. The heater kicked on and wafted the scent of her allure toward him. The steel in his backbone shifted directly to his lower brain.

Isla strolled to him and held open her coat. She stood in a tempting wrap dress. His lizard brain screamed, *One button at the waist, and she's an open book.*

A step closer and her coat dropped to the carpet. She was on the desk beside him and swinging her knee over to straddle his lap. "If we can't take the celebration home, may we celebrate here?" Her hands framed the scruff on his jaw as she nuzzled him with a purr.

Gerry drew her closer, enlivened by her sensual assault. Her heat connected with his fascination, and it was time to clock out figuratively if not actually. "What are you doing to me?" His fingers wove into her hair and held her close. Forehead to forehead they exchanged a breath.

With a daring bite to his bottom lip, her sigh undid him. He was up, she was in his arms and Gerry pushed through the tall, carved doors to the massive dining table they used for client meetings. The broad length of mahogany glistened under the chandelier as stately portraits of kings and queens silently scrutinized every transaction.

Gerry took care as he swung Isla onto the table, her feet dangling off the end.

She temptingly lounged back, her palms out to her sides. "What are you about to do?" Isla's words blew out on a soft moan.

"If I told you, the tension would be lost." Gerry demurred as he unzipped her knee-high boots and caressed her feet as their gazes held.

Isla's shoulders shimmied in reaction to his attention. His meticulous devotion began with each measured stroke of his finger. Her toes wiggled as her breath caught. Isla drew down on her elbows, still tracking his movement. When Gerry turned away from her and walked to the age-old wooden doors, she pouted. When he threw the lock, she drew her hands to her heart and dropped back, her bright-pink toenails a beacon.

"I think we're alone." Gerry loosened his necktie and thumbed open the buttons of his waistcoat. "Celebrations of two are," his gaze scanned the portraits as if to banish the watching spirits, "special." Without dispensing his shirt, Gerry unbuckled his trousers, recalling her past request for a strip tease. That he'd give her, for sure. Within the hushed walls of the old brick building, the wool of his trousers sang on their trip to the floor before he stepped out of his shoes. With a peppy hop that defied gravity, he was alongside Isla on the table. "I seem to have some issues with shirt buttons."

"But I have every confidence I can help." Her hands made light work of his shirt and she blushed furiously as she sent it to the floor. "You know, I didn't expect this type of service from a land development agent. Especially since you don't handle my claim." Isla's hands dove into the hips of his boxer briefs and held him there.

Shifting his weight over her, his hands out to her sides, he grinned. "Ah, yes... this type of service would be a supreme conflict of interest. However, ... since I am a full-service agent..." Gerry knelt between her legs and stretched to unbutton her wrap dress. A pale-lavender-lace brassiere greeted him. "I'm ready and..." He opened the front clasp and devoured her waiting pebbled nipple as his palm cupped her other breast.

Isla's body was as pleasing as a rushing creek on a summer's day. Her warm and welcoming flesh tested all of his switches. Without remembering who released it, the dress was apart and her nearly naked body issued a tacit invitation to plunder her feminine dips and curves. "Did you dress like this for me? The easy to reach button?" He hovered over her, the taste of her flesh on his lips. She was high octane and high voltage, a rare combination that with Gerry's controlled mastery delivered vibrations off the Richter Scale.

Isla's finger settled over her plump lips, and she shook her head, not answering him, but commanding him. "Gerry, love me."

So, he did. His desires unleashed, he wanted to savor every square inch of her. He wanted to explore the curve of her neck, to the insides of her wrists. The vampire's greatest hunger was to nuzzle the hollow of her thigh where her flesh turned dark and piquant. He wanted to lap at her lips as her hips bucked in his hands.

****

Isla couldn't contain her moans of pleasure. She was sure the monarchs spying down on them could hear them in the next world. *Such loose decorum!* She giggled at the fantasy. "I'm sure the Crown will have words with you about the unconventional ways you satisfy your clients."

Gerry raised his head from his loving work and smirked. "Let 'em watch."

Isla nodded. "If they asked me, I'd tell them." She gasped and lost focus. "Oh, my God." She felt his tongue breach her in a rhythm that left no intentions to the imagination. His strong hands held each round buttock in an immovable grasp as he lavished attention on her secret flesh.

Isla tried to squirm, but he held her fast. Her fists pounded the table and his fiendish laugh resonated through her. That wicked tongue of his sought and found the Devil's doorbell, which he rang repeatedly. Out of breath, she gasped, her back arching into him. "Please! Please, Gerry, please."

He mumbled the words through her. "Stop? You want me to stop?"

Her words flew out on a gasp. "If you do, I'll kill you." Her fingers wove into his hair and held him tight.

Gerry caught the morphing aromas of her impending climax and buried his face in her. His hands slipped to her thighs as she wailed his name to the twelve-foot ceiling.

****

Gerry didn't know what imp got into him. He felt compelled to pull her none too gently off that table and pin her up against the richly paneled wall. "Ever heard the expression, bang you like a screen door in a storm?"

Wide-eyed, Isla squealed when he pulled her to the end of the table, spun her around, and heaved them toward the wall.

Their bodies became two halves of a whole as Isla's palms smacked the wall. There was nowhere to go but deep as he voraciously sought her honeyed depths. The dim light of the crystal sconce sent fractals of a rainbow over her pale flesh as he rocked within her. The sensation of her cradling warmth overcame him with each deep stroke.

Held in place between his hips and the wall, Isla's hands smacked wildly in response to his unbridled strokes. As his body celebrated her welcome, that tell-tale knot of sensation crawled from his root. He let out a chuff of breath at her neck and fought his undead body's demand to bite and come.

Isla panted, her ivory hands flailing to seek purchase. Gerry heard the subtle crash of the cut crystal pendants dangling from the glass collar on the sconce. Isla's body leapt as her hand reflexively flew from the bloody crystal.

The electric scent of her pheromone-enhanced blood threw Gerry into abstraction. As his truly altered, if fleeting, state of consciousness drove his inner vampire to thrust to completion, his mind fought for self-control. In her spilled blood, Gerry read her fascination, her adoration, her devotion, and his teal eyes morphed into the opalescent gaze that accompanied his long fangs. *Thank the heavens she's up against the wall, eyes closed.*

Without missing a stroke, his steady hand caught her flailing fingers, and he soundly suckled the bleeding finger, hushing her sudden cry. There they were again, the emotions he read from her, buzzing in her blood. His free hand wrapped around her hip and danced his thumb at her delta to sweep her into another climax. Together they shuddered.

The room was silent, save for Isla's heaving breaths. Gerry's strong form still resolutely impaled within her, they reveled in their climaxes. If his climax shut down his impulse control to suckle her bleeding finger, the same sensation acted as a painkiller for Isla.

Chapter Nine

"Gerry?" Isla's forehead rested against the paneling as they came back to the reality of being naked, sweaty, and sated. She felt his chin resting on her shoulder, his tongue laving the sliced finger. Silence. "Gerry?" Isla's whisper rose as she shimmied out of his embrace.

Gerry's head hung as he steadied himself, falling back to the wall, one arm resting on the sideboard. As Isla sought his embrace, face-to-face, her hands reached for him. Her gasp caught in her throat when she recognized her blood on his lip and his tongue unconsciously wiping that blood away. When his heavy eyelids rose to meet her gaze, Isla's hands flew to cover her mouth. "What... is ... What are you?"

Gerry's forearm obscured his face as he turned away from her. When he straightened, running his hands through his hair he began pacing. "What am I?" His thumb slowly drew across his lips.

Isla clutched for her clothing and boots, rapidly working herself back into her wraparound dress. She pulled a chair from the other end of the table and sat to hurriedly stuff her feet into her boots. "You heard me." All the emotions of their coupling blurred reason as her fingers fumbled. Whatever ecstasy she felt was replaced with shock. She stared as the magnificently built man took a ponderous step toward her. Both hands up in an impotent defense gesture, Isla rose and pushed the chair between them as she retreated around the end of the table. She shook as she wrapped her arms around herself.

"Isla, please, sit down, let me…" He gestured back to his clothes on the floor. Hastily he dressed and then drew both hands through his hair. Gerry pulled out a chair at the other end of the table. "Will you let me explain?"

"Explain? Explain what, you demon?" Isla looked out the dark window at the street. The windows were locked. She glared at Gerry while gauging the steps to the double doors.

"Please... Once we talk, if you need to leave, leave." Gerry gestured to the doors behind him as he settled into a chair to don his socks and shoes.

Her back to the wall, Isla pulled out a chair a few feet from Gerry. He was 'Gerry' again as he buttoned the cuffs of his shirt. "Are you...?"

"Am I what?" His large hands covered the ends of the chair's arms. He nodded to Isla as if to commence her line of questioning.

"I don't know. You tell me." Isla covered her lower face with her hands.

"What did you see?" Gerry tilted his head in curiosity.

"You suckled the blood from my cut. You stopped the bleeding, but it was your eyes. They were... not your blue eyes, they were like glowing opals." Each word shook as her lips trembled. "You tell me what you are, I am not wasting all night guessing. Especially after the other morning."

Gerry folded his hands and rested them on his crossed knee. "Ah, yes, when you woke the undead."

"Undead? You witless, fucking cocksplat, are you telling me you're a bloodsucker?"

"The lady has guessed it!" Gerry raised his hands in applause, and she jumped at the sound of the smack.

"Okay, Bela Lugosi, we are done." She held up a Girl Guide salute and shook her head. "Let me out of here, let me out of your life or whatever it is. I promise to keep your secret as long as you stay away from me."

Gerry shifted in the chair. It squeaked and Isla jumped. "You promise? Do you believe it's that easy? You throw up a scout sign and think that seals the deal?" He leaned his elbow on the chair arm and then rested his face on his palm. He was the image of calm control.

"My family knew I was meeting you. If anything happens to me, they'll point to you." Her voice grew strident.

"Isla, you are in no danger. I would step between you and any danger."

"You would?" Her gaze narrowed as she regarded the soft tone of his voice, the melodious baritone soothing her. "But I don't get it. You are a…"

"Vampire." They said the word together and then stared at each other in tense silence.

"It happened so long ago, except for my unusual dietary constrictions I don't think much about it. I was always a night owl."

Isla balled both hands into fists. "Dietary constrictions?" She suddenly caught both sides of her neck as her eyes widened. "Have you bitten me? Are you using mind control? Am I turning into a vampire, too?" She bolted from the chair and held on to the back of it like a shield.

"I'd never forgive myself if I lost control and bit you against your will." Gerry stretched his long legs out in front of him, letting his head fall back on the chair as his expression grew dreamy. "Although you are delicious, I've been tantalized by your taste." Isla's hands covered her clothed feminine parts as she shook her head. "Are you certain you don't have questions before you leave me forever?" Gerry slowly lowered his gaze from the ceiling and refolded his hands in his lap.

"Why me? Don't you have your own kind? Oh, dear God, how many of you are there?" Isla wrang her hands, her wild curls dancing over her shoulders.

"Because you fascinated me. You're fire." He kissed his fingers. "Why would any man ask you out? They do, don't they? I didn't deflower you, did I?"

"That's disgusting." Isla retreated to the window and stared blindly through the mottled glass. "You stay away from me. What do I need a wreath of garlic?"

Gerry swung the chair right and left. "Silver."

Isla stared, nonplussed. "Silver what?"

"Aerosolized silver, solid silver, silver jewelry, utensils…" Gerry pointed to the sideboard. "Please, rather than asking me to give a demonstration with the cutlery, just go." He threw up his hands in resignation.

Isla backed along the wall as Gerry retreated in the other direction to watch her go. As she dodged out of the room and swept up her scarf and coat, Gerry watched silently. He pocketed his necktie, returned to his desk, and sighed. *I wonder what Rick's doing tonight?*

****

Out on the street alone and shivering, Isla asked herself where to go from here. The answer didn't take her long. As if the church on the corner was having a redemption sale, Isla ripped open the heavy door and fled to the empty confessional. *God will hear me, that's all I need.*

"Bless me, Father, for I have sinned. It has been God knows how long since my last confession." She drew a deep breath and readied her next volley. "I was seduced by the devil. I had impure thoughts, I slept with him, and I know it was the devil because it felt so good. Every time, it felt so good."

Isla hushed when she heard footsteps on the marble floor and then the opening and closing of the priest's door. He sat, made the sign of the cross, kissed his stole, and donned it.

"Oh, cheese and crackers, do I have to start over again?"

"No, my child. I heard you from behind the altar. Go on." There was silence. And the priest spoke kindly. "You know, whatever offense this man has done to you referring to him as the devil is blasphemous."

Isla's heat bubbled up. "But he's not…" She thought about it. Was she honestly going to tell a priest she slept with a vampire? "You're right, Father. I spoke in anger."

"Ah, one of the seven deadly sins caused you to bear false witness against your brother."

104

"False witness? Right, I guess. But is that worse than…?"

"Lust?" The priest nodded. "And have you foresworn this activity and repented?"

Isla buried her head in her hands. "Whatever it takes, Father."

"As there are the seven deadly sins, there are also the seven virtues, chastity, temperance, charity, diligence, patience, kindness, and humility. To purge your transgression from your soul, for your penance the Lord requires you to perform an act of kindness daily, starting with yourself."

Tears sprang to her eyes. "Myself? Can't I just say Our Fathers, some Hail Marys?"

"No, I think kindness is needed. After all, you called him a devil."

"Yes, Father. Thank you, Father." She watched his lips move as he made the sign of the cross and gave absolution. *Kindness? If he only knew.*

****

Gerry left the office high and dry and drove to Ayrshire Manor. Music spilled out of the foyer as Rick greeted him at the door. "How are you, dear boy?"

Glenn Miller's orchestra threatened to deafen Gerry. "Have I interrupted a party?"

Anna slid across the foyer to Rick. "Fitz, I have to start the record over. Hi, Gerry? Do you dance?" Rick threw his arm around his mate.

"Yeah, Gerry, do you dance? Cupcake and I were cutting a rug."

Gerry's hands dug into his trouser pockets, and he shrugged. "I don't feel like dancing. I did a dumb thing tonight."

Anna and Rick flanked Gerry as they led him to the lounge where the rest of the gang played cards and drank. Heads came up all around and Anna lowered the music.

She nodded to the kitchen. "Ladies, I have something I need to show you."

Cat and Willow nodded knowingly and left Gerry to the mercy of the men.

Rick poured him a stiff drink. "Dear boy, now is the time for Everclear and O Positive. Who among us has not done something dumb?"

Matt raised a hand. "Don't get me started." He glanced at Adam. "Don't sit there all innocent, Sparky."

Adam grimaced at his friend and looked to Gerry. "Come and sit with us. You're among friends."

Gerry carried his glass with him to the empty loveseat. He looked up at the ceiling fresco where angels danced. "You know how you get when you catch that whiff of blood and maybe it's just a scratch..."

Three pairs of eyes watched Gerry attentively. Rick nodded. "Go on." He shook his head and covered his face before Gerry spoke.

"We just had the best--" Gerry abruptly stopped.

Matt inhaled deeply. "We all know what you just had."

Adam's aqua eyes narrowed. "I get that scent mixed up when one of them is mortal. I can read you two." He gestured to Rick and Matt. "But when a mortal is involved, I miss the other half. But I digress. Go on."

"Her hand hit the sconce and she sliced open a finger. I thought because she was up against the wall..." Rick grinned and waved him on. "I didn't think she could see my eyes."

Matt shook his head. "But she did and now you're blown."

Adam lowered both hands in a quelling gesture. "You had relations with the woman and didn't tell her what you are?"

Gerry nodded miserably. "Isla."

All three men groaned. Finally, Rick spoke. "How did she take it?"

"She called me a demon, then a witless, fucking cocksplat. She left with her panties and bra stuffed in her coat pocket."

Matt winced. "That's never good."

Gerry gulped his drink. "The trouble is, I think I love her."

Rick raised his glass. "To witless, fucking cocksplats everywhere."

Ever the psychologist, Adam fingered the rim of his glass and looked up grimly. "You've committed a serious breach of trust, Gerry. Sometimes there's no going back from that."

Rick waved away the thought. "Oh, have a little hope. I flew across the continent to get Anna back. Scotland is a small country, the size of South Carolina, you could crawl back to her."

Matt stared at Rick and waved 'no.' "Gerry, we have a situation with the entire Cathcart clan."

Gerry emptied his glass. "What?"

Matt took the floor and explained how the Moreaus came to exploit the Cathcarts. "The Moreaus are the last of a criminal undead dynasty. Rick took out their Poppa, I took out their sister and we sent them to prison for sixty-five years. They're banned from the United States, but they're proving they don't have to be on North American soil to complicate our lives. Their little escapade nearly imprisoned Willow. We fear the Cathcarts are in mortal danger from them."

Gerry looked bleakly at his empty glass. "I'd like to be the hero of this story, but she's going to paint me with the same brush as the Moreaus. We're all vampires to her."

Rick took the glass from Gerry and as he made another drink, over his shoulder, he quipped, "Oh, the Cathcarts don't know who they're dealing with. It will fall on us to deal with the Moreaus before they kill the clan."

"I should have told her weeks ago when she woke up next to me and I was…" Gerry lamented as he accepted the second drink.

Rick nodded. "Yeah, being blue and cold, that's a deal-breaker, ask Anna."

Adam shook his head. "You need to find an effective way to apologize. Not in person. Something thoughtful she'll appreciate."

Matt looked incredulous. "What? Flowers, candy, silver jewelry?"

Gerry shook his head. "Adam, could you petition the Crown with Rick's evidence? If I could swing the title to the Cathcarts, she'd know I was sincere."

Chapter Ten

Isla rose the next morning after sleeping fitfully. The first thing she looked at was her hand. *Did last night happen?* There was not so much as a thin, red line. Whatever he did, not only stopped the bleeding but healed the cut entirely. *Who knew vampires could be medicinal?* What else didn't she know about vampires? *He lied to me. He acted normal. Undead is not normal.* Gerry was never normal. Gerry was phenomenal. She'd never kept the company of a man who knew how to lavish his complete attention on her. He was like someone out of another age. *How old is he? If he looks thirty, is he three hundred? Dammit, I thought he was 'the one'.*

She slogged out of bed and dragged herself to the kitchen. The family milled around her as they went about their normal morning. She moved in a fog. The ache in her heart rose to her throat. She choked back tears at the slightest glance from her family.

Bram bumped into her by the toaster. "Head's up."

Her hurt look stopped him. "You take my toast. I don't want it." She walked off to take her shower. Mechanically, she readied herself for the big meeting with Dr. Clarke, the hematologist. *Oh, God, Caitrin is going to act the fool with that man. I can't bear it.* While she dried off there was a frantic knock on the door.

"Isla, you bleeding slow poke, I have to get ready to see the doctor." Caitrin's haranguing got on her nerves.

"You want some cheese with that whine?" Isla threw open the bathroom door and steam rolled out. "I used all the hot water. You need a cold shower anyway." She bumped shoulders with Caitrin on the way out.

Caitrin looked back at her and invoked an insult. "Cow!" She slammed the bathroom door.

****

By eleven AM, Cat, Matt, and the Cathcart family sat reading magazines in the hematology lounge. Matt gazed over the family as they nervously killed time bickering about the answers on the medical history.

Matt caught Cat's hand and smiled sweetly at her. In subtones, he said, "Nifty sign, hematology lounge. It makes it sound like this is a blood bar."

Cat playfully slapped at him. "Well, it is. Only not for us."

The cocoon of the sterile and hushed hematology lounge was shredded by the sounds of every kind of siren. Matt and Cat stood back, wincing at the sensory overload from the varying frequencies and decibels. Cat futilely covered her ears with her hands. "What is that? Armageddon?"

Drew looked up from his clipboard. "That's the sound of the police and fire emergency critical response team. I wonder if someone robbed a bank."

Ian went to the window. "I've never seen a convoy this long. They're hauling ass somewhere. Look at that. It's probably every available ambulance."

The din passed shortly, and Dr. Clarke arrived. "You've all finished your histories? Gentlemen, the three of you, please follow Terry." A man in a lab coat carrying a tablet raised his hand and the Cathcart men followed. "Ladies, if you'll come with me."

Caitrin bumped ahead of her two sisters. "Yes, indeed. Isn't this a pleasant day, Dr. Clarke?"

Aiden gazed doubtfully out the window at the cold and windy weather. "Mmm."

Cat slid back on the sofa with Matt and waved Caitrin's scent toward him. "She's got it bad. How perceptive are dragon shifters to mortal pheromones?"

Matt stifled a laugh. "I don't think he needs pheromones to understand this one."

Caitrin caught up with the handsome doctor. "So, are you seeing anyone?"

The door closed, leaving Matt and Cat to speculate on Caitrin's success.

****

Within an hour, Cat sat beside Dr. Clarke nodding sagely as he passed lab slips to each of the Cathcarts. "You can see for yourself; the results Mrs. Brenner and I have certified. None of you is positive for hemochromatosis."

Matt paced and gazed out the window as three ambulances screamed toward the hospital. Cat reinforced Dr. Clarke's words. "There is no doubt, absolutely no question this Dr. Ortega misled you on behalf of Samuel and Jonas Moreau. They used his ruse to continue drawing your blood daily."

Drew grew red-faced. "What the hell were they doing with our blood?"

Even as a vampire of only six years, Cat scented a variety of emotions. Anger, frustration, confusion, and betrayal. She and Dr. Clarke shook their heads. He answered for both of them. "I have no idea why. There is no clinical reason for it."

Matt turned from the window and gave a flat answer. "They want your property. Why?" He threw up his hands. "The distillery?"

Drew's fist pounded the table. "The spring. It's the water."

Cat looked up at Matt. "They did have environmental teams there taking soil, water, and air samples."

The door flew open, and two police officers stalked in. "Sorry to interrupt, sir, are you Dr. Aiden Clarke?" The people at the table turned at the officer's question.

"I am."

"Due to a suspected crime, your expertise is needed urgently in Accident and Emergency Services."

"Of course."

The Cathcarts nodded understandingly. He looked at Cat regretfully. "I'm sure Mrs. Brenner can field any other questions."

Matt stood behind Cat and his hands landed gently on her shoulders. "You've got this, right, baby?"

Cat swallowed deeply and was rescued by the flash of breaking news in urgent throbbing letters crawling across the bottom screen of the television on the wall.

Caitrin pointed with a laugh. "That's the convent our mother always threatened to send us to."

Isla's smile faded. "The Hermits of the Holy Blood?" She wrapped her arms around herself and shivered. "What is going on?"

Matt grabbed the remote and unmuted the sound. The anchor appeared rattled as he read the release. "At ten-forty-seven this morning a call was made to the police resulting in an investigation at the Convent of the Hermits of the Holy Blood. Police found all eleven sisters in the chapel, dead or dying. The massacre was discovered by a local parishioner delivering food. When the Mother Superior did not answer, as usual, Mrs. Ferguson made to use her key, but found the door unlocked."

The Cathcarts chattered among themselves, and to Cat's relief she was off the hook for questions. She rose in agitation and gathered her shoulder bag to seek Matt. He stood staring hard at the television. She embraced him from behind and spoke in subtones. "This is horrible. What are you seeing?"

Matt bit his lip and sighed. "See the decorative ironwork? Notice anything?"

Cat's jaw dropped as she noticed the chapel's line of clerestory windows interrupted by bent metal bars and broken glass. "That's about twelve, fourteen feet up?"

Matt sunk his hands in his trouser pockets and dropped his head. "Yeah."

"The Moreaus?"

"Probably."

Completely out of vampire character Cat's cheeks flushed. "They could have tiptoed into their cells and drank from them without murder." Her hands flew to her cheeks to cool her face. "Why did they slaughter them?"

Matt's face was ashen. "For sport."

****

That afternoon at teatime, the team of four vampires and two shifters made the trek to the Cathcart farmhouse. The family was in varying degrees of agitation. Drew paced the length of the front porch as the visitors arrived. "I'm for calling in the law. This is assault. How dare--"

Matt laid a friendly hand on the man's shoulder. "As a matter of fact, we've already called for the law. The authorities should arrive within twenty-four hours. Let us handle this, Drew. You don't need to suffer any more than you have."

The stubborn Scot stood, feet apart, arms folded over his broad chest, chin up. "This assault was against my family. This is my duty." He was ready for war.

Rick shook his head. "With all respect to your honor. You don't have the right ammunition for that group. We do. We've dealt with them before. It's as simple as that."

"If you've dealt with them before, why are they back?" Drew's eye twitched with tension as he stared Matt down.

Matt looked away for a beat and inhaled a calming breath. "We've dealt with their father and their sister. This will be the end of it."

Drew shook his head. "I don't know why I should trust more outsiders. But this morning, you delivered the truth to us. Mr. Hiatt has saved our title. Do what you need to do."

The magicals exchanged long looks as they followed Drew into the home.

Like clockwork, the phlebotomist arrived, and Matt met her at the car. "I'm Dr. Brenner. I've examined the family and I'll do today's draw and bring it out to you." The wary tech surrendered her tote and reached for her phone. Matt extended his hand and gazed directly into her distrustful eyes. "You won't need that. I'll take it and return it with the draw. Just lay back and relax."

Thralled, the tech's expression softened, she placed the phone in his hand and reclined the car seat for a nap.

While Adam and Rick spoke to the family about legal redress on the Moreau contract, Matt drew six vacutainer vials of Willow's Pegasus blood. He marked each with a Cathcart name and winked at Willow. "Let's see if it's true what they say about Pegasus blood."

Before returning the tech's phone, Matt cloned the history and returned everything to her. He made direct eye contact with her, and reinforced, "The family was pleasant today when you drew their blood. Nothing of interest to mention."

The tech nodded, accepted the tote and her phone, and keyed the ignition without a blink.

Chapter Eleven

The mossy flagstone path at the Moreau compound was perpetually damp. Jonas cautiously stepped outside for the first time this evening and halted at an aroma on a strong gust of wind.

His head swiveled as Samuel bumped into him. "Fool, keep moving."

Jonas narrowed his gaze at his brother and shushed him. "All this open land... I thought I smelled a virgin."

Samuel shook his head. "Doubtful, they're as rare as a new angel. Move along, I would like to enjoy my meal while it's body temperature."

They shuffled into the barn turned laboratory and watched Ortega split the Cathcart draw between two drinking glasses. His head came up at the sound of the brothers arriving. "Instead of IVs, I want to see if your absorption rate improves when you drink your dinner."

Two brandy snifters sat under the harsh lighting. The competitive brothers walked as quickly as their steadily aging bodies allowed. With their usual greed, they eyed each glass trying to decipher if one possibly held a drop more than the other. They reached for the same glass.

Ortega stepped away from this evening's bickering. Samuel took a haughty sniff before he visually inspected the blood. Having it in a large snifter glass made it easier to see the rich color. His expression darkened as his nostrils flared and he noted the uncommon scent. "What is this?"

Ortega took a step back from the other side of the table and flipped through a lab book. "I detected increased HCG in Maisie's blood last night. She's pregnant. The HCG will increase in the next two weeks then taper down."

Jonas rolled the fluid in his mouth and swallowed. "I can't say anything for the mum, I can only hope the infant is tastier." Like a child with castor oil, Jonas held his nose and drank down the glass.

Ortega sniffed. "You don't expect to make a meal from an infant. They can only lose one or two milliliters daily."

Samuel finished his glass and immediately shook his head, working to release his necktie and shirt collar. "If heat transmits youth, I'm going to be thirty again shortly." He moved around the warren of medical equipment and stored bankers boxes of research. Rolling his shoulders, he stared enraptured at the clerestory windows near the ceiling. "Ahh, the moon."

Ortega's gaze traveled to see the awesome sight, but it was only a waning crescent. "Nothing fantastic that I see, sir, what do you find so fascinating?"

Jonas's eyelids fluttered as he shielded his eyes from the bright overhead lighting. "Has the ceiling always looked like that?" Jonas gawked upwards at the ancient wooden beams.

Ortega shot a glance up and dismissively shook his head. "This barn is ancient." He kept working, methodically recording his research.

Jonas shrieked and shivered. "How do snakes keep a building upright?"

"Snakes?" Samuel tsked at his brother as he ran his hands over his bare chest. It took him all of a minute to wrest out of the scratchy clothing he'd put on at dusk. "Have you lost your mind, brother? Anyone can see the animals are doing their best tumbling games. See the donkey on the back of the deer?"

Ortega now took two steps away from the brothers and kept his mouth closed.

Samuel smacked at the thermostat. "This is hot as Hades you have it so high. I feel like I'm in a jungle." With that comment, he dodged something he thought he saw out of the corner of his eye. He grabbed Jonas. "Beware, the ostrich will peck out your eyes."

Ortega turned to the tech. "Did you put something in their blood?"

The flippant phlebotomist shook her head. "Just blood in the blood." She watched the men avoiding unseen things as they hopped from floorboard to floorboard.

Samuel held one foot up as he balanced on the ball of his other foot. "The lava, I'm burning. Doctor, do something."

Ortega watched the tech retreat out the back door and zoom away as best her beater of a car would carry her.

Samuel, now stripped naked, pointed angrily at the doctor. "You're the one making this lava flow."

Jonas hopped to the tabletop and crouched. "The lava doesn't concern me as much as the snakes dropping from the ceiling. Brother, the doctor has trained them to drop on us."

Ortega tried logic. "No, I--"

Samuel pointed. "You're trying to kill us. You want it to look like an accident."

Ortega led the tripping vampires to the two medical recliners. "I need to check some levels on each of you. Lie back, close your eyes and imagine something beautiful."

Warily, Samuel sat and extended his arm. Dr. Ortega began the venipuncture process and with the first stick of the needle, Samuel screamed. "A stake! He's trying to stake us." He broke Ortega's arm. As it hung uselessly from the doctor's shoulder, Samuel saw his sister's corpse superimposed over Ortega's body. "You should burn in hell, my sister." He delivered a fist to Ortega's chest and crushed through the sternum to retrieve the doctor's beating heart. "Ah, the jewel of darkness." He held up the dripping organ and Jonas jubilantly danced over to grab a piece of it.

"Brother, do you taste the darkness?" Ortega's body collapsed in a bloody heap. "This heart is nothing like the good women we plundered last evening. Ah, that was good, virgin blood."

Jonas cackled. "Those ancient nuns put up a better fight than this sorry excuse for a mortal."

Samuel crouched, hands out to the side feeling the air. "Where is that young lady?" He darted looks around the lab, stopping at the tech's station. "Where is she?" He ran his bloody fingers over his lips, his tongue flicking like a lizard. "I require the soft luster of a woman's blood on my lips."

While Jonas writhed as he fought off imaginary snakes, headlights skimmed outside, and an engine stopped. The hallucinating Moreau brothers raised their heads in curiosity and stood still, detecting the incoming scents.

Samuel beheld his naked self and cleaned the doctor's blood off his hands at the sink. "Look alive, Jonas, we have visitors." He stepped behind the bookcase and turned off the lights.

Jonas smacked both hands over his mouth in a rapturous sigh. "Look how the lights break like glass, watch where you walk."

The barn's double doors flew open. The faint moonlight dimly illuminated the silhouettes of two hulking vampires in the doorway. The shorter vampire's voice echoed off the rafters. "I know you're here, Moreau, I can smell your vile odor." A mouse skittered in the newly darkened barn. Outside an owl hooted. In the distance, a truck's brakes whined as it ground to a stop. The sound of shuffling settled in the rafters. "Samuel, you and your idiot brother have taken us for the last time. The Fentanyl in the sulky was traced back to us." The husky man spat out. "We've been marked by Interpol. You owe us."

High-pitched juvenile laughter bounced off the rafters. "You'll never get us."

A beaker of sulfur flew past the taller vampire. "No games, Moreau. Come out like the man you pretend to be."

Samuel pressed his body against the bookcase. "Come in and get me if you are up to it. Is it you, Dong Shan?"

The taller man growled, and Samuel heard their footfalls. There was a flutter of wings in the darkness and the crunch of a squelching grip as Dong Shan thought he caught the neck of his nemesis. The owl dropped to the floor dead.

Jonas cackled. "Oh, how I'd like to deliver the serpents from the ceiling to you, Mr. Shan. You would recognize them as brothers." Shan headed in the direction of the voice, watching the ceiling for snakes.

Like the vile predator he was, Samuel crouched in wait until Shan crossed his path. The flamboyant fractals of moonlight kaleidoscoped as Shan stepped into its path. Samuel froze in adoration of the psychedelic designs. He saw the world through a medley of danger in shades of blood red and poisonous green. As Shan turned in his direction, Samuel sprang from his crouch and toppled his opponent to the floor.

With vicious blows, Samuel stunned the intruder. While the felled vampire lay splayed on the floor, Samuel sank his fangs into Shan's neck and cackled as he raised his head from his prey. Under the influence of Pegasus blood augmented by the drug dealer's blood, Samuel's energy knew no bounds. With a victory shriek worthy of a banshee, Samuel tore Shan's head off his shoulders and bowled it toward his horrified lieutenant. The double doors flew open, and Shan's enforcer bolted for his life back to the car.

Samuel and Jonas stood and scented the air. Recognizing the driver headed in the direction of the main road, the Moreaus bounded out the back door to face the car.

Jonas stood, hands on hips in the driveway as the rental car struck him head-on. Once he rolled under the car, he grabbed the undercarriage and held the vehicle in place long enough for Samuel to pull the driver out through the window.

Shrieks shattered the evening's peace as the brothers worked in tandem to draw and quarter their prey. The sounds of agony were replaced with the sloppy slurping of too many body fluids.

****

Matt, Rick, and Adam sat stock still watching the morbid tape in real-time and listening to the screams outside the building. Adam glanced at his two companions. "Anyone want to make bets on who is screaming?" The visual on the feed picked back up when Samuel and Jonas stumbled through the doors with half a torso.

Matt shot a finger at the monitor and bit his top lip. "I'm thinking it was the driver." The tape ran out as the brothers knelt over the headless body and drained Shan like a zebra killed on the savanna.

****

The Security Council of the Vampire Nation sat stunned as the video concluded. Rick addressed them via video call on a secure line. "My Lords, you can see from this recording why we implore immediate action against the brothers Moreau. They have always been indiscreet. Witness their admission to killing eleven nuns only one night ago. Now, this bizarre mutilation of two vampires. Can there be any doubt they are a liability to the family?"

"Thank you, Sir Richard." The head of the assembly acknowledged. "We will take this under advisement."

From behind the monitor Matt waved at Rick with a vicious frown. He pantomimed rocking a baby.

Rick leaned into the camera. "Advisement? This city is on alert due to the bloody murders at the convent. If they resort to infants and children, next there will be torch-bearing mobs. You cannot put off their punishment." The diplomats around the able exchanged aggrieved looks and the screen went black.

Matt stomped around to Rick's side. "I call bullshit. This is why I won't get involved with your damn politics."

Chapter Twelve

Isla looked at her lonely twin bed as her thoughts gravitated to Gerry. She reminisced about their moments in his luxurious curtained bed. Then she remembered waking up to a dead man... She'd had such hope and for what? It was never to be. How strange to think that a week ago, vampires were creatures of fiction? How could her heart ache for one so deadly?

Weariness drove her under the sheets and smothered beneath the heavy quilt, she closed her eyes and her long day appeared like a film strip in her mind. Gerry McIntosh is a vampire... *Surely, there were other vampires? He couldn't be the only one. The Moreaus wanted their blood daily... but her family had no blood disease... Why? What were they doing with the blood?* Her exhausted body fell into disturbing dreams.

Ian's cries woke the entire house before sunrise. His heavy footfalls tracked each hallway as he shouted. "Maisie, if you've fallen call out."

Isla and Caitrin collided in the third-floor hall tightening the belts on their robes. Lights came on all over the house. They hurried down the stairs to the first floor. "Ian, what's wrong?"

Ian paced, his hand swiping agitatedly through his hair. "I can't find her anywhere. Her car is here, she's not in bed. I came home from the distillery and she's not here. The window in the bedroom is wide open."

Isla half sleepwalked up the stairs and into the second-floor bedroom to see the casement window cast wide open. She shivered and thought of closing it, but then considered her fingerprints. Using the sleeve of her robe, she caught the handle and cranked it back into its channel to staunch the ice-cold breeze. "Did you check the basement?"

Ian's eyes were wide with alarm. "Of course. You think I'd be making this racket if she was here?"

Drew caught his brother-in-law by the neck and steadied him. "Brother, is any car missing?"

Ian sagged. "No."

Bram questioned. "The barn?"

"Not there," Ian confirmed.

Drew frowned and reached for the phone. "We need to call the authorities."

Isla volunteered. "I need to dress. I'll come back down and put on the coffee."

As she drew on heavy jeans and a thick sweater. Thoughts of the nuns haunted her. They were drained of blood. Intuition tweaked her sanity telling her she needed to call Gerry. She ruthlessly ignored that thought.

****

By noon, a full contingent of police searched every building on the property, including the castle's warren of cellars. The damp, dank and dark recesses were off-limits for safety's sake, but they were a perfect hiding place.

The police family liaison officer addressed the Cathcart clan waiting in the kitchen. The woman dressed warmly for the day was empathetic but firm. "We came out because of your wife's condition, Mr. Bruce. She's an adult and we have to respect the fact that she may have decided to go off on her own. Pregnancy can plant funny notions in a woman's head. If she's not home within forty-eight hours, file a missing person's report."

It took all Bram's strength to hold Ian back. Isla bit her thumbnail as she watched her family's responses to the army of police constables retreating to their cars. With a deep breath, she turned from the family and poured herself a tall coffee.

"Funny notions? What the hell? She's preparing the nursery. She's revamped our kitchen to cook all the right foods." Ian slammed his fist on the table. "She learned to knit. Is that the sign of a woman with notions? The window was wide open, and she's gone."

Isla sipped silently thinking. *The second-floor window.* She slipped out of the house while her family tried to calm Ian. Underneath Maisie's bedroom window the grass was flat while the dew fell, leaving it mashed with large footprints. *Do these belong to the authorities or the kidnapper?* No signs of a ladder. The intuitive tweaking she'd felt all morning was now a scream. *I have to talk to Gerry.*

She returned to the kitchen and stood in the doorway, everyone turned. Isla shrank back. Walking purposefully to her purse and keys, she announced, "I have to go and talk to someone."

Drew postured, hands on hips. "Now?"

"Yes, right now." She stepped around him and palmed her keys. "I'll stay in touch. Call me if you get news."

"Isla..." Closing the door cut off their protests.

Isla kept the car radio on as she fought through afternoon traffic hoping and fearing she would hear news of Maisie. She immediately found a parking space outside Gerry's apartment building and stewed remembering he entered a code to get in. She pulled a shopping tote from her back seat, tossed her purse inside as if it were groceries, and waited. She watched a woman with a baby stroller approach the door and jumped in line behind her, slipping through the entrance with ease. The mother claimed the first elevator and Isla killed time at the bulletin board, wanting to stay as anonymous as possible.

As she rode up to Gerry's penthouse her anxiety increased with each floor. The doors whooshed open, and she froze momentarily. *What am I going to say?* Isla wrapped her hands around the silver letter opener in her bag. *He did say silver could hurt him.*

She pounded furiously on the door. She leaned into the doorbell. She pulled out her phone, dialed his number, heard the ring, and sighed.

It took maybe a minute before Gerry opened the door dressed in his robe, a day's beard on his jaw. He blinked at her. "I knew it was you before I opened the door." She tilted her head at him and narrowed her eyes. He tapped his nose. "Vampire sense of smell. What do *you* want?"

"I think the Moreaus have Maisie. Are they vampires?"

Gerry regarded the echo in the hallway. "Come in."

She stood just in front of the closed door. "Are they vampires?"

Gerry gave her a bewildered look. "Samuel and Jonas Moreau?"

"Yes, does that mean they *are* vampires?" She gasped.

"I've heard they are. I don't know them. It's not like we have a big clubhouse where we all hang out. Tell me what happened."

By the time she finished the explanation, he'd coaxed her to sit.

She wrang her hands, trying to hold back tears and fear. "Gerry, Maisie's pregnant. What will they do to her? Please help me."

"Of course, I'll help you, darling. I don't know what's going on. I will find out and I have friends."

****

Isla called her family while Gerry dressed. "I'm with someone who's going to help us."

Drew's voice rang with doubt. "We'll meet you, where?"

Isla half-listened to Gerry preparing in the bedroom as she walked through the living room taking notice of every knickknack she hadn't noticed before. "No, stay home in case Maisie comes back. I've got this."

Gerry emerged from his dressing room wearing outdoor gear with hiking boots. His wool jacket and flat cap contrasted with his tartan flannel shirt.

Isla pointed at his layers of clothing. "I thought the cold didn't bother you."

"Lass, the cold doesn't bother me, but I'd stand out like a duck on the sidewalk if I wore body armor." He checked his pockets for his wallet and keys in front of the large mirror in the foyer.

Again, Isla tilted her head in confusion. "I can see your reflection, what's up with that?"

Gerry waved the question off. "Today's mirrors aren't silver-backed." He grinned close to his image and checked his teeth. "Look, ma, no blood."

Isla rolled her eyes. "You find humor in this?"

"I do when it comes to helping someone who called me a demon." He palmed his car keys and led her down to his auto.

Once they were on the road, Isla settled and took a deep breath. "About that demon thing. The priest said calling you that was blasphemous."

Gerry gave her the fisheye. "Did he know why you called me a demon?"

"Uh, no."

He nodded. "I see. What else did the priest say?"

Isla took another deep breath and kept her gaze on her lap. "He said I should be kind." She looked over to Gerry. "It's very kind of you to help me after the things I said."

Gerry nodded to her while his gaze stayed on the road. "Of course I would help you in a situation like this." He paused and shifted uncomfortably. "I probably should have told you what I was before we got involved."

Isla snorted. "I probably wouldn't have believed you."

Gerry took his eyes off the winding road for a moment to gaze at her. "Would you believe me if I said you took my breath away?"

Her face down, she wiped at a tear that opened a stream of hot tears down her cheeks. "Is that why you didn't tell me about yourself?"

"Yes, partly. I wanted to be normal just a little longer. I've found that when women know what I am, they begin to expect things from me."

Isla's head swiveled in disbelief. "Like what?"

Gerry shrugged. "Within the family, as we call it, we have quite a lifestyle. It's exciting, even for a mortal looking through the keyhole. And then there's the whole sex thing."

She winced. "Sex thing?" Now she sat with her back to the door studying him. "Yeah, Gerry, you're good, on the high end of good."

Gerry's reaction caused him to brake too hard at the traffic light. "The high end of good? Do you mean great? But you have to understand, you haven't had sex with a vampire yet."

Isla waved a finger at him. "Did you send in a surrogate? Who did I sleep with?"

"I was saving the big show for when you knew what I was. Believe me, there's a difference."

Isla looked around the familiar countryside. "Wait a minute, this is the road to Ayrshire Manor."

"Aye, it is."

"Your friends are at the manor?"

"They flew in to help with your title."

Isla sat gobsmacked. "The Hiatts and the Brenners? Is this how you know the Hiatts?"

"Oh, I've known Rick and Matt for decades."

"How many decades?" Isla pressed fearing the worst. "Before you answer, how old are you?"

"I'm older than you think, I wouldn't want age to put you off."

"So, how many decades have you known them?" Isla swallowed hard.

Gerry hemmed and wiped at his dry mouth. "Ah, about two... decades."

Isla sat back in the car seat and stared at the beautifully landscaped manor. "So, they're like you?"

Gerry cleared his throat. "Well, they're not Scottish. Rick is Irish, originally."

Isla's eyes widened. "No wonder he spoke of historical figures as though he knew them."

Gerry pulled up to the front door in the circular drive. "Just a bit of undead decorum, don't ask how old they are or how they became vampires."

Isla raised a brow. "Is this vampire protocol?"

Gerry hesitated. "Remember when your mum told you to respect your elders? These folks are the ones she was speaking of."

Isla covered her mouth and sighed. "Right."

Willow answered the door. "Gerry, what has you up at this hour?"

He frowned and shook his head. "Isla's pregnant sister has disappeared. We thought we'd beg your help."

Willow's hand flew to her mouth. "Come in, Adam will wake the rest of the family." Kindly, she wrapped an arm around Isla and led her to a spacious kitchen where she put on a tea kettle to boil. "They'll only be a few moments."

Isla fingered the spoon on the saucer. "You aren't like the Hiatts and the Brenners?"

Willow's smile softened as she put the tea box before Isla. "If you believe the Wizard of Oz, I'm a horse of a different color." Isla caught Gerry and Willow smirking behind her back.

"Oh, yes, I'll catch up with that when this is over."

****

While Isla unloaded on the vampires, Matt paced back and forth in front of the hearth, head down, hands deep in his pockets. Rick sat like the lord of the manor in a tall chair eerily unmoving, his hands resting over the chair's plush arms. Anna and Cat sat on the love seat, their gazes moving from person to person.

"The Moreaus are vampires, aren't they? I think they've got Maisie."

Matt stood with his back to Isla and aimed an accusatory glare at Rick. In subtones, he spoke. "You and your damned vampire council protocol. The responders are still twelve hours out."

Rick rose "Excuse us, Ms. Cathcart." He led Matt to the pool table at the other end of the thirty-foot room. Casually Rick rolled pool balls back and forth as he spoke. "Clearly, we can't wait for the responders. I think she's right, they have her sister, and we must intervene *now*."

Matt leaned on the pool table rails and huffed out a breath. "What's our plan of attack? We have three vamps and a dragon shifter."

Rick rocked on the balls of his feet and looked back at the women. "There you go, dear boy, pissing off the women."

"After what we saw on the monitor last night, you think I'm allowing the Moreaus near my mate?" He made eye contact with Cat and by her expression, he knew she would not stay idle. He shook his head in resignation and turned to Rick. "The women will need to provide the very important role of calling for cleanup."

Rick drew back at that comment. "Dear boy, I know I prefer being the lover, but I've got a few battles left in me. Plus, we have a dragon. What did Tony Stark say? We have a Hulk. Could Hulk breathe fire?"

They looked over at Adam being the sensitive therapist sitting on the sofa holding Isla's hand as Willow sat on the other side, nodding in agreement to whatever they were discussing.

"He doesn't look high octane at the moment." Matt leaned over to get a better view of the rest of the crew.

Rick waved Matt off. "He comes through in a clutch." Rick looked back at the group watching the two vampires. "Gentlemen and Willow, could we strategize a moment in the library?"

Willow gave the ladies a wondering look as she rose and walked with her mate and Gerry to join Matt and Rick down the hall.

****

The Grandfather clock struck three. Cat smiled warmly at their guest. "Would you like more tea, Isla? Have you eaten? I'll bet you haven't eaten all day."

Isla covered her neck with a hand. "You have food here? I thought…"

Anna p'shawed. "We have mortal friends. Remember Willow and Adam are not vampires."

Isla looked down the long dark hall and whispered. "What are they?"

Anna and Cat chuckled. Cat replied. "Well, that's a funny question. What do you know about shifters?"

Isla's expression darkened. "Are they werewolves?"

Anna waved that thought away. "Oh, my goodness, no."

Isla nodded actively. "Well, that's a good thing because tonight is not a full moon, they'd be no help."

Cat nodded in agreement. "Absolutely. Adam is a Dragon shifter and Willow is a Pegasus shifter."

Isla put her arms out to her sides like wings. "Pegasus?"

Cat went on. "Wait until you see her, she's beautiful. Well, he is, too, come to that."

Isla squinted into her memory. "Pegasus, like in Hercules?"

Anna led them into the kitchen, rested her elbows on the island and laughed. "Oh, she's prettier than that. I know you've been upset, but you have to keep up your strength. Let's get you a sandwich."

As the women circled the large island Isla studied each of them. "When was the last time you ladies had a sandwich?"

Cat opened the large refrigerator and smiled. "You mean how long have we been vampires?"

Anna chuckled as she opened the bread box. "I haven't had a carb in six years."

Cat nodded agreeably. "Seven for me." The two vampires put together a sandwich from the food they kept. "Salmon, onion, and crème cheese on brown bread, okay?"

Anna held up the tea kettle. "Ready for a refill?"

Isla nodded and waggled a finger between them as she accepted the sandwich and tea. "You two don't seem very sensitive about my curiosity."

Cat and Anna gave her quizzical looks. Anna shrugged. "Why would we be? Are you sensitive about being mortal?"

Isla looked back toward the library. "No. Gerry said…"

Cat laughed. "Gerry's a bit oversensitive around you right now. He was very upset when you had your… er… little falling out."

Isla ate two bites and sat the sandwich down. "This is truly delicious, but I just can't eat right now." Her eyes teared as she pushed the sandwich away. "Can we wrap this half for Maisie, I know she's going to be hungry."

Anna and Cat nodded somberly. Anna placed an arm around Isla, and she looked up mournfully. "They think something terrible has happened to her, don't they?"

Cat's blue eyes filled with unshed tears. "Every moment they keep her alive is a plus. If I told you all the scrapes Matt has gotten out of, you'd think I was spinning fantasy."

As Anna finished bagging the sandwich, a piece of fruit, and bottled water, they heard the library door open.

Rick stood in command mode. He strode behind Anna and wrapped his arms around her waist. "Cupcake, you and Cat get your tattie field clothes on and fire up your Land Rover. Isla will ride with you. Everyone else will ride with me."

Chapter Thirteen

They parked under a copse of trees near the Moreau compound. The rural scene was typically bucolic. Rick checked his thigh holster for his machete while Matt unlocked his katana. Gerry smiled innocently as he withdrew an odd, sheathed weapon.

Adam gawked. "That's one wicked-looking thing. What does that do?"

Gerry held it to the dying afternoon light and the sun glinted sharply on the sickle hook's razor edge. "It chops, it cuts, it trims, it prunes. It's my pal." Gerry expertly swung the unique weapon.

Adam nodded at the men. "It's the twenty-first century and your weapons are *so* medieval."

Rick gave him a sardonic look. "Well, Sparky, our bodies don't make fire."

Adam began dropping his clothes. He looked over his shoulder at Anna's Land Rover. "Are they ready for this?"

Gerry's hand fell over his undead heart. "I don't know if I'm ready for this." He pointed to the half-naked Viking in front of him. He turned to Matt and Rick. "Are your wives used to this?"

Rick nodded in the direction of the Land Rover and three pairs of inquisitive female eyes watched with interest. "I don't think so."

Just then the air moved with a magical aura. A striking black and white pinto horse emerged from the woods. Rick's jaw dropped. "That can't be Willow, the last time I saw her she was like a delicate Arabian."

Adam held out his hand and Willow's Pegasus moved beside him. She now stood seventeen hands of sleekly muscled war steed. His fingers threaded through her thick mane affectionately. "My lady has been working out. Impressive, isn't she?"

Gerry stood back as Willow shimmered her wings into existence. He gaped back at Isla in the SUV, and she stared back spellbound. *After seeing this, vampires will be so yesterday.*

By the time Willow tested her fully emerged wings, Anna was out of the car walking to meet her, an apple in her hand. Gerry could have sworn the horse smiled and nibbled daintily on the treat. Anna petted her nose affectionately and positioned a camera between Willow's ears. She synced the camera to her tablet and nodded at Willow. "Okay, you're cleared for take-off." The Pegasus tested the camera's stability and pranced off. Gerry turned when he heard Isla's gasp and looked in the direction she pointed.

Adam's dragon stood grandly. His muscular arms were now front limbs ending in three vicious claws. Ominous curved horns grew from his skull. His cool Nordic coloring transformed into shades of carmine and gold. His aqua eyes burned like fire. The scales down his spine glistened and moved with the sound of articulated leather. His haunches rippled with muscles as he flexed his back legs.

Gerry retreated as Adam reared on those powerful back legs and released his leathery wings. The moment froze in time as Willow fluttered toward the towering giant and they touched noses. As big as she was, she was dwarfed by her dragon mate. He snorted a tiny trail of smoke.

Rick shook his head. "Get a room. Only you can prevent forest fires." The dragon snorted and a stream of fire died in the air a few feet over Rick's head. "Okay, point taken." He turned to the very ordinary-looking vampires. "Everybody ready?"

****

The women gathered around Anna's tablet to watch the mayhem. From Willow's camera, they could see the three vampires easily vault the fence.

Isla blinked. "Did they just jump twelve feet, straight up?"

Cat nodded, still watching her mate disappear behind the compound walls. "Twelve feet is nothing, it's fun."

Adam stayed behind out of sight, as much as a two-story-tall dragon could crouch behind the fence. Willow gracefully flew to land on the barn's roof, supporting her weight with an extended flutter of her wings. She took a panorama shot of the buildings. Isla could see the farmhouse, the barn, and two storage warehouses.

They watched their men slide open the barn door and enter while Willow fluttered down to a fallow garden area in front of the farmhouse. She whinnied high and strong repeatedly. The drapes drew back an inch in the front window. Back drafting her wings, Willow reared on her hind legs, whinnied again, and trotted a spirited circle in the weed-riddled garden.

The front slowly opened, and two faces peeked out through a crevice. Willow turned her back, kicked mightily, and then took off at a trot. With what looked like a short leap, she was airborne but hovered a few feet off the ground. The door opened fully, and Samuel and Jonas Moreau gawked.

Isla saw the rejuvenated vampires. "They were in their sixties when we met them. But now, what are they in their fifties? How can you age backward?"

Cat put her arm around Isla. "Honey, it was the Cathcart blood. But it couldn't get them back to their twenties, so they went berserk. They thought younger blood would be the answer."

Isla stared at Cat in horror. "That's why they kidnapped Maisie?"

Cat nodded. They watched Willow fly back to the barn roof and the Moreaus threw open the barn door. Willow lightly trotted to a skylight and aimed the camera through the dirty glass.

Anna angled the tablet. "There's Maisie. She's handcuffed to the gurney."

Isla squinted into the tablet. "It looks like she's moving, that's a good sign."

Cat reasoned. "They aren't going to hurt her if they want that baby."

Isla collapsed against the car. Cat caught her and looked over her head at Anna. "That was too much info." She fanned Isla. "We're going to get her out of there." She nodded toward the tablet. "Look, there's Gerry now."

Isla saw the Moreaus stalking the room, their chins up as they scented the air for intruders. Isla's hand flew to her face as she peered between her fingers. "Oh, my God, they're so ghastly. Look at their eyes."

The brothers' heads jerked as they spied Gerry at Maisie's side snapping the handcuffs.

"Oh, he looks like them... No, Gerry." Her cries turned to sobs.

Cat soothed. "He's ready for battle. He can't fight other vampires in his mortal form."

Isla's sobs continued as she watched Maisie shrinking back from all of them.

Freed from the gurney in a second, Gerry got Maisie on her feet. He stood between her and the Moreaus. "You don't come to Scotland and attack our women."

The Moreaus, now undead monsters, bared their fangs and hissed. The energy required to hold their ferocity reduced them to primal creatures. They grunted and snarled in a show of rage. Their hands morphed into clawed fingers as they hulked before Gerry. Maisie's breath hitched as she cowered and sobbed behind her rescuer.

Gerry nodded. "Look alive, gentlemen. You have guests."

Rick and Matt descended from the rafters behind the brothers. And when the Moreaus turned to them their ferocity slipped, drained by the energy they expended taunting the intruders.

Rick widened his stance and bounced battle-ready. "Aren't you two full of sound and fury signifying nothing!"

The Moreaus looked at each other. Samuel's growls became words. "He reads, how nice."

Jonas cackled, looking more like a fishwife the longer he menaced.

Gerry tucked Maisie behind him and backed out of the barn while Rick and Matt kept the brothers at bay.

Willow now stood pawing the ground impatiently. Gerry ran Maisie to the Pegasus. "You ride bareback, Maisie?"

Maisie pushed back tangles of hair and stared at the winged horse. "I'm dreaming." She looked back at Gerry. "Sure, I ride."

Gerry threaded his fingers into a step and Maisie vaulted onto the horse's back. He patted Willow's neck. "Hold on, Maisie. Hold tight."

Maisie squeaked as Willow's wings unfurled and they rose majestically in flight. She giggled until she saw a dragon. Then she hunkered close to Willow's neck and closed her eyes until she was on the ground again.

"They say pregnant women have odd dreams. This is one for the books." She slipped off the Pegasus right into Isla's arms.

****

Gerry ran back to the barn as soon as Willow spirited Maisie safely away. He saw the evidence of the Moreaus' previous carnage as Rick and Matt battled with the true demons. It was a life-and-death struggle complicated for the Moreaus by the fact that their usual vampiric strength waned with each desperate swing of their weapons.

With a silent shared nod, the brothers dropped their machetes and pulled out .44 Magnums. Samuel boasted, "You watch movies, you know where this is going. You brought knives to a gun fight."

Rick chuckled. He leaned against the wall and rested one foot over the other. "No, we brought a dragon to a gun fight."

The corner of the wood barn ripped away by a punch of three mighty claws. The roof sagged as old, dry wood complained.

Jonas's hands went up, still holding the gun that was far too powerful for an inexperienced shooter. As more and more of the walls flew away, his trigger finger let loose. Pigeons fell dead from the rafters, and he screamed like a fish wife confronting a rat.

Matt and Rick dropped back as Adam's magnificent dragon stalked forward. Samuel hid, crouched behind an upended worktable. Adam flamed and the table burst into ash. Samuel cursed and ran for the door. Adam shot a single stream of fire, and the vampire was no more. Poof, he was ash.

Jonas tossed his gun far away and dropped to his knees. "I implore you. I never like him. He bullied me. He made me do these things."

Rick stuck his head around what was left of the barn. "Sparky, Matt, and I will take this one. But stand by, we're not done."

Jonas dropped back on his heels. "You're not done? What will you do with me?"

Matt circled the defeated demon while he weighed his katana in one hand. "In 1922, Veronique Moreau crossed my path. It was like the superstition about black cats. To this day, I prefer black cats." He leaned over the quivering man. "It's time for you to join the heavenly choir immortal."

Rick rushed up at vampire speed. "Oh, dear boy, you've got that wrong. Where he's going, it's not heaven." Rick smacked the broad blade of his machete on his palm.

Rick nodded to Gerry in the background. "Dear boy, I'd say this victory belongs to you."

Jonas's head swiveled from vampire to vampire and before he could turn to lock eyes with the Scotsman, Gerry caught Jonas's hair from behind and the hooked blade sang through the air. Jonas's body fell forward, and Gerry dropped the head.

Rick motioned to their dragon. "We're going to skedaddle. For safety's sake," Rick made a large lasso-like circle with his hand, "…everything must go."

The hulking dragon stalked toward the house and in moments flames consumed it. Rick, Matt, and Gerry pushed open the compound gate as the building crackled, sputtered, and began its implosion. The sounds of gas lines rupturing, and water steaming echoed in the calm night air. When the dragon's tail swept the ground and he turned to the old wooden barn, his gust of fire whooshed up the rafters, igniting a roaring blaze.

As the group reunited, they watched in tremulous awe as the buildings sizzled and popped. Their senses were assaulted by the chemicals and the fertilizers stored in the back. A crop's worth of potatoes went up with the storage building.

Gerry pulled people back. "Guys, we need to get out of here. It's like a college bonfire now, but it's about to blow."

Anna led Gerry to join the women in her car, and Isla turned and sniffed. "Suddenly, I'm craving baked potatoes, how about you, Maisie?"

Maisie huddled under a light fleece. "Yeah, when I wake up from this dream, I could eat."

Gerry chuckled and put an arm around Maisie. "Just sleep, darlin'."

Maisie nodded her head before she rested it on Gerry's shoulder. "This started as a nightmare. It's okay now, this was fun, kind of. I liked the flying horse."

The convoy returned to Cathcart Castle while sirens wailed past them.

****

Isla called home as soon as they hit the road. Her family stood on the front porch, Ian pacing and anxiously awaiting Maisie's return.

As the car turned down the long drive. Isla whispered to Gerry. "How are we playing this, Mr. Vampire?"

Gerry's brows knit as he drew a finger to his lips, he glanced down kindly at a sleeping Maisie.

Cat turned from the front and spoke softly. "In situations of supernatural intervention, we always find it best to let the mortal express what they've seen and reply with a mundane explanation."

Isla nodded. "Does this sort of thing happen a lot?"

Cat was about to open her mouth when Gerry cut her off. "No."

Isla must have felt his words like a slap. "Just asking." Isla smiled and waved to the family bolting down the porch steps.

Gerry exited the car with Maisie in his arms and delivered her to her smiling husband. Ian's knees bent accepting his sleeping wife. "You're a strong one. Gerry. Want a job in a distillery?"

Maisie woke and stretched. "Oh, Ian, put me down. I'll break your back." Ian let her slide gently to the ground. "Nonsense, you're light as a feather." Isla watched Ian and Gerry exchange a smile.

As Rick, Matt, Adam, and Willow emerged from the second car, Caitrin waved "Is Dr. Clarke with yee?"

Adam grinned. "Not today, I'm afraid."

Caitrin looked disappointed but carried on. "Where was she? What happened?"

Maisie leaned into Ian's embrace. "All I remember is a dragon and a flying horse."

Cat stepped forward. "She was with the Moreaus. They drugged her. We were able to give an antidote on the way home."

Ian looked up with concern. "And the baby?"

Cat waved away his concern. "Will be fine."

Isla motioned. "Let's get out of this chill wind."

Ian turned to Gerry. "Where are those doctors now?"

Gerry nodded solemnly. "There was a terrible explosion and they died in the fire."

Caitrin gasped as the group stood together on the porch. She fanned the scent of smoke. "Sounds about right considering how you all smell like a charcoal grill."

With an air that clearly said, 'go now,' Isla extended her hand to Gerry. "Thank you all for coming to our rescue. You must understand our need for privacy."

Rick Hiatt stepped to Isla. "I'm glad you understand the need for discretion. We're happy to respect your privacy and take our leave."

As the head of the Cathcart family, Drew ushered the visitors down the front steps "I expect we'll hear from the authorities soon."

Matt grinned softly with a shake of his head. "We've kept your names out of this."

Gerry stopped and turned to Isla. "Your car is at my place."

Isla bruskly replied. "I'll have Bram pick it up." She dropped her chin and returned to Gerry with a wan smile. "Thank you, Gerry."

Chapter Fourteen

By ten o'clock, Ian fell asleep on the sofa 'guarding' the house. As Isla closed up and locked the doors, she smiled that Ian was down for the night. *The poor chap is finally getting some rest.* Isla was supremely serene knowing Maisie was upstairs asleep in her bed. She made her way to the bedroom where she put another log on the fire and stopped to watch her sister.

As she approached the bed, Maisie raised the covers. "Climb in bed like we did as kids with Mum. We can cuddle until we fall asleep."

As Isla's head hit the pillow and she saw Maisie's eyes flutter closed, her mother's habits flashed through her memory. Isla went to sleep thinking of Mum's tall tales.

The creak of the floorboards and fierce blowing wind and rain woke Isla. She saw Maisie's silhouette as she slid into her slippers and robe. "Did I wake you, Isla? I just need a hot cup of tea."

Isla glanced at the clock on the mantle. "At three in the morning?"

Maisie smiled sweetly, her hand low on her still flat belly. "Yes."

Isla groaned and got up, reaching for her robe. "Alright then. I guess I'll join you."

Downstairs the women tiptoed past Ian still sleeping on the sofa. Maisie contemplated him fondly. "I'll get him up when we go back to bed."

Drew sat at the kitchen table lit by the dim hood light over the stove. He raised a mug to them as they entered. "I couldn't sleep. Care for tea and a little more?" He held up a bottle of their whisky.

Maisie walked to the stove for the tea box. "Just tea for me, please."

Isla reached for a glass. "I'll have her share of more."

Maisie brought back the tea ball and played with filling it. "You know what I've been thinking about?"

Isla braced herself. "What's that?"

Maisie nodded to Drew. "Remember that fantastic tale Mum used to tell about Ibrox?"

Drew's expression soured. "Dad said that was all nonsense and we were not to speak of it."

Maisie gave him a rebellious look. "Well, Dad isn't here." She carried on as if he'd never interrupted. "Mum said she was rescued by a man with glowing eyes who fed her something red."

Isla stopped mid-sip. "What?"

Drew shook his head. "Well, you know right there, it's fantastical. Of course, when a doctor wears a mask, the light reflects off his glasses." He chuckled. "A doctor treated Mum."

Maisie pouted and turned her back on him to retrieve the whistling kettle from the stove. "But I did a school report on that disaster. There was no medical help on sight. Mum said she saw him pull the railing up from her chest. It was superhuman."

Drew shrugged. "She'd been knocked on the head. She didn't know what she saw."

Maisie was emphatic. "Dad and Mum made an acquaintance with three people behind them. One of them was the man who gave them that ratty old Rangers blanket. I will always remember Mum saying she thought she was seeing angels when the man named Gerry told his friend to work on her first."

Drew dipped his chin and looked up at her over his glasses. "You're balmy."

Maisie threw her hands up in disgust. "Mum has pictures from that day."

Isla's gaze narrowed as she balanced her chin on his hand. "Where?"

Maisie pointed in the general direction of the living room. "In the oldest photo album when Das and Mum were teenagers."

Isla was up and at the overstuffed black album on the top shelf. An old-fashioned album with black pages and white corner protectors, it held pictures with dates written in white ink. She brought it back to the table and set it before Maisie. "Where's the picture?"

Maisie flipped past school photos of teens on Vespas and bikes. School days showed faded color photos of dances and graduation. When Maisie turned to the photo of Da standing at the Ibrox gate she slowed down, and her finger trailed to locate the faces. Before Maisie's fingers stopped Isla gasped. Her mum had taken several candid photos of a long-haired Gerry McIntosh.

Maisie pointed at the cheering young man. "This was the man called Gerry." Her finger trailed past a young woman to a blurry image of another man. "This is the man who did it."

"Did what?" Isla asked excitedly.

Maisie lowered her hands to calm Isla. Her finger returned to Gerry's face. "This man told the blurry man to help mum first, he wasn't as bad off."

Drew curled his lips. "Neither one of them was that bad off if they were up and talking by the time Dad got back."

Maisie's gaze went to the ceiling, and she closed her eyes. "Mum said there were people on top of her. She couldn't breathe, this man was..." She concentrated to retrieve the name. "Conall... and he started yelling to clear people so he could bend the bar off Mum. She remembered him laying her on a table and she heard Gerry say, 'help her first'."

"That's good." Drew snorted. "And I guess his magic wand did the rest."

Maisie gave him a shake of her head. "I believe her."

Drew looked disgusted. "Well, you came home telling us you'd seen a dragon and rode a flying horse. So, I am sure you do believe her."

Isla looked down at the two open pages of discolored Kodachrome photos. Her mum had snapped a few pictures while Gerry cheered his team alone. Isla recognized the girl was enamored with the blurry friend. *Could this have been when he was made a vampire? What else happened that day at Ibrox?*

****

The following day was Saturday and Isla rose, did her hair, applied careful makeup, dressed in her best casual clothes, and added a light but alluring perfume all the while convincing herself the careful grooming had nothing whatever to do with Gerry.

She passed up breakfast with the family except for a cup of tea and told Bram, "If you'll take me to my car, I'll drive home after some errands."

****

Isla watched Bram leave before she turned to the building entrance. *Following a resident worked once.* Isla watched an older woman with a teacup poodle. The doggie moved faster than the woman, but Isla beat them both to the door, offering to hold it open after the woman slowly entered her code.

"You're so sweet, Boodles and I thank you." The white-haired woman nodded and headed to the open elevator. Isla killed time at the bulletin board waiting for the next lift.

****

Gerry hung in that limbo between going to ground and turning off his mind. Sometimes the fact that vampires don't sleep was so annoying. He waited for the switch following his circadian rhythm of the Moon rise and set to kick in. *So why is my brain overriding that rhythm?* It was that troubling subject of the Cathcarts.

What's the deal with this family? Why me? First Lyra, then Isla, then Maisie. Has the Universe declared me the family savior? Vampire logic is that we share a bloodline. Although Lyra was not made, she carried a small amount of Conall's blood line and passed it to her children. Gerry twisted and turned at the thought. *Is it incestuous that I'm attracted to Isla? This isn't in the books. At least none of my books. It's probably best we don't see each other.*

He was alone again. He wasn't loving work recently. What did Rick Hiatt say about reinventing himself? *America is nice, is it large enough to elude my ex? Ireland is close. Have I pissed off anyone in Ireland? If Adam and Willow are moving here, perhaps there's a position at Erne Castle.*

His solitude was invaded by a heavy fist on his front door, and then the repetitive drill of his doorbell. Luckily, his phone was set to do not disturb and Gerry could only imagine the number of hang-ups Isla would try before she got in her car and drove home.

Best we don't see each other again.

****

Frustrated with unsatisfied curiosity, Isla's cellphone rang in her purse. Thinking it might be Gerry, she pulled the car over on the country road to dig it out and safely answer. "Isla Cathcart."

The cheerful voice that greeted her was a vampire, but not the right one. "Hi, this is Anna Hiatt. I have a cup of tea with your name on it if you would like to join us this afternoon."

"Oh, Anna, have the papers arrived?"

"Yes, as a matter-of-fact Rick has some things he'd like to go over with you."

Isla glanced up the road. "I'm not far. But isn't this early for you?"

Anna laughed musically. "Oh, we lead a varied schedule when we travel. Come on over."

"I'll see you in ten minutes." *So, is Gerry playing possum, or can vampires 'ghost' you?*

****

Isla's ring at the door was answered by the housekeeper who escorted her to the kitchen. *For people who don't eat, they spend a lot of time in the kitchen.* When she came upon them, Rick, Anna, Matt, and Cat sat with tall mugs. Isla had no desire to see what filled them. Adam dug into a monstrous dish of bacon, sauteed mushrooms, tomato, a tattie scone, and eggs with coffee. His hand dwarfed his coffee mug. Willow daintily ate porridge with mixed fruits and tea.

As Isla entered the kitchen, the men stood. That was one for the books. That hadn't happened in her house since her parents died. Willow pulled out a chair and asked, "How is Maisie doing today?"

"She's feeling well. She's a little ticked off that the family thinks she hallucinated a dragon and a flying horse, but she's not sure about that herself." Isla looked at Rick. "I hear the papers have arrived?"

Rick toasted with his cup. "The package is in the study, but there's something we'd like to discuss first."

Here it comes. What debt do I owe? Isla wrapped her hands around the tea mug after Willow placed it before her. "And what is that?"

Rick's gaze was direct. "You've heard of Consort Group International Resorts." Isla sniffed and before she could say something derogatory, he continued. "As it happens, Consort Group was formed in 1922 by three like-minded vampire investors. Matt and I teamed up with Venus Aquillius in Los Angeles. Through the decades it went international and recently, Adam and Willow have become partners."

Isla shifted in her seat and wondered if this was a multi-level marketing spiel. She crossed her ankles to keep her knees from knocking. Her mind flittered past every remark she'd made about sex clubs in their presence as she sought words. "I... umm... 'er...'"

Rick waved away her awkwardness. "We know you have some misgivings about what we do at our resorts. I have to say you're misinformed." He sat back; arms folded over his chest with a smug expression.

Isla sighed with relief. "So, they're not sex clubs?"

Matt's crooked smile emerged. "Well…"

Adam crossed his silverware over his empty plate and pushed it forward to make room for his hands on the table. "Isla, you're a sophisticated woman. I think you can stand a little frank talk." Isla swallowed hard. "Vampires need blood. When willing donors allow the vampire's bite, it is orgasmic. Therefore, to stop unnecessary feeding accidents vampires recruited the most likely donor pool. At the Gaoler, the 'sex club'," he made air quotes, "that pool is made up of submissives."

As Adam dove deeper into the club's rationale, Isla could feel her face flame. *What's a submissive? The question must have flashed across my forehead.* Isla's gaze roamed from Anna to Cat to Willow. They were all so calm.

In her wonderful educator style, Willow explained. "There is a lifestyle within the fetish community made up of Dominants and submissives, describing men or women who are submissive to their partner."

Isla shifted uncomfortably. *This is worse than my mum's sex talk.*

Rick picked up the narration. "Vampires are natural Dominants. Much as dragons are natural Dominants. Dom/sub couples who wish to define the relationship form an agreement about what is acceptable, and you know what?" The question hung in the silent room for Isla to answer.

She blinked hard. "What?"

"This contract gets partners talking about what they like and don't like... in bed or at the Gaoler."

Anna caught Rick's hand in hers and smiled sublimely. "Plus, it's incredibly sexy to discuss sexual rewards... and punishments openly and out loud with your partner."

Isla felt her forehead crease. "And I need to know this why?"

Matt slid back in the chair with his manspread slouch. *What is that smile about?* "Because the sub is in charge. They set the limits. The donors who feed vampires are excited, they're pleasured. Subs come back as often as they can."

"And how often is that?" Her words leaked out of numb lips.

Cat smiled sweetly. "If you went to the blood bank, every fifty-four days. With vamps? It depends on how much blood they take.

When a donor feeds a vamp, they tap a pint by way of fang on flesh. If you're a mortal in a relationship with a vampire and they bite to achieve orgasm, they take a sip. You still go multiorgasmic but without much blood loss."

"Vampires have to bite to orgasm?" *Gerry never bit me, what are they talking about?* "So, that's why it sounds like you have a sex club?"

Matt sat up straighter and bit his bottom lip. "Well... It's hard to explain. Willow, can you share anything?"

Willow ran her hand through her hair. "You just love to remind me about my first night at Erne Castle when you and Rick had to oust someone who was playing rough."

Matt shrugged. "You could have admitted you knew about BDSM; we could tell by the look on your face you knew."

Isla's hands flew to the edge of the table to push back her chair. "This is sounding a lot like a sex club to me. What's BDSM?"

Anna gave the magicals a censorious glare. "BDSM is an acronym for bondage and discipline, domination and submission, sadism and masochism between consenting adults."

"They consent to that?" Isla's brows rose into her hairline.

Rick nodded. "It sounds far worse than it is. Nothing is done without both partner's agreement."

Anna's gaze swept her peers. "We're off the point. Isla, the only way you're going to really understand the resort is to be our guest at Erne Castle. That doesn't mean you have to participate in any way, but you are welcome to watch anything."

Cat could barely contain herself. "Oh, Anna, will you let Rick give a feeding demonstration?"

Rick's face turned stony. "Will *she* let *me?*" His expression switched back to charming, and he turned to Isla. "The point is donors/subs and vampire Doms use the gratification of sexual ecstasy to feed. No one gets hurt. Everyone goes home happy. No Dracula games unless you're into role play. Once vampires killed to feed, now we thrill to feed."

Isla squirmed in her chair. "So, if a vampire, say, bit me, it would be pleasant?"

Cat and Anna looked at each other with glee. "Oh, yeah." They both nodded.

Isla glanced at Willow and Adam. "Have you two ever been bitten?"

Willow tossed an assessing glance at Rick and Matt. "Not so far. But Pegasus blood is hallucinogenic for vampires.

Isla turned her gaze to Adam. "You?"

Adam glanced up at Willow from under his lashes. "Err... I'm older than I look and before Willow, ah... yes. I've been bitten."

"And was it good?" Isla's expression drilled down on Adam.

A slow sexy smile crossed his handsome face. "Indeed, it was."

The manor's air hung heavy with the chill of the stone walls and the scent of woodsmoke. The silence was deafening. Isla's hands covered her face as if in prayer. "I appreciate this in-depth explanation, but why are you telling me all this?"

Rick rose, walked to the sideboard, and uncorked a bottle of Cathcart Royal Wildcat. As he poured a wee dram into her tea mug, he flashed his most winning smile. "Can you imagine Cathcart Castle restored to its original brilliance as a twenty-first-century luxury resort? Thousands of people could enjoy the royal lifestyle of your home."

Adam broke into the scenario. "Isla, the reason Willow and I bid on the property was because of her work with abused and neglected animals. Before we knew about your distillery, we envisioned a resort featuring five-star dining, spa services, and top-notch equine experiences. The Gaoler and feeding vampires are a small segment of my envisioned business plan. Once I saw your distillery, I wanted to partner with your family to provide liquor for all our resorts and clubs. We want a partnership."

Rick walked behind Adam and placed a hand on his shoulder. "May I cut in?" Adam nodded. "The Moreaus offered you a contract only beneficial to them. That's not how CGI does business. We can offer you a truly equitable contract, and frankly, we're bigger than the next three resort corporations combined."

Isla's hand shook as she sipped. "That's a lot of vampires."

Rick's laughter rumbled through the room. Cat raised a hand. "Lots of magicals and lots of mundanes mean lots of weddings, parties, and money. You like money, right?"

Rick tented his fingers in front of him. "You would be part of the CGI clan and we would provide for all of you. Come to Erne Castle, see what we really do. If you like what you see, invite your family."

"You mean, I'd come alone and no one else would know about it?" Cat, Anna, and Willow exchanged glances. *Do they realize I'm thawing out?* "What do I tell my family?"

Rick pulled out a portfolio and slid it before her. "Tell them you're going to Dublin on business."

The portfolio cover featured Erne Castle under a rainbow with all the summer flowers in bloom. A fairyland of thatched roof outbuildings, stone cottages, and huge barns surrounded a stunning castle. Isla opened the cover and saw suggestions for planning a wedding.

Who am I kidding? She could see Cathcart Castle restored to this majesty. She shook her head and tried to come back to reality. "But you know, we're on the water in a bitterly cold country. You'd only have tourists in for a few months a year." She closed the folder decisively.

Rick shook his head. "Vamps don't worry about the cold. We love it. Our donors will be kept comfortable. So, what do you think? Look at the last page of the portfolio." Rick reopened the folder and slid out the pages of amenities. "This is my jet," he pointed at a photo of a 737, "it's at your disposal. When do you want to come over?"

Isla shivered at the sight of the 737's interior outfitted in cream leather. "When are you leaving?"

Rick looked at Matt and Adam. "We would want to be there with you, so you tell us."

Isla pulled out her phone and looked at her calendar. With a wry smile, she quipped. "I don't have to worry about those pesky blood draws anymore. How about tomorrow?"

Rick bit his lip to stifle a laugh. "Our driver will pick you up at dusk. We'll fly out together. If you don't have it at the house, we'll get it for you. Bring your bathing suit."

"Bathing suit?" Isla scratched her head.

"The indoor pool is heated, its looks like a beach," Anna explained.

"How long will I be gone?" Isla pressed back in the chair.

"How long do you want to stay?" Willow smiled.

Amber Anthony's Blood Legacy

Chapter Fifteen

Sunday evening, Darla, Erne Castle's administrative assistant, rang Rick at his desk. "Mr. Hiatt, I have a Gerard McIntosh on the line for you."

Matt prowled the office while Rick sat at his imposing desk. "Ah, our man in Glasgow, wonder if he caught a whiff of the fair Isla being here?"

Rick bobbed in his chair with a chuckle. "Darla, put him through."

"Rick?"

"Good evening, dear boy. What's on your mind tonight?"

There was a hesitant silence and then Gerry's words ran like a river. "You talked about reinventing yourself. I think I'm at a fork in the road and you know how pointless forks are for vampires."

Rick glanced at Matt with a mischievous smile. "And?"

"I canna do this job anymore." Gerry's frustration thickened his Scottish brogue. "I'm ninety-nine percent sure I have a co-worker going through my desk, that's especially annoying because he's family!"

Rick chuckled. "You, dear boy, have led a sheltered life. The family has a few rotten apples on the tree. What else?"

"I canna talk to one more entitled aristocrat about their property."

Rick glanced at Matt with raised brows. "My, my, some of the finest people you know are aristocrats."

Matt gave him side eyes and spoke up so Gerry could hear him. "Don't listen to him, Gerry. He's a royal pain in the ass."

"Oh, hello, Matt. I was wondering if CGI might have a position for me? I'm flexible, I can move anywhere." Gerry's tone implied more exasperation than flexibility.

"I hear you need a change. Of course, CGI could use a man with your talents. I'll tell you what, we're having a Tudor Masque this week, lots of management from our other clubs will be here. Great time to chat yourself up."

Gerry's tone grew hopeful. "When's the Masque?"

"Thursday night. Be brave, give your notice and tell them you need a couple of days off." Rick's laughter was infectious.

After Rick closed the call, he turned to Matt. "Do you know what I love best?"

Matt strolled in front of the tall windows watching the purple sky turn to indigo. "AB Negative?"

"Dear boy, you are so basic. I love when people's lives become a poker game."

Matt turned and cocked his head. "Some people have no poker face."

Rick leaned back in his chair and tented his fingers. "That makes the game all the more fascinating to watch."

****

Anna opened the heavy door of a tower suite and ushered Isla into a wealth of comfort. "Rumor has it that this bedroom set was used by Richard Fitzgerrald's mother, the Duchess of Erne." Anna ran her hand over the patina of the chest.

Isla trailed about the room like a cautious cat. "Really, when was this?"

Anna thought for a beat. "The family erected Erne Castle in 1512 and sadly she died in childbirth in 1513. Rumor has it this color was her favorite." Anna drew back the heavy rose-gold draperies to reveal the mullioned windows overlooking the pond. "If you are curious, her diary is on display in the library."

Isla's jaw dropped as she realized the ceiling was illustrated with animals of the era between ornately carved plaster medallions. "I've never seen a place this splendid outside a museum. I've certainly never stayed in one."

"When Fitz brought this castle back into his family, he wanted it the way he remembered it." Anna leaned against the wide mantle at the end of the bed.

Isla stopped short and turned to Anna. "The way he remembered it?"

Anna nodded as if talking about a man who grew up in the nineteen nineties. "He lived here most of his childhood until he was sent away to foster. He returned as a young adult." Anna walked closer, and her tone turned conspiratorial. "And I can show you the room where he was turned."

Isla's expression muddled. "What?" She shook her head in confusion. "But when was that?"

Anna seemed to count in her mind. After a beat she replied. "I'm pretty sure it was 1534."

Isla dropped onto the hassock as she ran the numbers in her head. "Fifteen you say? 1534?" Isla's hands covered her face and she cast them off explosively. "That means he's ancient."

Anna grinned. "You're as young as you feel."

Isla leaned to Anna. "I know this is rude of me, but are you from here, too? Oh, no, you told me you've only been this way for six years."

Anna waved off Isla's serious expression. "I'm a farm girl from Pickerington, Ohio born in the twentieth century. If you want to get under Fitz's skin, ask him who is the real Duke of Erne."

Isla grinned. "Does that make you the Duchess of Erne?"

The partially closed door pushed open, and Player and his doggie entourage padded in seeking their mistress. Isla was bowled over by a Sheepdog puppy.

Anna knelt and ruffled the young dog's ears. "When we refurbished the castle, we had a dear old gal named Bridget. This is Bridget the 2nd." She turned to the Dandy Dinmont posing like a prince. "This is the General and this is the smartest Rottie you'll ever meet. He is my dear companion, Player. The reason why I talk about them like they are family because Willow can communicate with them. I told you on the jet, we'd blow your mind."

Isla pushed back into the soft chair and let the animals sniff her. "Mind blown, you're right."

Willow stuck her head in the room and clapped her hands. "Alright you three, are you supposed to be upstairs?" All three dogs sat and lowered their heads. Willow laughed and turned to Isla. "They are so nosy. They want to meet everyone."

****

After Willow let Bridget and General outside, Player herded her to her office. Sitting face to face with the Rottweiler, Willow met his gaze. "What's on your mind, that brain crease over your forehead is deepening."

The formidable dog yawned and smiled. The telepathy began. "Isla needs a friend. She's hurting. Her heart is broken. What can I do?"

Willow narrowed her gaze. "What do you want to do?"

Player nodded. "I want to cheer her up and keep her company."

Willow's smile twisted with humor. "Are you going to tell her who you are?"

The dog's large head dipped. "We'll see how it goes."

"So, I'm assuming you'll occupy your room in the castle? Do you have your costume for the ball? When will you meet her?

"Did you say she promised to go out to the stables?"

Willow nodded. "She's coming to the cottage tonight. Adam and I are going to light the fire pit. You can drop by."

****

As Willow put the finishing touches on a dessert and charcuterie tray, Adam opened a bottle of Malbec. "You're siccing the puppy on her?"

"It was Trevor's idea. He read her heart and decided she needed a neutral friend. He's such a dear thing."

"Yeah, he's six foot three, two hundred pounds of walking, talking loyalty." Adam leaned against the specially built doorframe in their stone cottage on Erne Castle's property. His being six foot six meant all the dimensions of the home were more generous.

Willow placed the wine glasses on the kitchen island and Adam abruptly turned. "You are not giving that dog wine... you know what happened the last time."

Willow narrowed her eyes at her mate. "It didn't happen while he was shifted, it happened when he shifted back."

Adam rolled those gorgeous aqua eyes. "I had to hear Rick bitch about dog farts for a week."

"Trevor will be occupying his apartment until Isla goes home." Willow walked to the living room and fluffed a pillow.

Adam trailed along lighting fragrant candles. "When will you share with Isla that Trevor is a dog?"

Willow turned to Adam and flattened her hands on his broad chest. "I won't tell if you won't. Remember this woman was traumatized by the undead. We don't need to poison her mind about shifters."

The doorbell rang and Adam headed to open it. Willow ran two fingers from her eyes to him. "I'm watching you."

Adam flung open the door and grinned at Trevor Nagel on his doorstep bearing a paper-wrapped bouquet of tulips and irises. "What a pleasant surprise, Trevor, these are Willow's favorites." He stood aside for Trevor to present them to Willow personally.

"I'll always remember the first time they bloomed for her. She was so proud of that garden. I buried a truly tasty bone there."

Adam touched Trevor's shoulder as he passed. "Buddy, while you're like this." Adam gestured to Trevor's mortal form. "Hang back on the dog talk, okay?"

Trevor looked him up and down and his nostrils flared. "Right, you never brag about lighting campfires, sure. How did you light the fire pit tonight?"

Adam crossed his arms over his chest and lowered his gaze. "It's a little tight in the backyard to shift when I can easily use a lighter."

Willow arrived in the foyer. "Are you playing well together? Isla has had enough stress. I want you two on your best behavior."

Trevor soothed. "Willow, you're always the voice of reason." He extended the bouquet to her.

"Thank you." She held them to her heart. Before Adam could move, she playfully slapped her palm in the middle of his chest and held out the flowers. "Put these in water, won't you?"

"Yes, dear." Adam slunk off as Willow placed a sisterly kiss on Trevor's cheek. They followed Adam back to the kitchen island.

"Wine, Trevor?"

The dog-shifter touched his flat belly. "Uhm, no. Do you have that thing with the beef bouillon and Worcestershire sauce?"

Willow smiled. "Yes, I do. Of course." The doorbell rang and Adam left the flowers in the vase to answer the door.

He put on his gracious host persona. "Good evening, Isla. Welcome to our cottage."

Isla crossed the threshold and gaped at the twelve-foot ceilings of the spacious country home. "Cottage? Nice."

Adam led her back to the kitchen slowly explaining, "When Willow became the stable manager Rick had this cottage built for her. I married up."

Isla twirled around in the massive living room. "Do the horses live here, too? This is huge."

Willow and Trevor emerged from the kitchen. "Their barn is just as spacious but a little more to equine liking."

Isla smiled shyly at Trevor. "I guess Rick thinks of everything."

Trevor stepped up without introduction. "Rick has a heart of gold, he's just a guardian angel. I was…"

Adam intruded. "Trevor was employed in a bad situation in LA." Before Trevor could speak further, Adam made introductions.

Willow blew out the candles in the living room and waved everyone out the side door. "The patio is out here, the fire's lit, and I have blankets over the chair backs if you want one. Shall we?" She picked up the tray of food and Adam carried the basket with utensils and plates.

Adam turned to Trevor. "Would you mind fetching the wine along with your drink?"

Trevor narrowed his eyes. "I see how you're playing this, Sparky. Won't you mention again how you lit the fire pit?"

As Willow spread a blanket out on the loveseat glider she glared back at the men in the doorway and turned to Isla. "Those two always taunt each other."

Trevor handed Isla a glass of wine with a courtly bow. He turned to the Adirondack chair next to hers and walked around it once before he put his glass on the arm and shook out the wool blanket. He carefully fluffed it into a poof on the chair and sat down.

****

Isla waited for everyone to sit. "Trevor, what do you do, are you affiliated with CGI?"

"I'm Matt's top dog in security." He spoke proudly.

Adam snorted and Isla missed her mouth with her glass. "Adam, the two of you are hilarious together. You're as bad as my brothers." She turned to Willow. "Why are men so competitive?"

Willow began plating cheese and fruit for herself. "Men, can't live with them, can't banish them to a barn. They're too comfortable there."

Isla admired the tall brawny man beside her as he chose chunks of cheese and bacon-wrapped water chestnuts. She noticed he was particular in his selections, and he wasn't drinking wine. "What's in your glass, Trevor?"

Caught in the act of sniffing at the bacon before he dropped it on his plate he looked up. "Oh, it's a retro cocktail. Like a Bloody Mary, but you switch the tomato juice for beef bouillon."

Isla nodded with a forced smile. "Oh."

"Adam makes the best Bulls Shots, want to try one?"

Isla raised her wine glass. "I'm good with Malbec. So, I hear there are lots of entertaining things to do here and that employees get to enjoy them. How do you spend your spare time?" Adam's head dropped back as he chewed. *Is he star gazing?* Isla looked up for a comet perhaps.

Trevor sat his plate in his lap and his brown eyes lit up with joy. "I'm in heaven here. You can play all kinds of ball."

Willow leapt into the conversation. "Trevor is a real athlete. I dare say there's not a game with a ball in it that he doesn't play. Especially with the horses, he gets out there and tosses the horse ball with the best of them."

"Horse ball?" Isla swallowed a canape. "They make balls for horses..."

Trevor sat up enthusiastically and gestured. "Mephisto loves a twelve-inch ball, it has a handle on it, I fling it to him, he flings it back. It's like catch."

"Ahh." Isla caught a couple of chocolate-dipped strawberries. "So, CGI takes care of their employees."

"My bed is soft. My food is great. I have a job I enjoy. What's not to like? What do you do, Isla?"

Isla sagged back into the chair. "I'm at a crossroads and I'm here this week to think about bringing our family distillery into a partnership with CGI."

"How does your mate feel about that?" Trevor picked back over the beef sausage slices and rolled a few on his plate.

"Oh, I knew the conversation would come to this. I was seeing a gentleman I thought was special, but we had our differences. My family is large and only one sister is married, so we're all loose wheels."

Trevor winked at her. "You have sisters as beautiful as you?"

"Yes, one is married, one is pining for a Glasgow doctor and then there's me." She began popping the sugar-dusted pecans into her mouth.

"So, you're a loose wheel? May I offer to escort you around the grounds, I know all the best places."

Adam poured more wine into the glasses and chuckled. "He does, he really does."

Isla looked at Willow. "Anna told me you have a Clydesdale. I love them. Before we stopped growing our own barley, we had a Warm Blood/Clydesdale mix who plowed our fields, and we kids pampered and rode him as often as we could. When Fergus passed, I guess none of us could bear plowing with another, not even Dad. From then on we imported all our mash."

Willow smiled softly. "I am sure Mephisto will love you. He adores beautiful women. And you cannot possibly give him too much attention."

Trevor rolled his large brown eyes. "That's the truth." The deep dimples in his copper skin punctuated his grin.

Isla watched the motes of ash rise from the fire as they danced over their heads. She stretched out closer to the fire pit. "I've been spoiled since I arrived. That dinner was out of this world. Now your hospitality, Willow and Adam, I'm sure I look like I'm flagging."

Trevor sat up. "May I walk you back to the resort? I love walking in the moonlight."

Isla scooted forward in the comfy chair and folded up the blanket. "Thank you again for a wonderful night." She turned to Willow. "So, it's you and me at the stable tomorrow?"

As the four of them walked to the cobblestone wall's gate, Adam spoke up. "The path to the castle is well lit. Trevor, don't take the shortcut through the grass."

Trevor shot a finger at Adam. "Righto, Sparky."

Adam returned the gesture. "Okay, Buddy."

Chapter Sixteen

Gerry walked into the Royal Estate offices early, fully intending to give his notice. Was it because he carried his resignation letter that he heard and felt every trivial sight and sound that grated upon his vampire senses?

He sloughed them off as he slipped out of his jacket and dropped his keys into the drawer as he had done for the last five years. Randall's desk sat vacant, and that did not displease Gerry. He would not miss that judgmental snit of a vampire. *Weren't most vampires live and let live? Not Randall. His beaky nose was in everyone's business.*

With a dismissive shake of his head, Gerry settled into the familiar creaky chair, and the receptionist buzzed his desk. "Mr. McIntosh, royalty on line one for you."

Gerry leaned around the wall separating his area from hers. "I'm not usually here, who is it?"

She screwed up her face and did not use the intercom to answer, "The Duke of Erne," she said as if he should have been expecting the call.

Gerry's brows waggled and a smile spread across his handsome face. "Ah, thank you, Gemma."

He picked up the phone and his body language switched into business mode. "Gerard McIntosh, International Desk, how may I help you?"

The pleasant Irish brogue flowed sweetly to Gerry's ears. "Good afternoon, Mr. McIntosh."

"Good afternoon, sir."

"Rick Hiatt is a particular friend of mine, he called on me and presented copies of the letters patent that are currently being considered on a land claim. He is confident of their authenticity and after looking over the documentation, I quite agree. I'm recommending to the Crown they approve this title transfer to the Cathcart family."

Gerry sat stunned. He was aware of Rick's connections. This was one for the books. *If they only knew.* "Your Grace, I'm surprised to hear from you. The Cathcart's claim is not in my purview."

The duke chuckled. "Mr. Hiatt says you have a particular interest in this transaction."

Gerry's emotions washed down like rain through a spout. "Yes, I did, sir. I'll be happy to pass this news on to Ms. Browne, their agent. The family will be delighted. So kind of you to call."

The duke closed, "I'm always happy to accommodate Mr. Hiatt, he's done so much for my family home. Good afternoon."

Gerry tapped his headset and leaned back in his chair. *'My family home' if you only knew.* He slid his letter of resignation into his top drawer and strolled to the other side of the room to Ms. Browne's desk. "I'm going to make your day, Noelle."

Isabel looked up from a desk covered with a day's worth of work. She waved a hand dismissively. "Unless you can make all this disappear before five, you're useless." The dark-haired woman leaned back and stared up at Gerry as she ran the dagger-like nail of her index finger up and down the pad of her thumb. *If a look could emasculate...*

Gerry stepped back and folded his hands before him. "Ahh, is that the Cathcart file front and center?"

Noelle's face creased in agitation as Gerry scented her frustration mounting. "Yes, and I am waiting on that harpy's daily phone call."

Gerry winced at her comment. "Oh, well, would it improve your disposition if I told you the Duke of Erne is recommending approval of the Cathcart claim?"

Noelle's chair reeled around to Gerry. "Who plucked his strings?"

Gerry made a dismissive gesture and smiled. "A businessman with some sway spoke on their behalf. You know the letters patent are being certified." He shifted his hands deep into his trouser pockets and looked at Isabel from under his eyelashes.

Noelle's thin lips straightened. She obsessively repeated stroking her thumb with her ring fingernail. "Some university history buff has succeeded in pulling that off?"

Gerry shook his head. "That's unbecoming, Noelle. Who do you need to speak with to call the Cathcarts and give them the good news?"

Noelle returned to her keyboard and fired off an email. Gerry took a seat on the edge of her desk and ran his thumb over his bottom lip. The heater fan kicked on and fluttered a leaf of the pothos on Noelle's bookcase. In his mind, Gerry reran Isla's last visit when she banged fruitlessly on his front door. His shirt collar grew tight, and he ran his finger around one side and crooked his neck.

"Are you waiting on this?" Noelle waved a dagger nail at the open email account on her monitor.

Gerry checked his watch. "Four-forty-five, it could happen."

Noelle shuffled other files closed and dropped them into a side drawer. The clock over the reception desk ticked to four-fifty-five like a cheap alarm clock. Noelle's phone rang. "Ms. Browne... Yes? Of course. Thank you, sir. Good afternoon." She turned an incredulous gaze to Gerry and then her watch. "It's a go. I'm done with the dragon lady." She slid the file to Gerry. "Go ahead, make the call. I have a dinner date with a former equerry to the Prince of Wales."

****

The office was at last quiet after the day crew left at five. Gerry found a telephone number for the Cathcarts and made the call.

He closed his eyes and considered using another accent, something less Scottish but when they answered the phone there was a different voice. A relaxed, happy woman said, "Hello?"

Without giving his name, he smiled at the phone and spoke. "This is Ms. Browne's assistant at the Crown Estate Scotland. Is Ms. Isla Cathcart there?"

He heard the woman hush the people in the background. It sounded like a kitchen extension. "No, she's in Dublin on business. Is there a message?"

"Am I speaking to a member of the Cathcart family?"

"This is Maisie Cathcart Bruce."

"I see. We're calling to inform you that the letters patent you presented on the estate have been reviewed and approved. The final paperwork should arrive by certified post within thirty days. At this moment, you may consider the property yours."

The voice on the other end went up at least an octave in excitement. "Oh, that's wonderful news. Thank you so much for calling."

****

Gerry hung up the phone and sat back, clicking his fountain pen cover off and on. *In Dublin? Why? Did Rick convince her to visit Erne Castle? Rick knew this was going down... But if she's there, why didn't Rick let me know?*

If I did ingratiate myself to the CGI organization, am I going to bump into her repeatedly? Is this what I want?

****

Gerry's boss was not pleased with his resignation and was even less pleased that he was taking the rest of the week off. Spreading his suitcase on the bed he began considering what to pack, he wanted to dress to impress any potential employer. On the other hand, with Rick's recommendation behind him, he could walk in wearing a feed sack.

What had Isla said about loving his tweed waistcoat? *She said she liked my ivory sweater best. What does that matter?* Gerry sat down in front of the tall windows in his living room and dialed Erne Castle. "Ms. Isla Cathcart, please."

There was the musical voice of the resort operator who asked him to hold and then the Muzak played. The phone rang twice, and Isla's voice was a stunning confirmation. *She's there, alright.* He hung up, thinking, *what is Hiatt's plan? Has he brought her around to see the undead in a kinder light? What did I do with that ivory sweater?*

****

Isla decided on a wonderful salmon souffle while her dinner companion insisted on the largest steak, 'rare and blood running.' Trevor carved up the thick piece of meat like a surgeon and savored every bite. "I can always count on a fine meal here. It's funny," he leaned across the small table, "for a vampire resort, the mortal food is delicious."

Isla chewed with consideration. "After what Adam and Rick told me, don't you think the vampires taste what people eat? You are what you eat."

Trevor chuckled. "That's what I hear."

Isla looked around the half-full dining room and whispered. "Have you ever been bitten?"

Trevor looked up with surprise. "Me? No!"

Isla sat back again, relaxed. "Do you want to be?"

With his mouth full, he shook his head. Reaching for his drink, he smirked. "I have been such good friends with Anna and Rick, it wouldn't seem right between us."

Isla nodded. "As a mortal, how is it to work with CGI? There are vampires and dragons and Pegasus shifters and what else could there be? I mean, what other kind of shifters are there?"

Trevor readily replied. "In my experience, they are far better to work with than mortals. Mortals don't have a perspective on the long term. Vamps play the long game, that's Rick's favorite strategy."

Isla enjoyed the light texture of the souffle and sought to dig deeper. "If they are good business partners, have you ever dated one?"

Trevor sat up in alert. *Did his dark skin blush?* "I'll be honest, I was right there in the middle of Anna and Rick's meeting. She was kind of my girl first."

Isla's jaw dropped. "How can you still be friends? Isn't that uncomfortable?"

Trevor shrugged. "We never had that kind of relationship, and you don't choose who you fall in love with."

Isla sat down her fork. The corners of her mouth sagged. "That's the truth. Have you ever fallen for someone who wasn't who you thought they were?"

Trevor put down his utensils. "Like how?"

Isla took a long sip of her iced tea. "I dated a man, I thought he was *the one*, but he wasn't honest about what he was."

Trevor's face softened; his huge brown eyes drank in her reticence. "Go ahead, he is a…"

Isla nodded her head. "Yeah, he's a vampire."

Trevor sat up in alarm. "Did he hurt you?"

"Not the way you mean. His dishonesty hurt me, and I behaved accordingly."

Trevor nodded. "Ah, tit for tat. You hurt me, I'll hurt you."

Staring down at her plate, Isla nodded. "You've got that right. No wonder you're in security, you know a lot about people. The worst part of it is, when I really needed help, he came through, no questions asked. When the crisis was over it was good-bye."

"And you wanted 'hello' again?" Trevor renewed his attack on his steak.

"At that point, I knew more about vampires and if I could start all over again, I wish I could." Isla pushed her half-eaten meal back and rested her elbows on the table, with her face in her hands.

Trevor looked up and caught her hands in both of his. "As long as you live and breathe, there are second chances." His gaze sought hers and she felt a flow of strong unconditional love. It was as much healing as disturbing.

"How do you reverse harsh words?" She rested her hands within his while they sat.

Trever smiled all the way up to his eyes and shook his head. "Well, all you have to do is talk to Anna." He shook her hands in warm emphasis. "She smarted off to Rick in a way no one in their right mind would taunt a vampire." He raised a brow. "And she lived."

Isla slipped her hand out of his and covered his hands with hers. With a friendly pat, she nodded. "Then, I have to have a chat with Anna."

****

After checking into Erne Castle, Gerry strolled to the bar outside the conservatory dining room. He ordered, "Glenlivet with A Positive, please." Presenting his room key for his purchase, he turned to lean back against the bar and before he could swallow his first sip, he had something uncomfortable to swallow.

Isla and a handsome young man sat at a table for two. His hands gently held hers as they stared into each other's eyes. *Hope you're mortal, mate.* Rather than stand and sip, he downed the drink like a shot and left the bar. *It didn't take her long.*

As Gerry exited the bar, Adam came around the corner. "There you are, we heard you'd checked in. Why the long face? Is something amiss?"

Gerry nodded toward the dining room. "See the cozy couple by the window. Recognize anyone?"

Adam nodded. "That's Isla and Trevor, one of our security agents."

Gerry scowled. "Sure he's not a bodyguard? They look pretty friendly to me."

Adam shrugged. "Don't worry about Trevor, he's everyone's best friend. Why don't you come down to my office and we can talk about that job?"

****

Gerry paced in front of the wall of security monitors trying not to look too closely. "You've got twenty rooms that could be active at once. How do you stay on top of everyone?"

Adam leaned back in his desk chair and chuckled. "So to speak?"

Gerry shook his head. "Yeah, so to speak. But seriously... I was a young guy during the sexual revolution, I was a Mod in swinging London. But I just can't get into this stuff, it's not my kink."

Adam gave him the therapist once over. "I would love to know what your kink is... But I digress. I'm not talking about making you a Master Dom. You don't have the training or the interest. I need an assistant manager to cover nights while I cover days."

Gerry tilted his head. "I thought Rick covered nights."

Adam laughed. "No, not here. I'm ninety-nine percent sure Isla will recommend that the Cathcarts partner with CGI. That means we'll be breaking ground on the renovation of the castle by August."

Gerry spun on his heel. "Not there." His hand flew to his face as he shook his head.

Adam sat forward in his chair. "I'm sorry, mate, but that's where I'll be and where the need is."

Gerry folded his hands in prayer and aimed them at Adam. "What about here?"

Adam nodded judiciously. 'So, you'd be okay with working the day shift, because you're right, Rick has the night shift."

Gerry hooked his thumbs on his belt and examined the carpet. His head shook as he shifted from foot to foot and recognized Adam's logic. He huffed out with disappointment, "Yeah... but does the family know about us? Can you be sure after what they went through, they'd consider working with vampires? You're sure you don't have anything here?"

Adam gestured Gerry to a chair. "You could be instrumental in convincing the family to partner with us."

Gerry felt lost. "You're going to out me on the chance I can wrangle this deal?"

Adam nodded. "This is your step up from where you are. This is your chance to come into your own. How long have you passed in the mundane world? It's been lonely, hasn't it?" Adam swiveled in his chair and shook his head. "I didn't realize the freedom I had to be myself until I worked with other magicals."

They shared a solemn gaze for a beat and Gerry chuffed out a breath. "You've been dealing mostly with a willing donor population.

I don't think you understand the bias most mortals have against vampires. It's great if you think Isla is coming around to understanding, but it doesn't mean all the Cathcarts will. In that case, the deal is off."

Adam nodded. "Rick, Matt, and I do have some experience in making these deals. But let me suggest this, if we try with the Cathcarts, put our best foot forward, and they decline, so be it. We found this property, we can find another, and the deal will be the same. I'll manage and you'll be my assistant at night." Gerry nodded in slow agreement. "But, Gerry, what if they say yes? We are perfectly situated in so many ways."

Gerry's mood continued. "What about Isla?"

Adam cocked his head. "Well, mate, I guess it will either work or it won't. Are you telling me there's such bad blood between you that you couldn't work together? Because I didn't get that vibe when we were rescuing her sister."

Gerry scoffed. "We were saving their asses. Of course, she was amenable. Afterward, it was like, thank you very much, goodbye and good luck."

Adam continued to study him like a therapy subject. "Are you telling me that you are so wounded by her refusal that you're incapable of working in the same general facility? Because I feel bound to point out you'll meet hundreds of stunning women, both mortal and magical in doing this job. Surely Isla's not the only woman you could love?"

Gerry propped his elbow on the chair arm and ran a thumb over his lips as he stared at a couple on the screen. "You're right, it has been lonely." He shrugged. "Maybe I shouldn't prejudge the situation. If I speak on behalf of CGI with the Cathcarts, I will be putting myself out there more than I ever have."

Adam nodded. "Fortune favors the bold. Who knows, she might come around... It might be the best thing you ever did."

Gerry bit his lower lip. "And if they hate me, we find another location the same deal?"

Adam extended a hand across the desk. "That's the plan. Are you in?"

Gerry extended his hand. "I'm in."

****

Isla walked beside Anna while she pointed out notables in the portrait gallery. "We have costumes for all the paintings shown here. The Tudor Masque is kind of a tradition. We do it every year. I think you'd be perfect as Elizabeth I."

Isla looked at Anna's flaming locks down to her waist and gawked. "Me? You should go as Elizabeth. You could use your own hair."

Anna shook her head. "No. Been there, done that. It's your turn. You'll be gorgeous. I'm going as a Milkmaid by Vermeer this year." Anna pointed to the painting. "It's a joke for Fitz."

Isla turned, curious. "Who is Rick coming as?" Anna laughed and drew her to a life-sized Holbein painting. "It's... it's Rick!" Isla stared amazed. "But... is this painted in the style of Holbein? Is it a joke?" She turned to Anna wide-eyed, seeing her friend transported in time.

"Oh, no. Rick always comes as his former self," Anna assured her. "Holbein painted this in 1534, the month before Rick was turned. He'd just been made the Duke of Erne after his brother was imprisoned. See the family dirk at his side? Look over there." She pointed to Fitzjarrald family relics encased in a museum-quality glass display. "Who's the real Duke of Erne?"

Isla gaped. "That's real?"

"You bet it is," Anna confirmed. "He'll be wearing it Thursday night."

"Wow!" Isla admired the painting of Elizabeth I. "Well, if you're not going to, I'd be happy to come as the Virgin Queen. That gown is gorgeous." She studied Anna. "There was a lot for you to learn about Rick, wasn't there? I mean, Trevor let slip you two had something of a rough courtship."

"Trevor, huh?" Anna chuckled. "He did have a ringside seat." She led the way out of the gallery. "I need to get some notes from my office downstairs. Will you join me for tea there? I'll give you the secrets to dating someone with a past."

Isla grinned. "Sure. I'd love to hear your take on it." Anna led the way to an elevator that required a palm scan to enter. "What's this?"

"We're going down to the Gaoler. That's where my office is."

Scandalized, Isla gaped. "You have your office in the... the... sex club?"

Anna gave her a surprised look and laughed. "Yes. It's quiet there most of the time. Things don't get going until midnight. C'mon. I'll show you around. Cat's probably there now. We share the office. Willow might even be in Adam's playroom." She chuckled again at Isla's gasp. "Lighten up, my dear," she teased. "Let me show you around. You'll see it's not as debaucherous as you think." Anna knocked on the doorframe of the office she shared with Cat.

Cat looked up from her monitor. "Oh, visitors, it has been too quiet here. Have a seat, it's almost snack time." Isla's hand flew to her neck. Cat shook her head and doubled over with a feminine giggle. "As long as I live, seeing that response will never get old."

Isla dropped her hand, flummoxed. "You say snack just as I arrive, how am I supposed to feel?"

Anna ushered her to a sofa at a coffee table between their shared work area. "You're supposed to feel that you have not asked us to feed on you and therefore, we wouldn't do that. But would you like to watch?"

Isla stuttered as she sat against the sofa's back. "I... I... isn't that kind of personal?"

Anna walked around to her chair and picked up the phone handset. "We have dinner parties, and we dine along with Adam and Willow all the time. Was it personal when you had dinner with Trevor last night?"

Isla's face went blank. "That was just dinner."

Cat leaned back in her task chair. "And this is just a snack. So small, we have invited one donor." Cat leaned across her desk. "He's really delicious." Anna and Cat nodded giddily. "I'm going to ask you, Isla, to move over to this chair because we like the donors to be relaxed and able to lay back. Rick explained the process, but do you have any questions?"

Isla moved to a chair in the corner and sat like a mouse with her hands folded in her lap.

Anna pressed a button. "Will you send Alex in, please?"

A mountain of a man tread gracefully into the office. His startlingly white teeth accentuated his devastating smile. Isla was floored. *How can he be smiling? How can he walk around this castle with no shirt on?*

With a resonating bass that struck the chords of her heart, the long-haired man stood before Cat and Anna and nodded. "Thanks for working me in."

Cat rose to greet him and ran her hand down his muscular arm. "How is your physical therapy going? How soon will you be back in the game?"

This tan, broad-shouldered man took up so much real estate that Anna had to stick her head around his other shoulder to speak to Isla. "Alex is an Olympic-level martial arts competitor and he's taking a few months off from an injury." Anna cupped her hand at her mouth. "Vampire blood is very restorative, so this is symbiotic."

Isla's jaw dropped. "Oh." *Vampire blood does what?*

Cat gestured to Isla. "Alex, we have a guest from Scotland, this is Isla. She's just getting acquainted with vampires in general. Are you okay with having her watch us snacking on you?"

The genial man gave a luminous grin. "Are you ready for this?" His voice was one part mellow, one part hypnotic.

Isla blushed furiously. "I don't know."

Alex looked at Cat. "The monitor is right outside if Isla gets lightheaded."

I'll drop dead here, but I'm not leaving this room. She nodded. "Thank you for having me." Then Isla thought about what she just said. "I mean thanks for letting me watch."

Alex gave her a nonchalant smile. "In these situations, nothing you say will come out right. I know what you mean." He grinned. "You're welcome. After seeing this, you might want to try it yourself."

Anna patted the sofa. "Did Rick ask you to say that?"

"My lips are sealed." The athletic man sat on the sofa dwarfed by his height. He pulled up the crease of his trouser legs and got comfortable with each arm out to the side. Isla did not hear their transformation, but when Cat and Anna sat down and raised their heads they were fanged, and opal-eyed. Truth be told, their fair skin was pearly translucent, and they were stunning to see.

Anna ran her fingers through Alex's hair. *Is she looking at his neck?*

"Thank you, Alex, for sharing yourself with us." She waited for Cat to make a similar greeting and at Alex's nod, each vampire picked up a hand and scented for the bite.

Cat tilted her head as she inhaled at Alex's wrist. "You've been sampling the Guinness Nitro Cold Brew Coffee, haven't you?'"

Alex tilted his head onto the sofa's back and closed his eyes. "You would know, Mrs. Brenner."

Anna caressed his inner forearm. "Oh, you had our truffle fries with your salmon souffle, didn't you? Emm."

"Ms. Hiatt, you know me too well."

Isla sat forward, hiding her stiffening nipples, and focused on the rise and fall of Alex's well-sculpted chest. She rested her elbows on her knees and leaned on her folded hands. She expected the sound of their fangs puncturing flesh when they bit, what she heard was a passionate sigh that melted Alex's body into the sofa.

Each vampire held an arm as their lips sealed around his wrists. Their insistent sucking was so entrancing, Isla reminded herself to breathe. She squirmed in her chair when she noticed Alex's black drawstring trousers tenting. He smoothly shifted to give himself more room as his length filled out the left side of his pants leg.

She blinked and then worked hard to not think of what he must be feeling. Her belly tightened and she felt heat rising in the damndest places. It didn't take his sensual moans or his relaxing deeper into the cushions to spellbind her. It was the entire tableau of these two gorgeous women cleaving to him like sensuous bookends. She would never forget this. *Good God.*

It was over too soon, heralded by Alex's long gasp and heaving chest. With a lick of her cupped tongue, Anna sealed whatever puncture she made and pulled a small hand towel from her side. Cat did the same courteous gesture and Alex appeared oblivious to it all. Both vampires rose with their fingers to their lips. "If we tiptoe out, he'll nap for a bit."

Once they were outside the office, a monitor entered with a tray of fruit, juice, and cookies. Cat and Anna led Isla to a room and gestured her to enter. Cat was amazingly pink, so was Anna, they almost looked mortal. Isla found a seat and shook her head. "You're both glowing. Is that the blood?"

Anna smiled. "That's what good blood will do."

Cat brought a tray from the sideboard and placed it before Isla. That was when Isla realized they were in what looked like a hotel suite with a huge canopy bed and all sorts of kinky-looking stuff. "Are you ready to be amazed?"

Isla plated some of the goodies and stopped before she took a bite. "You just amazed me in the other room, what else is in your bag of tricks?"

Anna sat beside Isla. "Willow and Adam want to show you something."

Isla covered her eyes. "Do I want to see it?"

Cat waved that away. "They're fully clothed and they engage in Shibari. Willow likes to fly even when she can't be a Pegasus, this is their kink."

Isla's gaze darted from Cat to Anna. "Where do they do this?"

Anna picked up a remote. "I'm going to press this button and that frosted glass will clear. They're just getting started."

Isla nodded mutely and began a little stress eating.

One large downlight shown in the all-black room. If Cat had said they were going to dance, she would have believed her. The stunning couple stood embracing and moving as if to a mutual tune. They lowered slowly to the floor where Adam's hands skated over Willow's lithe body. She wore a sheer jumpsuit with strategic patches over her breasts and mound.

Adam wore sleek leather trousers and a tuxedo shirt painted over his sculpted body. Ropes sat coiled at his feet as he moved from this loving inspection of her body to creating knots and wrapping her torso.

Isla whispered. "Can they hear us?"

Cat and Anna shook their heads. They sat as if they were watching the evening news.

Isla couldn't eat. The plate of snacks sat on her knees as Adam tied Willow into what looked like a rope corset and connected it to a hook from the ceiling. Adam began tying ropes around each hip and leg until Willow was suspended from three ropes. Adam stepped out of the spotlight.

Isla gasped. "He's not going to leave her there, is he?"

Anna chuckled. "That's not part of their kink, keep watching."

Adam returned with a tray of oddities, a wool pom-pom, different types of feathers, and then a worrisome-looking thing that looked like chains connected to a handle.

Isla covered her eyes. "He's not going to hurt her, is he?"

Anna shook her head. "Are you okay, do you want to stop?"

Isla looked back as a lock of Adam's blonde hair fell over his forehead and he leaned over to kiss Willow on the lips.

Isla sighed, "I'm good."

They watched in florid fascination as Adam administered increasing levels of impact play at the lightest end. Cat gestured. "Read up on impact play, Rick is phenomenal at it."

"What?" Isla looked at Anna unbelievingly. "He's not like that guy in that movie, is he?"

Anna nodded to Adam. "We only allow true Doms; we don't accept sadists masquerading as a Dom. And Rick is so good at it. Cat blew my mind with a story about Rick before he and I got together, but that's another story."

Cat slunk into her chair, her shoulders shaking in silent laughter. "You bet it is... talk about blowing my mind."

Isla leaned back and watched Adam and Willow's empathic responses to each other. Every sensation that Adam visited on Willow resulted in her flesh blooming a rosy shade. Her smile and apparent relaxation were mindboggling. Willow full-out giggled when Adam stood behind her and pushed her like a child on a swing.

Isla recognized Adam was as much into all of this as Willow was. Together they were replete with happiness. Adam stopped her swinging and held out a wand with dozens of fine chains draping off the end. He trailed it from her foot to her belly and up her torso. He leaned in and whispered something to her, and Willow flexed in the air demonstrating her anticipation. *First, she's hanging from ropes, now she's swinging from ropes and what do those chains feel like?*

All three observers were fascinated until Adam opened a drawer in a nearby cabinet. Anna held up the remote. "I think I know what's coming." Adam retrieved an interesting-looking vibrator and Willow shivered with a grin.

Isla gasped. "Will yah look at the size of that thing... Ah, jeesh."

Anna clicked the button and the glass frosted over leaving them to their privacy.

Cat sat up straight. "Have we blown your mind yet?"

178

Isla poured another cup of tea and drew it up to inhale the scent. "This tea is very relaxing." She nodded to the window. "That's nice for them if they like it... I can't see it for myself."

Anna nodded. "That's right, you know the old saying, different strokes."

Isla nodded actively. "Yeah, exactly. I'd just like to wake up next to someone who isn't dead." She gasped and covered her face, apologizing from under her hands, "I'm sorry..."

Cat rose and laid a gentle hand on Isla's shoulder. "I think you and Anna could have a good conversation about that. I'll leave you two and catch up later."

Anna offered a different location for that chat. "Let's go to the conservatory's butterfly room. The lightning bugs should be out."

As they walked shoulder-to-shoulder to the exquisite crystal palace, Anna explained she once found Rick looking quite dead and how it became a breakthrough in their relationship. "He told me he thought we could work through my fear if I understood he was undead, not dead. But to mortals, those two things seemed synonymous."

Isla looked down, processing the info. "Gerry could have told me."

"If he'd told you, would you have stayed?"

Isla had to admit, "I would have run screaming from his place, not necessarily believing it, but very sure he was nuts."

Anna nodded. "Common reaction. Maybe you can understand why having encountered just that kind of reaction before he was reluctant to tell you. He was smitten, he didn't want to lose you and then he did."

Isla stopped and faced her new confidante. "Now that I know about the undead... as much as I care for Gerry, I don't see how a vamp-mortal relationship can be successful."

Anna stifled her laugh. "Oh, my, you have Matt Brenner syndrome."

Isla's lovely face was serious. "I don't think Matt is wrong. Who wants to grow old and infirm while your lover remains thirty forever? There's a use-by date on this deal."

Anna's smile grew as she nodded. "I asked Fitz one night, what's my shelf life."

Isla nodded. "I don't want to become a vampire, sorry, but I don't. How do I look at this? In the future do I end it saying it was nice while it lasted?"

Shaking her head, Anna grew serious. "You broke it off. You're here this week to think about partnering with us. If you do, you're going to meet lots of vampires. You may be smitten like Gerry was with you. You can decide right now to be open and honest when you meet more of us and now your vamp radar will be tuned in."

Isla's mind spun considering her feelings. *Am I over Gerry?* Anna's frankness was refreshing. It felt good to get something so forbidden out in the open.

Anna and Isla strolled through the lobby when Anna caught her hand and sought her gaze. "Vamp and mortal relationships can get intense very quickly. You're the only one who knows if it's right for you." Anna accentuated that sentence with a soft shake of Isla's hands. "If you love him, it will be essential to suspend belief in every mortal myth you've been told about the undead. We're no better or worse than mortals. We just have lots of bad press."

Isla tightened her grip on Anna's hands as tears welled in her eyes. "Now you're making too much sense and I'm here alone with my guilt."

Anna released Isla's hands, patted her cheek, and parted with a sublime smile. "You never know. Things change."

The troubled mortal stood in the cavernous lobby until the elevator bell snapped her out of her thoughts.

Chapter Seventeen

Isla luxuriated in her suite's spa tub. This was definitely not a holdover from the original castle. She thought about the plans her family dreamed up for Cathcart Castle. *Don't kid yourself, unless we partner with CGI, Cathcart Castle will always look like a DIY network catastrophe.* As she soaked, she envisioned her brothers arguing about renovation companies. She wanted to submerge underwater and not think about it.

Another thing she didn't want to think about? The hang-up call she answered. Wrong number? *Aye, that's all it was. It couldn't have been Gerry.* What took her mind in that direction? *Is it my secret wish? What have I done?*

What's wrong with my life? If I listen to Caitrin, she will say I'm too finicky. But the truth is, Gerry was always the perfect man except for one thing... *Now I know that one thing is not how I envisioned it. Anna is a walking, talking poster gal for the undead. What did she call it? Just bad press? Every relationship has complications, doesn't it?*

Five hundred years ago it could have been about faith, a hundred years ago it could have been race or religion. A hundred years from now what will it matter? She paused with the startling thought, that she was thinking that far ahead. *What if...* Had she made an uninformed assumption? *How scandalous would it be to change my mind?* Oh, the irony that she was here without Gerry when he extended an invitation to come with him. *I wish I could see this place through his eyes.*

Isla toweled off with a bath sheet that felt like angel's wings. She found the ornate costume for tonight's ball laid out on her bed. The note beside it said her dressers would be there after the stylist and makeup artist had her powdered and painted. *My dressers? I will feel like the Queen herself.*

****

When Isla rode the lift down to the Masque, she feared she would be the only one to fit in the car. They probably used bolts of ivory and gold brocade for her costume. When she caught her imperial image in the mirror, she had to blink to recognize herself.

Although the ballroom's hum spilled out into the lobby, the only person in the lavishly decorated area other than the staff was Rick Hiatt, posed exactly as he was in his Holbein portrait. Her gaze went directly to the ornate livery collar encrusted with emeralds and pearls spread over his opulent mocha and ivory clothing. Leaning on the back of a wing chair, his right hand rested on the hilt of the Fitzjarrald dirk.

When Rick noticed Isla, he snapped to courtly attention, removed his feathered flat cap, and bowed. "Good evening, Your Majesty. I am your obedient servant."

Isla's lace-gloved hand flew to her mouth. "You have certainly made me feel like a queen during my stay. I want to thank you, your Grace."

"Ah, under all this velvet and wool, I'm just Rick...You're welcome." He extended his hand to her, and she found that when she placed her own on top of his in the Tudor manner they walked well together.

Earlier that evening, when they dropped the cylindrical farthingale over her head she wondered if that was Tudor birth control. *You can't kiss what you can't reach.* However, the Duke has his ways. *I imagine Gerry would, too.*

Rick continued his charming banter. "Elizabeth I favored immense ruffs. They created the illusion that she was a shining sun around which her kingdom orbited." His rich brown eyes flashed as he regarded Isla. "However, with your radiance, Ms. Cathcart, you are our shining sun." Speechless, Isla flipped open her fan and blushed behind its golden feathers. "Have you ever attended a Masque?"

Isla shook her head. "Nothing like this"

"As modern as I try to be, the traditional masque themes would be seen as chauvinism rather than chivalry and courtly love. I know for a fact women are strong, and men are vulnerable." Isla nodded, wondering what she was in for. "Although, the Tudors favored stories of male authority, I mix it up."

They strolled to the ballroom's open double doors and Isla gasped at the great thought paid to props and staging. She turned to Rick. "Every time I think it can't get more fantastic; you slay me with the next event."

Rick gestured to the cleverly designed model of the Mary Rose. "Bluff Hal," he gestured to the massive ship at the other end of the ballroom.

"Bluff Hal?" Isla blinked with curiosity.

"Ah, Henry's nickname, he was not born to be king." Rick ducked closer and spoke in a whisper. "He and I had a little in common. We were both destined for the church, but our older brothers died, thrusting us into a role we never expected." With a mutual nod, Rick continued. "He was an enthusiastic shipbuilder. His fleet grew from five to fifty-eight by the time he passed." He nodded toward the stage's replica. "The Mary Rose was his absolute favorite."

Before they crossed the threshold, Isla asked. "Why is there a Jolly Roger flying from her mast?"

"Aye, that remains to be the entertainment for the evening." He gave a courtly bow. "Come dine with us, your Majesty."

Isla looked askance. "Am I dinner, your Grace?"

"Indeed not, ma'am." Rick led her to her seat beside Adam dressed as a young Henry VIII and Willow dressed as Jane Seymour.

As Adam rose, Isla tilted her head in a bow. "Good evening, father."

The table chuckled at her humor. *That's because I'm queen, right?*

Adam played Henry to a tee. "Join us, daughter." He clapped his hands. "Bring in the feast."

Willow buried a laugh. "You know, this all ends at midnight, Cinderfella."

Adam pouted. "No jousting?"

"Only the horizontal kind."

Liveried servants bore golden trays filled with groaning platters of food. Some carried pewter mugs for the undead's meals. Isla was astonished to find the dishes for the mortals were traditional fare copied from Rick's family menus. They were dishes Isla had never eaten before. The castle dogs, collared with elaborate ruffs, wandered among the diners hoping for dropped food, snapping up the occasional treat. Musicians circulated playing the hurdy-gurdy, citols, strangely shaped drums, and recorders to entertain during dinner.

Isla had no idea what the conversation was like at the tables of the lesser royalty, but at the King's table, they joked about the fun of doing this once a year.

Willow leaned back and caught Isla's attention. "Save room, there are seven courses."

****

The mixed choral ensemble, dressed out in flamboyant costumes began the story of 'Plundering Mary Rose'. The ribald lyrics followed the pantomime of a handsome buccaneer as his most modest sloop, pushed by Tudor stagehands overtook the King's ship.

The women of the audience swooned at the emergence of the colorful pirate with his wily mustache and long, black curls that framed his lace shirt and blood-red doublet. His knee boots shone with a patina not likely for a man of this station, but he was devastatingly gorgeous even behind the gold half-mask.

The tenor soloist stepped up to sing the narration of the pirate's plight. "Cutthroat Damian, the Bold Cap'n Charming on this fare eve did scheme his way. Deprived of home and fortune, Cap'n Charming took his revenge on the Crown."

The audience tittered and applauded as the agile man led three cut-throats up the side of the ship and over the gunwale to seize the bridge.

A soprano stepped up and coyly sang. "Not only was this good ship the apple of the King's eye, but a beautiful virgin also stood beside the ship's captain. She watched with trepidation as their ship was overpowered."

The tenor continued the story. "It's not the size of the dog in the fight, it's the fight in the dog."

The soprano, once so serious, stepped in front of the tenor and belted out. "But size matters."

The sailors on the Mary Rose pantomimed jumping overboard or dramatic deaths until the captain surrendered and the tenor sang a song of sad defeat.

For a few beats of dark and menacing hurdy-gurdy music, the scene played out like a melodrama with the virgin and her ladies encircling her. The hoots and hollers of the audience increased the exaggerated acting until each pirate found his sweetheart.

The virgin and Cutthroat Damian ogled each other as she threatened to jump off the ship's bow. Damian's earnest appeal on one knee stayed her hand from grabbing a line and going overboard.

The choral group sang an extended ode to love and then the pirates and their newly won ladies began a lively gavotte.

Adam leaned back in Henry's persona and clapped as the pirates and ladies leapt about. He turned to Willow. "Do not expect me to dance like that."

Isla and Willow exchanged giggles. When the chorus receded to the ship, just the Cap'n and the virgin were left. A stagehand rolled out a rock grouping and the couple stood as if on land enjoying their lives together.

The soprano and tenor stepped to sing their sonnets. Cap'n Charming struck a bravado pose embracing the virgin as the tenor sang.

"My Fair Virgin, you inspire me to write.
How I love the way you dances and sings,
Invading my mind day and through the night,
Always dreaming about your comely lips.
Let me compare you to a youthful sprite?
You are more divine, special, and glowing.
Sure sun heats the dewy peaches of June,
And summertime has the light glow brightly.
How do I love you? Let me count the ways.
I love your royal burnished hair and eyes.
Thinking of your gorgeous gaze fills my days.
My love for you is my knightly desire.
Now I must away with a sprightly heart,
Remember my true words whilst we're apart."

Isla flipped open her fan and watched with interest how tenderly this Cap'n Charming regarded the virgin. *I'm no virgin. Is that my problem?*

After more exaggerated pantomime in which the virgin played a classic hard-to-get, the soprano sang as the virgin allowed Cap'n Charming to embrace her and sway in a dance duet.

"My the piratin' king, to you I write.
How I love the way you capture and loot,
Invading my mind day and through the night,
Always dreaming about the brave salutes.
Let me compare you to a daring tune?
You are more rakish, caring, and loyal.
Grave sun heats the growing peaches of June,
And summertime has the bobbing robin.
How do I love you? Let me count the ways.
I love your brash daring and seduction.

Thinking of your bold good looks fills my days.

My love for you is our mutual attraction.

Now I must away with a foolish heart,

Remember my crowned words whilst we're apart."

The tenor proclaimed, "Cutthroat Damian, the Bold Cap'n Charming begged her to sail with him. Instead, she returned to the Mary Rose no longer flying the Jolly Roger."

The soprano lamented, "This barren ship will sail like a ghost never to find a port."

Although the buccaneer hoisted a treasure chest on his shoulder, he mourned as he lamented losing his finest prize. As the stagehands pushed the sloop away from the larger ship, the swelling melancholy music crescendoed and the lights went down.

****

Isla finished watching from behind her fan. She looked to Rick on one side and Adam on the other. "What happened to 'and they lived happily ever after'?"

Rick put down his pewter goblet and thought a moment. "Oh, my Queen, art imitates life. One must create their happy ending."

She pointed at the empty stage. "But they were perfect together."

Rick conceded. "But could she live with a pirate?" With a flourish of his hand, his question hit home.

****

Isla felt Player at her knee, his large head resting there with huge brown eyes adoring her. "Oh, Player." She wiped a tear before it could trail down her cheek. "Do you need to go out?" She rubbed behind his ears as he yawned and threw his body against her. "Maybe we both need some air."

The volume of the room increased as people began circulating and dancing. Once the tables sat clear servers laid down trays of sweet and savory desserts and drinks. Did anyone notice her leaving?

Isla ambled the cobblestone walkways that wove along the privy garden, torches lit the way close to the castle but the further away she walked, the darker the night became. She walked in the moonlight. *Am I as foolish as the virgin? Have I thrown love and my life away?* Hearing Player's bark she looked up to find Cap'n Charming before her.

He swept off his feathered seafarers' hat and presented a leg. His baritone was soft English. "My Queen, what troubles you so?"

"Don't you know, Cap'n Charming? I fear I've lost my love forever and I cannot bear it." She turned from the burly pirate and dropped her chin, her face covered with her fan.

"Majesty, as a loyal subject, perhaps I can beseech this fool who would not return to such a fair lady."

"Thank you, Cutthroat Damian, some things a queen must do for herself."

"Pray, Madam, practice your words on me, who would you so beseech?" The moonlight cast long shadows on the two of them as Player circled them concentrically drawing them closer and closer until their silhouette had no light between them.

"I would say, my beloved Gerard, I was so wrong to turn you away. I don't deserve your forgiveness, but oh, how I would revel in it."

As they stood as close as two people in these elaborate costumes could, he spoke up. "Mayhap a pirate such as I could secret you to your love and bid the two of you speak. I would stand guard ready to run him through should he rebuke you."

Isla giggled and turned to the masked man. "Well, as stupid as I was, murder is a little over the top."

He placed his hand over his heart and bowed low. "Your Majesty is always wise." As the handsome stranger bent, Player jumped, snatched the long wig in his mouth, and bolted with it.

Watching the dog run away, Isla laughed and turned to apologize. "I'm sorry…" She stopped, stunned. "Gerry?"

Gerry stood with his dark hair matted to his head and eyes twinkling. His Scottish accent returned. "Majesty?"

She slapped him on the shoulder with her closed fan. "Did you write that masque?"

He stood back, his hand up in pledge. "I was given the script an hour before I dressed." He ruffled the lace spilling out of his jerkin. "Rick wrote it."

She shook the fan at him, now standing back with one hand on her hip. "Do you feel used?" She threw up her hands. "I feel used."

Gerry dropped his hat back on his head and caught her at the waist. "Did you mean what you said earlier?"

She wrested out of his hands and turned from him. Before her whisper, she nodded. "Yes, yes, I did."

"Then we should make merry at this happy reunion." He extended his hand, and she welcomed his embrace.

Showing only her fascination, Isla flipped open her fan and peered over it. "Have you seen the Duchess Suite?"

Gerry drew in a deep breath. "I have not... Is this an invitation?"

****

The ballroom was alive with music and dance. Adam played Henry with so much bravado that Rick elbowed him. "Next year, we reenact the Field of the Cloth of Gold. You'll King Francis I of France and I'll be Henry."

Adam stopped a beat and narrowed his gaze. "Were you on that field?"

"Don't be ridiculous, I was seven. My brother was there."

"If we have a joust, afterward, may I fly my dragon over the field like the tapestry shows?"

Rick considered, striking a pose, and tapping his chin. "Why not? We need something different."

Adam used his height to surveil the party. "We seem to be missing a Queen."

Willow snuck up behind Adam and covered his eyes with her hands. "Majesty, my spy brings news." She held up the pirate's wig. "Look what he brought back to me."

Rick, still with one hand protectively on the pommel of his dirk, turned to the diminishing crowd. "Are the private rooms filling up?"

Adam nodded, "You know who I don't see?"

Rick poked Adam with his finger. "Matt and Cat have already repaired to their…" Rick made air quotes, "'library.' I don't see the Queen or Cap'n Charming. But I must take my leave."

Willow hugged Adam's arm. "While you and the milkmaid are busy in the hayloft, don't scare the horses."

Chapter Eighteen

Between her restricting costume and unleashed emotions, Isla was breathless by the time she and Gerry cast open her suite's entry.

Before she could speak, he had her up against the closed door. His lips covered hers in a stunning kiss as his hands held her powdered face. "You didn't have to don this getup to attract my attention."

"I noticed plenty of lusty sighs from the audience as you cavorted on stage." Isla blushed through the heavy white makeup.

"Aye, but this pirate only seeks *your* booty." He spun her into the sitting area. "I can do the work of two dressers." He stood back and cast off his hat. "The catch? I only undress."

Isla advanced on him, her fingers working open his fancy jerkin. "Can we have *regular* makeup sex?" She had his velvet vest off in a heartbeat and worked on the ties of his ruffled shirt.

"Regular makeup sex? How does that go?" Gerry slanted her a smirk.

As her hands skimmed his collarbones, she raised a brow. "I've heard things about vampire sex... you never bit me. In order for you to come, you have to bite. What's with that?"

Gerry caught her around the waist and drew her closer. "I would have frightened you. I didn't want that. I hid the beast from you, I bit myself. You're right, I have to bite to climax." He spun her around and she wobbled as he began vigorously unlacing her.

"You know, when you think about it, vampires have a lot of rules."

"Yeah, but I have insane stamina. If I can't come until I bite...that means more time for milady's pleasure."

"Well, right now, it's going to be the old-fashioned way because I'm too impatient to get schooled on vamp sex." Her gown and layers fell away rapidly. "Is this what they mean by vamp speed?"

Gerry embraced her from behind and whispered in her ear. "Aren't you glad I don't do everything this fast?" He wiggled the farthingale. "I didn't know this was going to be a steel cage match."

Isla turned and whipped him in the knees with the contraption that held out her skirts. "Get me out of this. Now!" She turned her back to him for help. "Tell me, are you so practiced at getting women out of these because you've had prior experience?"

Gerry stepped back. "What is that supposed to mean? How old do you think I am?"

She turned around wearing only her shimmy. "You tell me. Rick used to be the duke of this castle for real. Were you somebody famous?"

"Before I was turned, they put me in a Carnaby Street fashion shoot as a lamppost."

"Lamppost?" Isla pulled the shimmy over her head.

"Yeah, I just stood there with Twiggy hanging off me."

Isla shrugged. "That's a certain kind of fame, I guess. What year were you born?"

"November 10, 1941, Newtonmore, Scotland. I was a war baby born at my Nana's farm."

Isla cocked her head. "What did Nana farm?"

As she talked, he undid his clothing at a mortal pace. "Ya know, I'm staring at your lovely naked body, and you want to talk World War II agriculture?"

"Not interested in talking about what Nana raised?"

He pointed to his rising flesh. "I know what you're raising." He grabbed Isla and carried her to the suite's bathroom. "Tub or shower, milady?"

Isla looked at the white makeup and wig glue around her hairline. "Shower, definitely."

He stepped into the shower's spray and extended a hand to draw her in. She came bearing a bath puff and a come-hither smile.

Lovingly Gerry sprayed her with the rain soft handset and dribbled bath gel across her shoulders.

Isla slammed him against the wall and grabbed his wrists. "Come on, Farmer Gerry, take me to the hayloft." Her white kabuki-style makeup melted down her neck and onto her body.

"Huh, so far I've been a pirate and a farmer. What a night."

Isla caught the corner of his mustache. "Is this thing real?"

Gerry moved his face as she pulled. "Wet me down before you start pulling on me."

Isla gave his body a long look. "What part are we talking about?"

Playfully, he swatted her derriere with a washcloth. "You know, my face. But if you want to pull on one while the other soaks." She reached for the mustache. "No, no, no, this part soaks while you tug on the other."

She stopped and put her hands on her hips. "There's no arguing in make-up sex."

"I didn't think you meant that kind of makeup."

In record time they bathed away their theatrical layers, leaving two very lusty wet bodies to wrestle in the party-sized marble shower.

Gerry caught her face in his hands and sought her gaze. "About the vampire stuff, let's have that talk later." His hands slipped down to her shoulders and arms to thread their fingers together. His oral assault began with playful nibbles along her neck. She giggled and shimmied out of his grasp. "Oh, if it tickles, I'm not doing it hard enough."

"I do like it hard."

Gerry insinuated his knee between her legs and slipped her into the corner of the shower. Flat against her, he growled low. "I can do hard." He drew her up on tiptoe against his body and her erect nipples stroked his. He reached for the back of her neck, and she drew his face to her breast.

Cool fire streaked through him as he closed his lips on her nipple and massaged it with his tongue. He suckled her blushing flesh and with his hand poised over her mound felt her small spasms taking wing like butterflies.

She leaned against his arm as the excitement built within him. Cupping the back of his head, her lips oohed her invitation, welcoming him. Her fingers meandered through his hair and penciled designs on his ear.

She released his head and arched into his hips. He gasped sharply as her wet hand caught his anxious flesh and stroked insistently. "Gerry, take me... please... now."

He nuzzled at her ear. "What about foreplay? I've been told twenty-first-century women enjoy it."

Her breath against his chest told her foreplay was dispensable. "I'm ready, believe me." Her breath against him grew shallow and fast as he slid facile fingertips down between her legs. She caught his shaft and cupped his balls.

"More, Gerry." With a hearty snarl, he had her legs around his waist and poised to go hilt deep. "Like this?" He thrust happily and caught a buttock in each hand. "I think I've got the right idea."

Isla moaned wordlessly as her head lolled with abandon. "Oh, Gerry, yes."

"You know, this could take a while." His thumb poised over her mound as he devilishly began stroking in rhythm with his hips.

Her breath caught as she thrust her breasts into his face with the desire to ride him harder. She caught his jaw and gasped. "I want to see you when you bite."

Gerry turned his head away without changing his tempo. 'Oh, darlin' what did I say about the talk?"

She pouted. "Not right now?"

He caught her around the waist, spun her around, and bent her forward. "You keep talkin' about vampires and I'm not going to get to do the things I want to do... things you'll enjoy."

She shook her head and stared around at his bobbling flesh. With a squeak, her hands flew out to the wall to catch herself. "Really?"

Gerry caught her hips and surprised her with a long lick down her back. She shivered and bowed into his kiss, inviting him lower.

So transfixed by her sweet flesh he found himself on his knees, licking, and suckling her, as his fingers found their way within her. "How's this?" His words mumbled vibrations through her. She giggled until his lips evoked a low moan ending in his name.

He rose behind her and trailed the head of his thick erection along her thigh. "You know, while you had me in exile, all I could think of was your mouth on me." He notched himself within her, evoking another low moan. As he began his loving thrusts, he kissed her shoulder and drew back a lock of wet hair from her ear. "And now I'm going to take you. Let's see how long you can stand." His hands held her in place as she grasped for balance.

The water sluiced over them as her body glowed from his attentions. He fancied the loud drumming sound was her excited heartbeat. When her breaths caught in halting gasps, he snared her hair and bent to her ear. "Come for me, Isla, and I'll come for you."

She almost slipped from his grasp as she turned to watch his metamorphosis. He wagged one long finger at her. "What did I say?"

Her head whipped around to face the marble as she pushed back into him. "Oh, God, just let me come."

With on-target instincts, Gerry delivered her to the land of lights and heat. Lowering his head and facing the wall his fangs dropped long and ready. The shower flushed the few drops of blood he shed as he thundered into her, his wrist at his mouth.

Gerry caught her around the waist and drew her back to the large shower seat. Still within her, he kissed her neck and brought up one delicate hand to suckle her fingertips.

She collapsed against him, and whispered, "I like makeup sex."

****

195

While Isla turned the hairdryer on her locks, Gerry ordered a wee 'night cap'. She heard the knock on the door and shut off the dryer to join him in the sitting room. "What did you get for me?"

Gerry's smile was rakish as he uncovered a plate of mini crème puffs. "I ordered a Decaffeinated Irish Coffee. All of the flavor and none of the pesky jitters." She tightened the belt on her robe and walked on air toward him. He held up one puff to her lips and winked at her. "These are my favorite. I want to taste them from you later."

She caught his hand as she chewed the delicacy. "Taste them? How is that?"

He embraced her in a robust hug and nuzzled her neck. "More about that later."

"What did you get for yourself?" She stood over the room service cart, hesitant to lift too many lids.

"Some warm blood. It's like warm cocoa for the undead."

"I'll take your word for it." She yawned hugely. "I have to confess. You wore me out. I've been up since six in the morning." She half yawned. "I may struggle to stay awake."

"Then let's go to bed." He nodded toward the bedroom."

She full-on yawned. "You won't mind? I know we have different hours."

He sipped at his mug. "Don't worry, I'll have things to do."

"What will you do?"

"I have a lot on my mind. I'm thinking of a career change. Being with you, I'll have some time for thinking and planning."

Isla was halfway through her Irish Coffee, and it was affecting her. She stifled another yawn. "You can turn on the TV if you get bored."

Once they were done with their bedtime snack, Gerry meshed his fingers with hers. "This is so unromantic, but before we turn in, I need some time for dental hygiene."

Isla shook her head. "There are new toothbrushes in the basket on the counter. Anna thinks of everything."

Isla enjoyed the normalcy of brushing their teeth side-by-side at the double vanity. It was like Ozzie and Harriet.

Once they climbed into bed, they luxuriated in the soft linen sheets. Isla stretched like a cat and rolled into Gerry's arms. Her head nestled into his shoulder, and she was asleep before Gerry finished saying goodnight.

****

Gerry watched the play of the moonlight across the floor and the bed imagining what form their lives would take in the future. Beside him, Isla's muscles twitched slightly. He watched her face as her eyes moved under her lids. She's dreaming. *Is she dreaming of us?*

Gerry longed to join her in her night's adventure, and he knew just how. He nuzzled her neck and carefully let the tip of one fang drop slightly. Delicately, he pierced her ear lobe gently enough to draw a drop or two of blood. Tasting it, he was instantly inside the dream with her. When he grazed his lip and pressed a drop of his blood to the nick on her earlobe, he completed the circle.

****

Gerry looked within Isla's dream to get his bearings. He was apparently already a player in this one. They sat joined at the hips on the comfortably lumpy flowered couch in her parlor. Spread across their laps was a traditional family scrapbook.

Isla pointed to the faded Kodachrome photo of two teenagers. They playfully grabbed at each other at a bonfire. "This was the night Dad met Mum."

"Looks like love at first sight." Gerry's finger traced over two pages of photos of typical teenage life.

"I don't know if Mum would call it love at first sight." She chuckled. "But Dad was persistent. He told her on the second date, he was going to marry her."

"They look very young." Gerry gazed at the wistful emotion on her face.

"Love is love regardless of age... I wish I'd found my love that soon." She sighed and turned the page.

Gerry's gaze drifted over the photos. He immediately recognized the set taken at Ibrox that fateful January day. Kyle and Lyra posed with frozen smiles holding up Conall's blanket. "I took that picture. I was behind them in the stands that day with a couple of my mates. Your mum couldn't get warm and Conall, being a vampire, was happy to surrender his blanket."

"That's how you met them? Were you like this then?" She was astonished.

"No, I was a thirty-year-old real estate salesman working my way up the agency. I didn't even *know what* Conall was."

Her jaw dropped. "So, you were just a guy with some other people who happened to sit behind them at the game?"

Gerry shrugged. "Life's funny like that."

****

She turned the page; and unfolded a sheet of newspaper. It was the front page bearing the headline and the tragic article. "Mum said she nearly died that day. If it hadn't been for a man pulling the railing off her like a Superman none of us would have been born."

"Right." Gerry nodded. "That was Conall. He, Fiona, and I were on the steps behind them when the crush hit. Your dad fell under the railing. He wasn't hurt. Your mum fell ahead of him, and the crush brought the railing down on her." Gerry tapped the article. "Because of vamp strength, Conall was able to bend back the railing and carry her to a ticket office. He fairly walked over the heads of the crowd to do it. I've never seen a man carrying an injured woman kick a door in like he did."

Isla's hands moved to cover her mouth; she shook her head in disbelief.

"Conall parted the crowd like Moses parted the waters."

"Dad was okay, how about you and Fiona?"

"Fi was a wreck, she went full-tilt hysterical, but she wasn't hurt. I was..."

****

Isla bolted straight up in bed. The hum of the heater was the only sound. She shoved at Gerry. "Wake up, I just had the most bizarre dream."

He rolled on his side and propped his head on his hand. "I'm up... because I don't sleep. Remember that?" He quirked a grin.

"Tell me how you met my mum and dad."

Gerry regarded the bedside clock. "At four in the morning?"

She stared at him, her adrenaline draining away. "Oh, I guess it is early. It just seemed so real." He gathered her close against him. "Someday, you have to tell me how you knew my parents." Gerry remained silent and she was quickly asleep again.

Chapter Nineteen

It was just after dark when Isla and Gerry got into his car at the airport. She smiled over at him. "So, we're agreed, no time like the present?"

Gerry shrugged. "Why put it off? They'll either agree with your decision about CGI or they won't."

Isla giggled. "If I were you, I'd be more worried about how my brothers will feel about us moving in together."

As Gerry drove, he nodded at her comment and clicked his teeth. "I think I can take all of them. I just don't want to. Helluva way to start a relationship with in-laws."

Isla's head snapped to him. "In-laws? Did I miss something?"

"Awe, you've been in love with me from the moment we met."

Isla made a screwball expression. "You're sure about that?"

Gerry nodded. "That's why I made you so mad. The opposite of love isn't hate, it's apathy."

Isla settled back in her seat and nodded. "Hmm. You realize we have maybe ten wonderful years... Fifteen if we're lucky."

"*You* realize the average marriage only lasts fifteen years. I'll bet we could go longer."

She gave him an arched look. "And then I could be referred to as your mother."

He reached across the console and squeezed her hand. "Or my cougar."

Her hands flew to her face. "I don't want to think about that right now. I'm too happy. They could drop a bomb tomorrow and we'd both be gone."

They gave the castle a long look as he pulled his car up to the family homestead. "In a year or so, you won't believe the change around here."

Maisie opened the front door, and they saw the family gathering around the dinner table.

Everyone pushed chairs closer to add one for Gerry. Drew waved. "We've just begun. Come in, join us."

The home smelled deliciously of pan-fried salmon and potatoes. Isla held up a hand. "We ate on the plane, thanks. But we'll sit with you."

Maisie bustled up and laid a decorative box of sweet Scottish tablet in front of them. "Then you need a wee bite of dessert."

Isla smiled at the sugary treat and picked one piece to savor. Gerry held up a hand. "Do you know what that stuff does to your teeth?"

Isla sucked on the delectable confection and spoke with her mouth full. "I can get dentures." Gerry tsked.

Drew passed the platter of salmon after he skewered a piece. "What's the verdict?"

Maisie leaned across the table in delight. "What sinful things do you need to confess after a week at Erne Castle?"

Isla laughed nervously. "Nothing I'd tell you. You're already pregnant. Seriously though, it's a wonderful resort."

Ian winked at his wife. "No blow-up dolls with handcuffs?"

Isla swallowed and poured herself a cup of coffee. "The rumors of rampant debauchery are highly exaggerated. Nothing happens there unless both parties want it to happen."

The Cathcart men looked up in unison and dropped their utensils. Bram's eyes twinkled. "So, there *was* debauchery?"

Isla exchanged grins with Gerry. "More like games. You know extended foreplay. You do know about foreplay, Bram?"

"Just because I'm the baby of the family doesn't mean I don't know my way around a woman," Bram defended.

If Gerry could have blushed, he would have. "Their golf course is PGA quality, and their stables are legendary. Their chef has eight Michelin stars. I tried to convince Isla to spend a day at the spa, but she spent the time negotiating with Rick on the terms of the agreement."

Caitrin waved a hand. "You can take me. I'd enjoy a spa day."

Isla rolled her eyes at her sister. "Remember we will be working... Cathcart Castle won't be a fifty-two-week vacation."

Bram winked at her. "Don't worry, Caitrin. She was more interested in the dirty sex room."

All eyes turned to Isla. "I've already told you, it's more like role play."

Drew turned a jaundiced eye on all of them. "What about the distillery and our liquor?"

Isla nodded with pride. "CGI has eighty-one clubs and resorts worldwide. That's a lot of scotch and we would be the preferred brand. We're talking millions."

Drew swallowed and frowned. "We aren't prepared to supply that much scotch."

"When you look at Hiatt's proposal for the plant, he wants to build for us, we can begin bottling at three years for their rail scotch. Believe me, brother, this is quite the opportunity."

Drew raised a brow. "And the castle?"

"Renovation will begin as soon as the architects get approval." She leaned across the table. "And for us, that includes a cottage for each of us on the property. When Hiatt says a cottage, they build a mini-mansion." She yawned, stretched, and stood. "I'm going to let you think about this a bit. I have another piece of news."

Gerry's chin ducked as he pushed back from the table. "I've asked your sister to move in with me. To my astonishment, she agreed."

Maisie who'd stayed quiet spoke up. "Oh, she has, has she?"

Gerry cleared his throat. "She has. We stopped by to get a few more of her things and let her share the news of her trip."

Maisie gave her a concerned look. "You've thought this through, darling?"

"Probably not the way you would have, but Gerry and I have already aired many differences and we come back to we're going to try this." Isla pushed in her chair and Gerry stood beside her. "Plus, Caitrin gets the whole top floor to herself."

Caitrin got up from the table. "Let me help you pack."

****

Gerry opened the front door to his flat as Isla barreled through with a copier paper box of pots and pans. He nodded toward the kitchen. "Just put them anywhere. It's rather empty."

Isla dropped the box on the long island. "Quelle surprise... I did need my favorite saucepan, my best knife, my chopper..."

"It's a good thing this room is a blank slate."

Isla halted. "I didn't even think to ask if cooking odors bother you... like garlic?"

Gerry spread his hands out on the island in rapt attention as she unpacked spices and the box seemed unending. He made the sign of a cross with two fingers. "In the Middle Ages they tried to ward off vampires with spices, I think they make blood more delicious."

Isla caught her peppermill to her chest. "Oh, that's a subject we'll have to cover."

Gerry circled the island and drew Isla into his arms. "I know I've been a hermit since I moved to Ayr, but I am far more comfortable with mortals than you are with vampires. I don't want you walking on glass. Talk to me whenever you have a question."

"I may stumble over that as we go. I'll ask as they come." She ran a hand down his face, stopping at his lips. "So, when are you going to bite me?" She paused and tapped on his lips. "Of course, what if I don't like it?"

"After moving all your stuff in?" He smirked and hugged her closer. "Oh, I believe you're going to like it."

Isla melted into his embrace and then stepped back. "I'm afraid that you will be offended by my scent... I'm a little road-worn."

Gerry caught her back to him. "That is the essence of your allure. I love you when you've come in after a full day. Everything about you is a delicious mélange of scents and spice." He nuzzled behind her ear and nibbled her lobe.

She melted against him, her cheek against his chest. "Yeah, but... next week I'm going to barricade myself in your spare room with a pint of ice cream and mugs of butterbeer."

Gerry's head dropped back as a grin grew across his face. His fangs dropped as his tongue slid across his bottom lip. "I know, I was waiting for that."

She pulled back and grasped his shirt. "You what?"

Gerry bent to nuzzle her forehead. "Yes, this schnozz of mine scents everything. Last month, when I scented your flow, it was all I could do to keep from throwing you down and licking you like a lollypop."

Her hands flew to cover her eyes. "No secrets, huh?"

Gerry caught her hand and led her to the hall. He pointed to the door on the left. "If you find my nature too much to handle, this could be your room." He opened the door to a lovely shabby chic room with a full-size bed and Tiffany lamps. "When my family had an estate sale, I was able to pluck a few of my favorites. This was my family's guest room and now, it is again."

"Oh, Gerry, I never gave a thought about your family."

He nodded, his smile bittersweet. "I kept in touch as long as it didn't look hinky. One day it didn't make sense to keep up the charade and I confessed to my younger sister."

Isla smiled sweetly. "A younger sister?"

Gerry nodded as he approached a picture framed in heavy wood. His finger traced the toddler's face. "Hazel is a trip. She lives in a senior community in Aberdeen and runs the entire show."

"She's an administrator?"

Gerry's smile twisted with irony. "No, she's just a fairy godmother. She'd get a kick out of you. She's been telling me for decades to settle down with a good woman."

Isla bit her bottom lip and yanked his belt buckle. "I don't know how good I am... you be the judge."

Gerry playfully swatted her behind. "Get yer bahoochie into our bed so I can properly bite you."

"Ooh, finally... Is it okay that I'm a little nervous?"

Gerry rested his chin on her head and drew his fingertips down her arm. "You know about my special skills; nerves are a thing of the past."

****

Isla held his face in her hands. There on the bed, they knelt, lost in each other's embrace, lost in the depth of each other's eyes. From where Isla knelt, Gerry was a rascal, a rogue of her very own. But his mischief? It was exactly what she wanted.

Tonight, his hair was thick and dark as the horizon at midnight. His bright-blue eyes seared through her. His perpetual fascination fueling his undressing Isla. He touched her like a precious, highly coveted gift plucked from under the Christmas tree.

How, in such a short time, did Gerry know she was his? His manner, his style, was pure sensual elegance, with the spirit of an eight-point buck. It was painfully clear to Isla was that deep within Gerry, his wild eloquence covered his past heartaches. No wonder it sounded like he was walking eternity alone.

In Isla's solitary years, she bore the scars of her lost dreams, the stars fallen like ash from her different ill-ended affairs. She saved them as if one day she could stack stars on stars and hold them together with wishes to build her dream lover. Tonight, she shook her head. Gerry was no dream; he was the reality born of attraction and possibility.

Each time they danced in his bed, more of their secrets seeped into the other. Unspoken secrets drew them closer and closer.

Exploring his flesh, understandably cool, she realized his time with her warmed him to downright inviting.

Kissing the tip of his perfect nose; paled in comparison to kissing the thick head of his cock. But it would be too soon to start there, she wanted a slow preamble to 'the bite.'

While a sudden storm whipped up outside, they cocooned within the draped bed. Their deliberate movements extended their pleasure as the backs of their fingers trailed across tight bellies. Sighs answered each other until their slow, passive lovemaking was insufficient. She needed to feel his bite. Her greatest desire was to push him over the edge into his ultimate need.

Gerry tapped the nape of her neck with a butterfly's touch. Isla giggled playfully and caught his hand to cover her breast. Inch by inch, she memorized these ethereal steppingstones to his bite.

Gerry's hands swept through her luxurious hair. His words were a whispered song. "So soft, fragrant, enticing... Oh, Isla." He put a finger to her lips and smiled.

They entangled wildly with each other until she felt undone by his pink beast of a tongue. His lips and tongue along her throat and behind her ear drove her to grasp for his hard cock. Her nipples pebbled as she stroked him. The inimitable flex of his muscles down his torso caused her to wrap her legs around his waist as they sat facing each other in the center of the bed.

Gerry touched the tip of her nose. "I want to kiss you there..." His fingertips walked to her nipples. "When we weren't ... speaking, you know what I missed? I wanted to feel the uncanny flex of your beautiful body every time you rolled your hips into me. I craved running my hands up your back to pull you closer, to hold you against me."

They shifted gracefully into these enviable positions and stretched like cats in each other's arms. Isla swept her hair across his shoulders. "When I can feel my nipples brush against your chest with every forward movement it makes me want to grind my pussy into you."

Gerry's chest rumbled at her saying 'pussy.' "But the ache in your tummy just gets more...intense, more acute." Gerry flipped Isla onto her back and crawled down to deliver the most delicate of tongue lashings. "Mmm." His tongue and lips worked her anxious flesh into a fever of neurons firing, and sizzling sensations. When her excitement was such that Gerry scented it in her cachet, he buried himself deep within her.

"Ahh, Gerry, so good, so deep... don't stop, please."

His kindling strokes built until she felt she was burning alive. She wanted to let go, she wanted him to never stop.

Gerry's back bowed, eyes closed, he buried his face into the crook of Isla's neck. "Oh, Isla, I want to forget where you start, and I end. I want you to know you own every part of me." His strokes filled her, their thrust and parry on perfect point.

"Gerry, I love you, you wild man."

Her words sent him into a starless depth and as his body took flight, his fangs dropped long and sharp. "Isla, I love you, my darling."

The dark side's energy crackled in a shadow as they met each other with animalistic abandon. As Gerry's well-placed bite drew, they relished the delicious burn that reignited Isla's orgasm. Entwined together, they shook. Bonded in this bite, they cried happy tears. Time passed and they refused to let go. Tangled up in sheets, tangled in the emotions, they stayed like this for hours.

****

Between the bite and slipping into sleep, Isla floated in a limpid pool of emotions turned to images. Every sensation of Gerry's bite moved through her, invigorated her fascination, and sated her completely.

When her eyes fluttered closed, Isla dreamed. They were some of the oddest dreams she'd had in a year. Yes, Gerry bit her. No, it wasn't what she expected. At the golden moment when she thought she'd pass out from excessive stimulation, he became the most beautiful creature. His look alone was spellbinding, but what followed was nirvana. She truly had to rethink that fifteen-year limit on their relationship. If she felt this divine every time they made love, she would cleave to him forever.

Forever? Did I just think that? Within her dream, every image cracked like a broken mirror and fell to the mists. She found herself alone sitting on a fluffy cloud, pondering romance as outside sounds began to interrupt her thought process.

She felt silky sheets, a soft pillow or two, and Gerry's cool body next to hers. *I will not shriek; I will not flip out. I'll just wake him with my lips.*

Isla slowly lowered her face to his resting flesh. Planting small kisses all along his waking length she heard a bass chuckle. He sighed an acknowledgment as she tongued his balls.

"Isla... I'll give you until twilight to stop that."

Circling the base of his cock with her talented mouth she relished nibbling him and hearing his reaction. It was hard to tell where he was most sensitive. His response to her holding his sac in her hand while she stroked and licked him, told her this was becoming one of his favorite treats.

"You better get up here... I know what you're doing. You're going to force me to bite you." She tongued harder and giggled, sending the vibration up his body. "I can tell by your scent; you've woken up ready to play."

Isla leered at him over the head of his cock. "Play? Oh, I'm not playing after last night." She swung her legs over his hips and filled herself with his hard length. She fell forward and leaned on her palms. "I don't know how we'll function. All I can think about doing is staying in bed with you."

Gerry's hands slid up her torso to cup her breasts. "I believe Adam is a severe taskmaster when he needs to be. I don't want him walking in here and flaming us out of bed."

Isla began her rhythmic assault, rising and falling on Gerry's thick length. "That would be freaky as hell. We could lose a lot of beds that way." She rode him harder and pointed out the window. "Can you imagine him, flying by and tapping the glass?"

Gerry's nostrils flared and he caught her around the waist pinning her on her back. "Less talk, more of this." He plunged deeply within her as his fingertips danced down her tummy. "Do we have appointments this evening?"

Isla moaned. "Yessss." She rose on her hands and gave as good as she got. "Like you said, no talking."

Within different positions and degrees of ferocity, they arrived at the agreement that Isla had to watch his transformation because that was so much of her initial turn-on last evening.

When her sweat drenched his sheets and her legs quivered around his waist, he dropped his head, returned as the icy-eyed amorist, and delivered the devastating bite delivering them to Eden.

Rush hour traffic sounds revved up while they lay wrapped in each other's arms. "What a horrible thing to be sitting in a car right now. I could lay here for…" Her word froze on her lips. Why was the word 'forever' in her dreams and on her lips? She closed her eyes.

Gerry's embrace teased her as he moved over her. He whispered. "Are you going to sleep all evening?" He gestured to the windows. "People should be eating dinner, aren't you hungry?

She startled. "We have that meeting with my family, what time is it?" She looked around for a clock.

"Vampires don't need clocks. We wake with the rhythm of the moon and sun."

"But you wear a watch, what time is it?" She was up and searching for her underwear and then she sniffed herself. "I have to shower. I smell like sex."

He picked up his old timepiece from the bedstand. "Well, you have about fifteen minutes before we jump in the auto to get to that meeting."

She squealed and ran to the bathroom.

Chapter Twenty

Isla and Gerry arrived at her family home in time for dinner. Walking up the steps, Isla turned to Gerry, carrying a stainless-steel travel mug. "I'm pinched with hunger. You're the devil you are."

Gerry caught her before she opened the front door, it was an impulsive adorable move. He drew her close, their foreheads touching. He whispered. "But you continually cried out to God last night."

Wresting out of his arms, her hand twisted the doorknob and she looked over her shoulder. "I did, didn't I?" She stopped to gauge dinner by the aromas. "I hope it's stew and lots of bread." She thought about Anna's comment about carbs.

The table was set for all of them. As her brothers and sister drifted in from the distillery and helped Maisie bring food to the table, the men were silent.

Bram nodded a good evening and whispered to her as they walked to take their seats. "You look like you've been pumpin' all night. Did yah just roll out of bed?"

"What?" Isla patted her hair and hissed playfully. "Sook off, Bram."

The family took their seats, said a prayer and the food started its circle around the table. Gerry sat his mug in the middle of the stoneware plate. He passed on everything with a polite shake of his head and Isla felt her family's scrutiny as they began eating while he sipped.

Drew nodded at the mug. "Whatcha got in there, a drinking problem?"

Gerry smiled with lips covering his teeth. "I'm on a new Army fitness exercise and diet program."

Maisie looked him up and down. "There's not an ounce of fat on yah. I can't imagine why you'd need a diet."

"Got to stay in shape for the new job. You are what you eat." Gerry hoisted his mug with a wink.

Isla nodded to the cast iron skillet filled with a flat loaf. "I'll have more bannock, I'm famished."

The conversation turned to the before and after photos of Erne Castle Isla had posted all week. The family agreed that, with CGI, the castle's restoration would be in good hands.

After they carried their dinner plates to the kitchen, Drew sat with shortbread and coffee. "Pending our attorney's look at the contract, the deal with CGI sounds profitable to us."

Isla refused dessert and nodded with a sip at her coffee. "It's very profitable. There's no doubt." She looked earnestly around each participant at the table. "I hope no one here is prejudiced."

Maisie thumped her hand on the table. "Lass, you've been in this house since your birth. It hasn't changed since you left with your man. You know we aren't."

Isla nodded and folded her hands on the table. "Remember you said that. Let's move into the parlor. Bram, will you fetch Mum's blanket?"

Bram scoffed. "You mean what's left of it. Maisie had to rebind it. It's falling apart with age."

Gerry buried a smile as Isla went to the bookshelf for the family scrapbook. He waited until she took her place on a loveseat and patted the cushion next to her. The family took their seats as an air of mystery filled the room.

Bram gave Gerry the once over. "Aside from bein' Americans, they're not criminals, are they?"

Gerry made a dismissive wave. "Oh, no, they answer to a much higher standard of behavior."

Drew tilted his head. "They're saints?"

Isla jumped in. "Not at all." She settled herself for the reveal. "There are beings in this world that most of us have thought to be mythical." Maisie closed her eyes and gasped. "Some of these beings are known to us as vampires, others are shape-shifters." Isla thought she could hear dust falling on the furniture and the house settling. *Are they breathing?* "Yes, I said vampires and shape-shifters."

Ian leapt to his feet. "You're daft. What, no aliens?"

Maisie looked up at her husband and said quietly but firmly. "Sit down." Ian turned to his wife. His mouth moved like a fish, but he sat down.

Isla continued. "The owners of CGI and many of their employees and guests are vampires."

Drew shook his head. "Come on."

Gerry smiled sublimely. "Would you like proof?" Isla placed a hand on Gerry's arm. "What, love, they aren't ready for this?" He drew his finger back and forth over his face, ending at his wide smile, full of sparkling white teeth.

"Ah, Gerry, I wouldn't ask you to expose yourself like that. It's not a parlor trick."

Bram snarked. "Now you're going to tell us you went to live with a vampire."

Incensed, Isla turned to Gerry. "Go ahead," She waved her hand in resignation, "Do it."

Caitrin dug between the cushions of the sofa and retrieved a paperback book. "This book here says…" her expression froze as Gerry's face transformed. "Saints above." She shook the paranormal romance novel. "This book is wrong." She tossed it to the side and folded her arms over her chest as her head swayed back and forth.

Gerry let his features normalize and Isla gazed into each face in the room. "Any questions?"

Maisie shook her head. "I have no questions. Now the dreams make perfect sense. You had your two mates with you, right Gerry?" She looked around the room at her still gobsmacked family.

Gerry conversationally answered as if they were discussing the price of petrol. "That's right, Maisie and you rode the Pegasus. Remember?"

"You saved my life that night."

Drew gathered himself. "Wait."

Isla shushed him with a stroke of her hand. "You're not the only member of this family Gerry has saved."

Maisie's head came up. "He saved you, too?"

Isla shook her head. "He saved Mum."

Drew stood. "You're daft. He wasn't alive in 1971."

Isla opened the album to the Ibrox pictures. She turned the album and tapped the photos. "Gerry took this photo and then his mate took a photo of Mum, Dad, Gerry, and his date."

Bram stood to pace with Drew. "You could have photoshopped that."

Maisie slanted her head at him. "Photoshopped a picture taken forty-some years ago, that we've grown up looking at?"

"Well?" Bram stopped to consider the absurdity.

Isla turned to Gerry. "Will you tell us the story of that day?" She looked up at Drew and Bram who seemed frozen in place. "Take a seat, you'll want to hear this."

Gerry began the story.

****

"I'm going to give you my perspective on the Ibrox Stadium tragedy. You know your parents were involved in that?"

He was greeted by nods from the family who still watched him warily.

"It was like so many other mid-winter days in Scotland, damp, grey, and cold. I was there with my girlfriend, Fiona, and a new chum from the university. His name was Conall."

The men in the family didn't quite rest comfortably. Each one had their nervous tell. Drew cracked his knuckles. Ian held his head in his hand as he stroked his brow and Bram sat rigid with his arms crossed firmly over his chest.

"It was a tight game, Rangers versus Celtics. I was pissed off, the girl I proposed to a week before hadn't given me an answer and there she sat, next to me but eating up every word Conall laid down. I noticed when I was chatting up Fi about her answer, the young couple in front of me began talking about their future. They were the couple I wanted to be."

Isla's expression turned bittersweet as she sat back with a tissue.

Maisie reminisced. "They were always in love."

Bram threw up a hand. "You don't know he's on the level."

Isla raised a brow. "Just like he's not a vampire?" Bram scowled but remained silent.

Gerry continued his story. "Your Mum was just a wisp of a thing and she was shivering under her Rangers jacket. Conall sat with a heavy Rangers blanket folded on his lap, I said 'How about you let the young lovers cuddle under your blanket?'"

Caitrin stroked the historic blanket, nodding.

"Your Dad said he couldn't keep her warm in the stadium like he usually did." The sisters blushed as the men shook their heads. "We took photos and chatted, and then they cocooned themselves for the game."

Drew pulled out his cellphone and started searching the web. Gerry nodded to him. "Are you fact-checking me? Want the score on the game? The day's temperature? How about the body count?"

Drew grudgingly put away the phone and grumbled. "Is that what you did?"

Ignoring the question, Gerry continued. "While the tension played out on the pitch, people started to leave thinking Celtics had it in the bag." Gerry shrugged. "I didn't care. The girl I wanted, wanted my mate. I was just as happy to leave. Conall gave your folks the blanket, but your mum was still freezing, and they decided to leave. They walked out and we followed them. That's why Conall was so quick to rescue your mum."

The anticipation in the room was palpable. Isla spent the time watching each of her family.

"While we were walking up the stairs, at first, your mum was telling your dad she looked forward to him being the best master distiller in Scotland. He said the same to her about being a graphic artist."

Drew sat forward and gnawed on his knuckle. His slow blink was a tell, as his defenses crumbled.

Gerry took advantage and pressed the point home. "They talked about graduating and coming home to take over the distillery."

Maisie wiped her eyes and Isla handed her the small box of tissues.

Gerry bit his bottom lip and wrung his hands as he went on. "Everyone knows about the wide steep stairway embedded into the earth embankment." He gestured the angle with a flat hand. "We were shoulder-to-shoulder, inching up for five flights. It was madness, we weren't far from the top when there was a stand-shaking gasp and cheers. Your dad turned back to me and asked what just happened?"

Gerry shook his head as if he were there now. "I said, 'I don't know, mate. It's getting tight in here. Look ahead'." Gerry nodded and waved ahead. "It was feeling too close for safety's sake. Before my next step, fans fell forward, like dominos. They were falling against the tubular railings." Gerry bowed his head and pressed the heels of his hands into his eyes. When he returned to the story, his eyes were red. "They fell on each other. The people behind crushed right over us."

Gerry stopped to catch his breath and regain his composure. "Your dad went down under one of the railings which gave him some protection. Your folks were separated by his fall, but she went down on her next step and the railing above her gave way. She was flattened beneath it along with the falling bodies. As I grabbed for her, some guy

as huge as a goalkeeper pushed me and I went down. I jacked my jaw."
Gerry jerked his head back, holding his neck.

The family held their breath and Isla gasped.

"Conall could see I was headin' to get your mum when my chin hit the step. I heard a crack, but I didn't know how badly I was hurt. It was surreal, the way the crowd moved away from Conall's outspread arms. I don't know if he vamped out or not, but people bolted from around us as Conall wrenched the tubular steel railing away from your mum's body. He had her up and in his arms in a flash. Your dad got to his feet and helped me up. There was a ticket office to the left and Conall carried your mum, kicking open the door and pushing things out of his way."

Gerry's hands scrubbed his face and now the resistance of all the observers was gone. "Your mum was grey, gasping for breath. Conall gently placed her on a large, cleared desk. He laid his ear against her chest and barked at your dad. 'She'll die without medical care. Go get it. I have field medicine training. I'll do what I can'."

Gerry held his neck, his face grave. "I offered to help, but Fiona was an hysterical wreck, and Conall had me push her down the hall in a desk chair. I went back to Conall and your mum. He could see I was in pain, by the way I stood, by my posture. He started to come to me, and I waved him away and spoke. 'I'll be fine, help the young woman'."

Maisie nervously drank from a glass of water as she passed the tissue box to Caitrin.

"Your Mum was barely conscious and Conall told me to push desks in front of the door to keep people out. He directed me back with Fiona... but I couldn't step away from them. When he said I didn't need to see what he was going to do, I didn't understand. I turned away but something drew me back. I saw Conall dripping something from his wrist into your mum's gaping mouth. I couldn't process that Conall was force-feeding her his blood. It's odd what shock will do to you."

Several hands flew to their mouths as a communal gasp went up in the room.

"I felt for the task chair behind Conall and lowered into it. But it gave way and went out from under me. My body hit the floor and I've never felt such pain. Everything went dark and I went numb. I thought the light developing behind my eyes was Heaven. When I couldn't force a breath, I wondered if I was dead."

Isla's clasped hands were white knuckled. "I had absolutely no idea vampires were real." He blinked and shook his head. "Conall was beside me in a nanosecond and I heard him say, 'You're not going to understand what's happening, but it's either this or lights out. Blink if you don't want to die.' So, I blinked, it was all I could do."

The family startled at the statement.

"Somewhere in my consciousness, I heard your mum breathing and moving around. I felt as if I was floating down a dark corridor. I drifted like that thinking, 'Where am I?' Conall said. 'In a minute, mate, this is going to be weird'. But I thought it was weird already."

Drew wiped at his mouth and barked. "What did he do to our Mum?"

"Vampire blood is healing to mortals. He was able to restore your mum's ribs and lungs with his blood without turning her into a vampire. My spinal cord was severed by the fall, and it was this," Gerry gestured to his vampire self, "or death."

Caitrin shook her head, holding the blanket to her chin. "My God."

"By the time your dad got back without help, your Mum was sitting up and sipping water. Conall shoved me into a closet to keep me from the light and mortals. Your dad took Lyra home and we never saw each other again."

Maisie clasped Drew's hand. "You remember what Mum said about that day. I know you remember. And Dad came home and said it was rubbish and we were not to play into it. He couldn't have known she was telling the truth."

Drew nodded. "All these years, we thought she was delirious." He wiped tears from his eyes.

Gerry watched them compassionately. "I tell you this so you will know, vampires were people first. Like so many mortal conditions, our nature isn't always our first choice. But I never regret what I am unless mortals reject me out of fear..."

Bram withheld his support. "But you're monsters."

Gerry nodded. "Monsters come in all forms. The Moreaus were monsters. The Hiatts and the Brenners came to my aid for Maisie. We're the good guys."

Maisie squinted out the window. "But I saw a dragon and a Pegasus."

Drew smacked his forehead. "There ya go."

Gerry chuckled. "Those are my shapeshifter friends, Willow and Adam."

Caitrin sighed. "Is Dr. Clarke a shapeshifter?"

Gerry smiled kindly. "Yes, he is."

Caitrin fell back against the sofa and grinned a moan.

Drew stood. "We have to talk about this, it's a family matter. Gerry, thank you for understanding." Drew reflexively walked Gerry to the door.

Isla followed catching up behind them. "Drew, he's going to be family one way or the other."

Drew and Isla stared each other down as he showed his sister and Gerry the front door.

****

Gerry keyed the ignition after they buckled in. They sat for a beat. Isla turned to the side and sought Gerry's gaze. "You left out some of the details when you told me the story."

Gerry gave an ironic smile. "Aye, it's not an easy story to tell, but I reckoned I should give it full-blown to your family. How do you think it went? I couldn't tell."

Isla smirked. "Men are always more hardheaded than the women."

"Oh, you think so. I know a hardheaded woman." Gerry laughed.

Isla looked out the passenger window and whistled. "I could use a drink after that experience."

"I have to go by the office to clean out my desk, so we can hit the pub afterward."

"When I was at Erne Castle, Trevor said alcohol doesn't affect vampires. Except for one kind."

Gerry nodded. "Everclear gives a bit of a zing. Remember the vitamins I put in my sherry?"

Isla narrowed her eyes at him. "Yeah. Vitamins in sherry?"

He flashed his lopsided grin. "We use a few drops of blood so we can taste the liquor, otherwise I wouldn't know how great your scotch is. Trevor, huh? You had dinner with him, didn't you? Did you get to say goodbye?"

Isla hedged for a second. "No, and he was so nice, I'm sorry I missed saying goodbye."

Gerry nodded. "He pals around with everyone, but he was there when we left."

Isla shook. "No."

Gerry laughed. "You know he's the dog, right? He shifts."

"Oh, Gerry, he's not. Besides, there are a few dogs there."

Gerry flicked his turn signal and watched the oncoming lane for a right turn. "Yeah, but the Rottweiler is the only shifter."

Isla stared in shock. "You're serious."

"It's a brave new world, darling. At least the teacups don't sing."

****

Gerry pulled into the Crown Estate car park and stopped next to a tiny red car. He nodded in its direction, there being only two cars in the lot now. "That little red Picanto there is Randall's chariot. He'll probably drive it until the wheels fall off. He's that cheap."

Isla squelched a smile. "I don't think you like him."

"Someday, I'll have to introduce you to Drucilla. She works at the Arcane Veil in Glasgow. How do I describe it? If Colonel Sanders and the Addams family opened a boutique with fast food, that's the place."

Isla raised a brow. "Not exactly Erne Castle."

"No, but it's the only place for miles that serves both vamps and mortals."

"Lovely, you must take me sometime, when there is no other food left on the earth."

They got out of the auto and Gerry clicked the key fob. "Ask Adam about the fried pizza." He draped his arm around her shoulder as they walked up the steps. "I left my key with my letter of resignation. I hope Randall lets me in." He twisted the Victorian brass doorbell three times and an agitated Randall arrived.

"I heard you on the first ring." He opened the door but blocked their entry.

Gerry stepped away from Isla and shook the change in his trousers pockets. "I have to clean out the remainder of my desk, would you be so kind as to let us pass?"

Randall rolled his eyes. "Make it quick." He stepped back and Gerry felt his icy stare all the way to his desk.

Isla sat in Gerry's chair as he hunted down a copier paper box and began sorting the contents of the drawer. He folded the twin photo frames safely in the bottom and retrieved his mug of fountain pens and ink bottles. There were two or three aluminum travel mugs in the bottom drawer and in minutes he recorded a parting message on his phone.

Gerry put the lid on the box and extended his hand to Randall. "They accepted my resignation immediately, so expect a new body in the chair."

Randall sniffed. "I believe they've already hired someone. It's not like you were difficult to replace."

Gerry shortened the handshake and sniffed. "Goodbye, old man." He restrained himself from staking the bastard and led Isla back to the car, where he dropped the box in his boot. "Time for sherry?"

Isla's purse muffled her ringtone. "Ooh, it's the family."

Gerry slanted a look, still holding the car keys. "The Addams Family theme?"

Before she answered, her smile was droll. "Drew came as Gomez to the family Halloween party, Morticia is no longer with us." Gerry winced. "Oh, no, they broke up on New Year's Eve." She held up a finger and took the call. "Yes, brother dearest... Oh, you want us back, so soon? Okay, we're downtown it will take a hot minute."

Gerry opened her door and walked around to seat himself. "It's like a trial when the jury comes back quickly. Is it good or bad?

Isla waved away his question. "We'll see."

****

The family sat around a cleared dinner table with different bottles of Cathcart liquor in the center. The only sober one, Maisie, nursed a mug of tea and her teapot.

Maisie jumped at the sound of their footfalls in the foyer, threw herself into Gerry's arms and hugged him soundly. "Thank you so much. You've saved two members of this family." She patted her baby bump. "Oops, three actually."

Gerry hugged her back. "It's my pleasure, my darling. We couldn't let anything happen to you or the wee one."

She held on to his hand and gazed conspiratorially up at him. "Are we related because of that man's blood?" She slanted a look at Isla and winced.

Gerry's brows rose into his hairline. "It's not quite like that." He pointed between him and Isla. "It's not even kissin' cousins."

They strolled into the kitchen and were greeted by well-liquored men. Ian raised his hand. "Have a drink."

"Aye." Drew and Bram encouraged.

Gerry took the open chair nearest the door. "What are we drinkin' to, lads?"

Drew held his thumb and forefinger about a half-inch apart. "One little thing."

Gerry rested his hands on the table's edge. Isla poured them each two fingers of their best liqueur, a blend of aged Scotch whisky, spices, herbs, and heather honey. "Did you bring your vitamins? I want you to taste this."

The family chuckled and waited as Gerry opened a small dropper bottle and dispensed four drops. They watched with fascination as the red liquid infiltrated the golden liqueur. They raised their glasses to the family. "What are we drinking to?"

Drew raised his glass, easily three fingers, and announced. "Given your, err... natures, given your state of being... We want to meet again with Hiatt, Brenner, and Lachlan. But we think we may have a deal."

Gerry glanced up at Isla who beamed. "You're not going to believe what's about to happen to that crumbled castle."

Gerry nodded. "I think Rick and Anna should invite them all for a weekend at the Erne Castle resort."

Chapter Twenty-One

Eighteen Months Later

On Cathcart Castle, a date stone above the entry door showed that in 1543, the original Isla Cathcart added a wing making it L-shaped. Once CGI began the restoration, they identified the foundations of a round tower built on the external angle and a smaller rectangular turret in the re-entrant angle. This expanded the resort's hotel accommodations into several spacious suites. The resort embraced its Tudor heritage featuring tapestry wallcoverings, grand portraits, and a gracious lobby of polished wood and stained glass.

When it came to erecting a recreation center, they built on to the gatehouse with a crystal palace inspired enclosed pool and gymnasium.

Willow and a few of her Kentucky Pegasus transplants worked the stables where they led trail rides, jumping courses, and horsemanship classes.

Adam and Gerry occupied twin offices in the renovated castle, while Isla and her family occupied offices in the new distillery directly behind the castle, still tapping into the precious spring water.

Restored to its 1970s appearance, the Cathcart family home held collectibles from the initial distillery. Family photos and examples of early bottles decorated the rooms. It was a pleasant beginning for guests exploring their castle. The family's individual cottages lined along the creek on the perimeter of the two hundred acres.

Isla walked through the mostly empty cottage she shared with Gerry. It was move-in weekend. His four-foot by eight-foot industrial freezer and their bed arrived before the rest of their furniture. The box springs and mattress sat in the middle of the master bedroom. She watched gardeners outside her window as they prepared the flower beds for next summer's climbing roses to grow over the stone fence. Two gardeners plotted wide beds of tulips and daffodils for next spring.

She tightened her sweater and cradled her mug of warm tea. November's weather was brisk. Checking the cast iron door next to the fireplace Isla thrilled to find freshly chopped wood. Throwing two more logs on the fire, she sat in the bay window seat and daydreamed.

The property was a beehive with trucks and workers putting the last-minute touches on the resort before the soft opening this weekend. Looking at her watch, a gift from Gerry, she recognized she was due at the main dining room for a tasting dinner in an hour.

November days were short, barely ten hours of sunlight. What a magnificent time for comfort food. She had not met the chef Adam brought in from his home clan. *Caitrin is tripping over dragon shifters, trying to meet every eligible supernatural being.* Kieran Russell moved from his Dublin restaurant, the Rustic Chef, to ride herd over the massive Cathcart Castle kitchen staff. *Another dragon shifter.*

As Isla locked the front door and fingered her golf cart key, she saw Matt's helicopter landing with Cat, Rick, and Anna. *He loves that damned thing. It's noisy as hell and Willow has fits because it spooks the horses, but he says it's a rush to fly one.*

****

After the group shared just about everything on the menu, Gerry pushed back from the dinner table and regarded the people he'd grown to appreciate as a second family. The Cathcarts occupied one side of the long dinner table, while the vampires sat across from them. That made serving easier for the new staff. Dinner was a huge success. The menu featured mortal delicacies as well as finely crafted blood-based dishes for the vampire guests.

Now with dessert wines, fine coffee, and teas, they sat reviewing the plans for the weekend. Gerry caught Isla's hand and kissed the back of it. "The restored portrait of the original Isla arrived yesterday. Since she's our family icon I thought we'd hang it in a little ceremony tomorrow."

Isla impishly slapped at him. "You promised you'd let me see it as soon as it arrived. Where is it?" She moved her chair back.

Drew waved her to stay. "We've barely finished dessert, settle down." Isla pouted. "There you go. Before you moved in with this guy," he hooked a thumb at Gerry, "you weren't used to getting your way every moment. He's spoilt you."

There was a general agreement that most of the CGI women were a pampered lot. Cat spoke up. "I'd like to at least see it."

Anna agreed. "Does she resemble you, Isla?"

Isla threw up her hands. "I have no idea. I haven't seen her."

Rick winked. "You will be amazed at the Cathcart antiques I discovered once I found your letters patent. I pulled that string and all things Cathcart materialized."

Willow stood. "I'd like to see her. Can't we sneak a peek?"

Gerry shrugged. "Wow, tough room. I can't wait to see you at Christmas skulking around the tree shaking the boxes."

The group meandered into the lobby only to find a heavy crate encasing the portrait. Isla rubbed her hands together. "Curses, foiled again. Everything is complicated! I'll run down to the woodshop and grab a couple of hammers."

The Cathcarts stood back and watched their animated sister dart off to the woodshop at the end of the property's carpark.

****

Though filled with the Cathcart family and the vamps, the lobby was still spacious. Drew ran his hands over the carved concierge desk. "This was made in the woodshop?"

Adam strolled over; it was a 'man thing' to touch the fine patina of the wood's grain. "Yes, and it's from lumber milled here. There were a few trees we had to clear out. The tree this is made of was about four hundred years old, and we thought it was a fitting transmutation."

The night shift security guard appeared and nodded to the party seeking Adam and Gerry. "Excuse me, sirs, did you receive a delivery from a man in a little red car?" They looked at each other askance.

"Delivery?" Gerry shook his head. "Perhaps he went around to the kitchen?"

The guard looked baffled. "No, sir, that's why I am asking. The car hasn't left the resort and I'm not seeing it on my patrol."

Gerry and Adam shared another look, now more concerned. "Have you checked the security cameras?" Gerry asked.

"My partner is checking. I'm waiting to hear from him." He tapped the radio on his shoulder, nodded, and stepped back from Adam and Gerry. "Unit two, this is unit one, please respond." There was only static. "Unit two, respond." He frowned. "Unit three, this is unit one, can you give me a location on unit two?"

Unit three crackled on the radio. "I'm en route to the carpark. That's where unit two headed. But he's not responding."

Gerry's hand scrubbed his face. "That's where Isla was headed, to the woodshop. I'll be back." Gerry sprinted out the door toward the woodshop.

Adam shrugged. "Probably a reporter trying to get behind-the-scenes photos."

The women stood along the tapestried wall talking design. Matt hung with the Cathcart men chatting scotch and their distillery process. Adam and Rick disappeared into the office behind the front desk.

****

As Adam circled the bank of security cameras, he shook his head. "I'm sure it's paparazzi trying to beat our reveal this weekend." Adam dialed to the multi-level carpark. "Rick, does that look like a shoe?" He pointed to a red car and possibly a body hidden behind it.

"More than a shoe, old man. That's your guard. I recognize the boot."

Adam bolted out the back door for the car park.

****

As cool as a five-hundred-year-old vampire could be, Rick strolled out to the group. Hands casually in his trouser pockets, he rocked on the balls of his loafers. "Folks, let's take a look at the library." With a sweeping gesture, he motioned them toward the room with no windows.

As Matt made up the tail, Rick spoke in subtones. "We've got trouble in the carpark. You'd better get out there. I'll stay with the mortals. Adam should be there already. Gerry is headed to the woodshop."

Matt nodded at Cat and Anna who pretended not to have vampire hearing. "Are you thinking of a bomb?"

"Could be anything. I know one guard is down."

Matt generated his mega-watt smile and wiped at his bottom lip. "Who did we piss off?"

"Brother, I have no idea. Watch yourself."

****

Gerry threw open the door to the woodshop and found Isla struggling to keep cutting tables between herself and Randall.

The edge in Randall's voice was as sharp as the tools on the wall. "...And another thing...You Cathcarts think you're sent from heaven above...You ruined everything." The perturbed vampire hopped on the table and dropped in front of Isla, grabbing her by the shoulders. With his wicked shake, she shrieked.

Gerry bellowed. "Randall, that's enough. Step away from Isla and you can leave."

Randall threw her aside and roared with rage. "You think I'm afraid of you, Mr. plaid waistcoat and manners? You may think I'm a wimp, but I grew up on the streets of Glasgow." Randall pushed up the sleeves of his jacket and hoisted his fists for a fight.

Gerry gave him a dismissive look. "I'm not going to fight you, Randall. What's the point of that? Just go."

"I had everything planned out. The Moreaus were paying me a fortune in commission on this property as well as a bounty for that baby. I would have been set for the next hundred years. What is it your friend says, play the long game? You put a boot in my long game."

Gerry eyed Isla along the back wall, recovering from slamming against a table saw. "Darlin', did he hurt you?" Gerry leveled an ominous look back at Randall. "Go, now."

The vampires heard Matt yell to Adam from deep in the carpark. "The guard is dead. Where is this guy?"

Randall looked around furtively as Gerry advanced on him. "You stay away from me." He grabbed a roughing knife left out on the workbench and waved it with a practiced stance. "One step and I'll have your lassie by the throat."

Gerry halted. The door flew open, and Adam's form filled the doorframe. Randall flexed and yanked Isla from the floor. With one arm around her neck and the other hand brandishing the knife he jerked his head toward Adam. "Who is this animal?"

Adam shook his head. "You don't want to find out."

Gerry took a tentative step forward. Randall whipped around toward him. "I'll kill her right now. I've already killed one of my own, what's a mortal life? What's it worth to you, McIntosh?"

Gerry dug deep for calm reason. Isla's gaze registered raw terror. She fought to breathe evenly. "Please, Randall. I've never been anything but nice to you. Please let me go."

Randall took another step back from Gerry and Adam and drew in a deep inhalation of Isla's scent. "You've been all over her. Do you know what else I lost when you flamed the Moreaus? Drucilla decided I wasn't rich enough." He glanced down at Isla. "I ought to kill your tart right now."

Gerry caught Adam's eye and pointedly glanced up at the exposed beams over the worktables. Adam nodded imperceptibly and kicked over a can of rags near the door. At the same moment, Gerry made a vertical leap for the closest beam, but it was too late.

For extra show, Randall spun Isla out as if releasing her. Gerry reached for her, but Randall yanked her back and with a swing of the roughing knife slit her throat. At vamp speed, the murderer dropped Isla to the floor and darted under Adam's arm braced against the doorframe.

In that same instant, Gerry was beside Isla, futilely trying to hold pressure against a deep and long wound cut ear to ear. Blood gushed between his fingers; no *drops* of vampire blood would reverse this. Gerry recognized his only option. "Matt," was his extended cry as he drew his bleeding love to lay flat on the floor. *Where to start?* As his fangs dropped long, he sank them into his wrist to start the flow of what could begin to heal her. *Will it be enough?*

Matt slid into the room and dropped to his knees, pushing up his shirt sleeves to expose his wrists. "Rick!" Matt roared before he bit his wrist to begin a healing flow to patch Isla's torn neck. As the dark vampire blood hit the fresh wound, healing began from the inside.

Rick bounded into the room and without question opened a vein on his wrist, he began patching the other side of Isla's neck with his blood.

The security guard arrived but stood in shock for a beat. Gerry began to falter. "It's not supposed to be like this. I'm supposed to drain her and feed my blood back to her." He pushed the bloody heels of his hands into his eyes and shook his head at what he needed to do.

With cupped hands, he caught as much of her blood as possible and drank it down. Matt narrowed his gaze at Gerry and Rick spoke up. "Damn fine thinking, Gerry, you understand you have to consume her blood and feed it back through your system for this to work."

Gerry leaned over Isla's body hoarding every drop of her blood that had not yet clotted. Seeing her neck wound healed, he returned to her gaping mouth and spilled his precious blood into her.

Matt lowered his ear to her chest. "I think I heard something, keep feeding her."

Gerry knew a normal, mortal heartbeat was around eighty beats a minute. Vampires at rest were generally two beats a minute. Waiting thirty seconds for that second beat was an eternity. What scared him most was how long her brain hung in limbo, unsupported by oxygen. *Can vampire blood heal that?*

Gerry knelt over Isla's body, pouring out his life's blood while Rick fed him. Matt continued to listen for signs of her undead heartbeat.

Somewhere in the far reaches of the resort, Gerry heard a roar, an explosion, and then silence. Matt raised his head. "I've got another heartbeat." He chafed Isla's wrist and spoke softly to her. "Open your eyes, Isla. Blink if you can hear me." He grinned up at Gerry. "She's with us, now."

When Isla's hands clutched at Gerry's wrist, he startled at the force. "Did you see that?"

Rick and Matt nodded with a chuckle. "I think she is with us."

****

Rick walked to the wall phone and hit the extension for the blood donor pool. "What chance is there of finding five or six healthy donors?" The voice on the line hesitated. Rick barked, "This is a crisis. Step it up."

"Sir, we have staff scheduled Saturday evening."

Rick turned and surveyed the bloody carnage in the woodshop. "Get into the kitchen, tell Kieran we need at least five mortal donors, or we're going to lose some good people."

Glancing over the bloody tableau, Rick drew in a calming breath as he saw Isla leaning against a haggard Gerry. The longer she suckled on his wrist, the more Gerry paled.

Matt bent over examining her healed throat. Standing he nodded to Rick. "I've got to get some of this cleaned up before her family barges in here."

As Gerry slid the two of them to lean against the wall, Rick and Matt swabbed the floor. The air was full of anger, fear, and the scent of copper as the security guard returned with Cat and Anna.

Cat grasped at the door frame as she absorbed the meaning of the shocking scene. Anna slid into her back. "Cat, what?" Cat stepped aside. "Oh, my God." Both vampiresses rolled up their sleeves.

Matt looked over from the mop sink and gestured, "Emergency turning, we spent half of Rick's and my blood to heal her throat. We're about to lose Gerry if we don't have someone to spell him on feeding Isla."

Neither woman hesitated as Cat lovingly pulled Gerry from his fledgling. "Gerry, we've got this." She offered her wrist to him and pulled him back from Isla.

Anna insinuated herself closer to Isla. Offering her wrist, she coaxed, "Let me see those baby fangs of yours." She spoke as if to a child." Isla's huge eyes blinked, not registering understanding. It wasn't until Anna forced her wrist into the fledgling's mouth that Anna felt fang on flesh. Sitting close to Isla, Anna wrapped her arm around the bewildered woman's shoulders. Anna shook her head at Rick. "Does she understand what happened? What *did* happen?"

As Isla's grip on Anna tightened, Rick turned to the guard. "Stand ready to spell us on feeding Gerry and Isla." Three kitchen staff arrived in their bright white uniforms. "No worries folks, your cleaning bill is on me. How many of you have ever fed a vampire?"

They shrugged and rolled up their sleeves. Anna regarded Rick slouched against the table. "Fitz, eat, now."

The unit three guard arrived with a six-pack of blood bags. "These are thawed and ready to drink."

Rick waved a hand. "Over here." He grabbed a bag like a juice box and sucked down the pint in one long draw. On the second bag he was able to sip more slowly. As Matt and Gerry made use of the other four pints, Rick explained to his horrified family, "A vamp slit Isla's throat. He damn near decapitated her. We had to heal the wound before Gerry could feed her. The concern is the gap between..."

Anna looked up at him. "We're going to need more blood, she's got a helluva draw on me." Anna flexed her fingers to feel circulation in her hand.

Adam returned barefoot wearing only trousers. Kieran was close behind. "Okay, mate... let's see what dragon blood does..."

Rick levied a suspect look at the two shifters. "Excuse me?"

Adam volunteered both arms. "Venus drank plenty of my blood, was that what made her so feisty?"

Rick pointed to Anna. "Come out, Adam's going in."

As Adam drew Isla onto his lap, her eyes filled with tears, and she curled into his chest. Her sobs were childlike and confused. He stroked her hair back from her face. "Isla, lay back, have some of this." He offered his large arm and held her tightly as she bit and suckled.

Beside the two of them, Anna watched closely and monitored Adam's heartbeat. One of the kitchen staff sat beside her and offered his wrist. She shook her head, bit her bottom lip, and admitted, "I'm sorry, this isn't going to be my best bite, she damn near drained me."

Cat rushed in between Anna and the staff member. "Bite me. I'll get you over the blood lust." The kitchen staffer jumped back a foot hearing those words.

As she fed from Adam, Isla's confused expression matured to awareness of the people in the room as well as her needs. She lifted her mouth from his wrist and wiped daintily. Anna nodded from where she fed from Cat. "Adam, time to trade places with Kieran. Our fledgling is about to be full."

Rick looked over at his mate. "Cupcake, I'll say the same for you and Cat. Let Kieran's staff feed you and Cat. He stood steady on his feet and moved in front of Gerry. With his hands on Gerry's shoulders, he sought his gaze and raised a brow. "How are you, dear boy?"

Gerry's gaze was coherent. "I could use a little fresh."

Rick gestured over one of the kitchen staff. "Gerry, make yourself comfortable. "As soon as we can find more volunteers, you'll be your old self again."

Matt swallowed the last of the bagged blood. "Gerry don't let him kid you. With a fledgling, you'll never be your old self again."

Cat licked the bite on the kitchen staff's wrist and leveled a look at her mate. "Oh, yeah? Are you about to tell him how his life is bound to improve?"

Matt smirked. "With or without a trip to see Khuno?"

Cat's brows arched at the memory of her own traumatic turn. With a smirk, she gave the room an assessing gaze. "Thank you so much for your donation. Why don't you go back to the kitchen and drink some orange juice and lay down for about an hour's nap." Cat smiled graciously at the kitchen worker who just fed her. She made sure the wound on his wrist healed. Although he was lingering in that post-orgasmic ecstatic state, he was able to wobble to his feet.

Adam turned his back on the group as he spoke into the phone. "Willow, I need you to keep the family in the castle." He listened and shook his head. "By Odin's missing eye, they've what?"

As the kitchen staffer ambled away from the woodshop in his bloodied kitchen whites there were gasps from outside. In seconds, the Cathcart brothers pushed into the room and froze.

"What in the actual bloody hell?" Drew held the remaining family back. "Isla, what's going on?"

Isla sealed the puncture on Kieran's wrist and nodded to him. "Did you hear what Cat said to your staff member?"

Kieran's eyes glazed over in delight. He ran a hand over his face. "I didn't."

Rick came by and offered his hand to help the big man up from the floor. "That's okay, we'll get you where you need to be."

Drew stepped into the room and barely avoided the remnants of Isla's lifeblood. He demanded. "What happened?"

Isla wiped her lips and put a finger to them. "Shh! Vampire hearing," She tapped her ear. "My ears are very sensitive."

Drew's stance grew aggressive as the other siblings moved around him into the large woodshop. Murmurs rose from the doorway. Isla waved her hands and yelped. "Enough! Be quiet. Shh. I'll tell you everything, just don't speak."

She sorted her thoughts for a moment. Drew grew impatient. "Well?"

"A man tried to kill me. Tried is the critical word. As you can see, I'm not *dead*."

Gerry's expression lightened for the first time during this melee. "Yeah, Drew. She's not dead, simply undead."

Bram pushed forward from behind and barked. "Who tried to kill you?"

Isla placed her finger over her lips. "Ssh… It's not important. What is important is my Gerry saved another Cathcart and he couldn't have done it without his friends." She looked up at the faces of her mortal family. "As a matter of fact, every vampire here except me could use some fresh donor blood because they've given themselves fully to my rescue."

Drew walked in silent inspection around the cutting tables. He winced at the discarded roughing knife still on the floor, his sister's blood dried over it. He paced and wrung his hands, looking back at his siblings and then the vampires. "I know next to nothin' about all this, but even I can see this was an extraordinary effort on their part. You say they need blood?" He turned to his family. "We have plenty."

Rick extended his hand. "You've proven to be an understanding lot since I've met you. Now I know how truly generous you are." The two men shook hands and Rick regarded the number of people, the room's general havoc, and turned to the Cathcarts. "Why don't you meet Willow back in the lobby, she'll take you downstairs and get you instructed on the feeding process." Rick watched the family move in a cloud of shock as they kept looking over their shoulder at their sister. "I don't mean to be common, but I believe I'm going out to the barn to hose off." Each vampire regarded their current bloody state and followed along.

Chapter Twenty-Two

The following evening, Caitrin wended her way through the resort property seeking Matt Brenner as though he was an addiction. She found him in the bar, directing the hanging of the family portraits. Matt painted the life-sized gilt-framed masterpieces in the Holbein style. He turned as she entered the room. "Ms. Cathcart, how are you feeling?"

Caitrin wandered to her portrait leaning against the wall. As one hand's fingers trailed over the frame's intricate carving, she bit her other pinkie. "When I posed for this portrait months ago, I had no idea how irresistible you are. Then last night when I fed you..." She sighed and sank against the wall like a fangirl.

Matt stood with his hands on his hips, his fingers splayed, and nodding pleasantly. "You know that feeling is an illusion, Caitrin?"

She shook her head. "No, it's real. I dreamt of you all night. Please don't tell me all your donors feel this way."

Matt winced and stuffed his hands into his jeans pockets. He began a slow shuffle around the bar. "Actually, they do. Vampires would never attract willing donors if it were a horrible experience?"

Caitrin shook her head, gobsmacked. "But you're all I can think about."

Cat and Anna entered the room each carrying large vases. Cat put hers down and moved toward Caitrin. "I couldn't help overhearing your reaction to feeding my mate." Cat hugged Caitrin like a sister and whispered in her ear. "Ask Anna how she felt feeding Matt."

Anna turned from placing her vase. "Cat... that was so long ago."

Matt moved back to sliding portraits along the wall. "Yeah, Cat, that was ages ago. But Cat's right, feeding vamps can be addicting."

Caitrin grinned at Matt. "When can I feed you again?"

"By the time you can donate again, I'll be back in Malibu painting for my show and enjoying my beautiful mate's company." He extended his hand and Cat curled into his embrace. They stood shoulder-to-shoulder.

Cat smiled sweetly, her arm around Matt's waist. "I understand Dr. Clarke is visiting this weekend. I don't believe he has a plus one. Perhaps you can keep him company?"

Caitrin's eyes lit up. "Oh, I've got to get a good night's sleep to be fresh for this weekend."

Passing by with bubble wrap in her hands, Anna enjoined Caitrin. "That's a good idea, I'll walk out with you." As they turned the corner, Anna gestured to a sign for the spa. "They're practicing some of their new pedicure aromatherapies. Why don't we drop in?"

Caitrin looked over her shoulder at Matt and Cat in a more than warm embrace. Caitrin's smile faded with her hopes.

Anna confided. "Been there, done that, and then I got my own vampire."

"Are they like swans, do they mate for life?" Caitrin's voice broke.

Anna nodded. "For the most part? Yes, we do mate for life."

****

As Gerry felt the pull of twilight, he nuzzled Isla in his arms. It was her first rising as a member of 'the family', and she was a tentative vampire. Her body's assimilation to her new nature was challenging. Gerry hoped to awaken her with what he lovingly thought of as true love's kiss.

When his lips touched hers, she stretched against him and let out a squeal through her covered mouth. Her hands flew to tickle his torso.

"Whoa, baby." Gerry threw open the freezer door and sat up. "You're frisky this evening. There is something you should know about our new bond."

She shimmied her shoulders and leaned into him. "How my flesh sizzles with delight when it touches yours?"

Gerry grinned as she groped for his manly parts. "Oh, yeah. Fledglings only need a breeze to kick start their libido. There I was thinking a couple of years ago that you were a little uptight and now, what have I created?"

Isla cocked her head, Gerry thought she was listening to some faraway sound. "About your creation..." She pushed to the opposite end of the padded industrial freezer and leaned her chin on her hand. She looked around the room with no windows.

Gerry chuckled. "No windows, but you can see me perfectly, can't you?"

She nodded. "It's crazy. Anyway, about that time between Randall cutting my throat and me being like this... What did *you* experience during the time you were being turned?"

Gerry gave it a thought and shrugged. "It's going to stick with you forever. I remember mine like it was yesterday." He paused. "You understand you had a very unusual emergency turn. If it had been just you and me, I couldn't have brought you back." They shared a somber gaze. "I probably would have joined you in the afterlife from trying to save you. You needed so much blood."

Isla's hand went to her throat. "I don't feel anything now."

Gerry nodded. "Not a mark on you."

"But I remember the burn of the knife, I remember the expression on your face. And then it was as if a giant hand reached in, grabbed my soul, and pulled me out. I was suddenly above everything."

"I have heard that before. It wasn't like that for me. The fear on their faces frightened me. Every experience is different." He reached out for her hand and meshed his fingers with hers. "Tell *me* about your crossing."

"I felt bad for Matt and Rick, they worked so hard over me. From the looks on their faces, I was frightened. Then I looked for you." His head dipped, and she paused. When she looked up at him, tears waited to fall. "Gerry, remember the first morning we were together?" He nodded with a smirk. "You said I had given myself a fright. Hah! If you think I had a fright in your bedroom, I think I gave you a terrible fright tenfold."

"You had me on the edge, girl, you did. Where were you?"

"I was out there." She waved a hand toward heaven. "I'm struggling to find words for something inexpressible. I was in a real place of exquisite beauty, but my body was lying on the floor of the woodshop. I felt as though I still had a body, but it was lighter and without pain. All the while I knew I'd seen myself bleeding out seconds before."

Gerry nodded as he traced a pattern on the back of her hand. "Did you hear my pleas to come back to me?"

She tapped over her heart. "I felt them... But it was as though it was very far away. I was in no pain. In fact, I met my parents in this beautiful place and I told them about you." She negated that with a wave of her hand. "Told them is not really it. It's like telepathy and I downloaded every wonderful thing about you and us in a nanosecond. They understood, and they helped return me. My mum was over the moon about us. She understood how badly I wanted to be in this relationship. She knew I wanted to see the resort blossom; I wasn't done... Then Adam's blood felt like jumper cables. That was crazy."

Gerry shrugged. "Wow, great. Matt and Rick are bandages, I'm what, chopped liver?"

"Oh, that's not what I meant."

Gerry drew her closer. "The lifeforce of a dragon is a thousand times stronger than mortals. I believe the fact that he'd just returned from a shift, his dragon blood was even more impactful."

Isla cocked her head. "When did he shift?"

Gerry's expression was tranquil. "While you were off visiting your parents and we were taking desperate action, Adam was apprehending your attacker. Randall had the bad judgment to think his roller skate of a car could outrun a dragon. Right now, do you hear the sound of heavy machinery outside?"

Concentrating, Isla closed her eyes. "I do. What is starting now? Don't we open this weekend?" Both hands flew to her face.

"Not to worry. It's just the soft opening. They're digging a nice deep hole in the north pasture to bury a lump of burned-up auto."

"Eww. Where's Randall?"

Gerry made a circular motion with his index finger. "Follow the process of a vampire driving to get away and a dragon flaming him." Her mouth oh'd. "He's ash." She grimaced. "Adam got him from behind, I don't think he even felt it."

Isla ran a hand through her hair. "I owe Adam a thank you card. Maybe a nice fruit basket..."

Gerry laughed. "So anyway, Adam's dragon was pumping. By the time he made it back to us, his sense of protection was still front and center."

Isla looked around the sparse room. "Oh, Gerry, half our house is mortal."

"Ah, well it's a good thing nothing else has arrived. We fit pretty well in my freezer. Will you share it with me?" He ran a hand over the padded interior.

She tried to react, and Gerry laughed softly, "I know from the look in your eyes, you're blushing. We'll right everything up -- have the windows done as you saw at Rick's place at Erne castle. You need a little time to acclimate to your vampire senses and learn how to control your strength and speed. But most importantly, feeding will be a big learning curve. Luckily, you're surrounded by some of the finest donors in the UK. We just don't want you biting anyone's head off from hunger."

Isla slid into his lap. "So, we're going to be together a lot."

"Yes, my dear, we will." Gerry's fingers dove into her wealth of mussed hair. "Right now, how about a nice cold shower and dinner?"

****

Two Weeks Later

Isla adapted beautifully to her new nature. She spent as much time as she could around the largest group of humans in her immediate area, her family. She didn't have even the slightest inclination to bite one, even when Bram got on her nerves.

Gerry worked almost nonstop the last three days because tonight was the official grand opening. He felt guilty rising a bit early to dress and get to the Castle.

The CGI dignitaries flew in last night. The platinum patrons landed with their entourages. The Cathcart family stood beside Rick, Matt, Adam, and Gerry to greet the VIPs.

The lobby filled with sharply dressed bell staff carefully managing bespoke luggage. As soon as a limo arrived, and the occupant's bar code scanned, the bell staff escorted them to their suite.

Since the informal reception was already underway, many elected to see their magnificent room and bounce back down for the party.

****

Isla arrived and took her place next to Gerry. *Wow, was he right!* She nearly tasted the perfumes and aftershaves. She could scent different shoe polishes and hair sprays. It made her feel like she had an attention deficit disorder. One scent would trigger a memory and she'd zone out for a second. She caught Gerry's arm as Rick and an older couple walked up to them.

Rick bowed, took Isla's hand, and turned to the older gentleman. "Marquis, may I present the newest member of the family, Lady Isla Cathcart."

The Marquis bowed and kissed the back of Isla's hand. "Your hospitality is even more gracious than we expected, and we expect a great deal from CGI. Helen and I will take advantage of every inch of this beautiful estate."

Isla nodded, her brain buzzing from all the names. Rick smiled at the older woman with the Marquis. "Helen, have you caught up with Anna yet? She's looking for you."

Helen, a mortal woman in her late sixties stood tanned and coiffed California style. "I can't wait to catch up with your Cupcake, but first I want to meet Isla." Helen stepped closer and gave Isla a head-to-toe inspection. She leveled a sweet smile at Rick. "She's not a bon-bon. She's not a cupcake, but she definitely is a buttery shortbread."

Isla stood with her hand in Helen's, looking at Gerry and thinking, *What's going on?*

Helen patted her hand. "In the dark ages, I fed Rick." She smirked at him. "I work in the Los Angeles office. Come visit us!"

Isla's relief returned with a calming breath. "What's this cupcake, bon-bon, shortbread thing?"

Quickly, Rick embraced Helen and spun her back to the Marquis. "Oh, Isla, a story for another day."

Rick says that a lot.

They moved the party into the grand hall. Adam and Willow stood beside Gerry and Isla before Rick and Matt stepped onto the orchestra platform.

Sharing accomplished smiles, Rick spoke. "Over a hundred years ago, our clever idea of thrilling to feed took off and here we are today with our eighty-second property. This one is special because of Adam --" Rick scanned the crowd and found the couple, "come up, Adam and Willow." Moving through the tight crowd, they joined Rick and Matt. "This one was Adam's idea. If you like it, tell me. If you don't, tell him. This site is the beloved homestead of Lady Isla Cathcart." He gestured to Isla and Gerry. "Her determination to bring the property back into her family opened it to the world. It's seemed like forever, but tonight we celebrate one family's persistence. "Isla, Gerry, get up here."

When Isla stood on the stage, her mind spun. Wearing designer clothing and Gerry's pampering did not hold a candle to the fact that her family history was vindicated by none other than a five-hundred-year-old vampire who rubbed shoulders with Henry VIII.

Rick gestured her to center stage where she nodded and smiled before taking the mic. "Mr. Hiatt gives me too much credit. I was the face of the family who interacted with the Crown Estate. Generations of Cathcarts have worked on legitimizing our claim." There was hearty applause from her family which spread throughout the room. "Please give a hand also to the men in my family. Drew, Bram, and Ian work every day to produce the finest Highland Scotch Whisky in the world. Perhaps the rest of the world has not met us yet, but when they do, they will love us." Isla smiled at her sisters. "My sister Maisie learned graphic arts at our mum's knee. Every time you see one of our signs or bottles, that's her artistry." The crowd applauded. "And my baby sister Caitrin and I will wear your ear off with our sales pitches."

****

The band played on, but the mortals drifted off around three in the morning. Isla experienced as much stimulation as a fledgling could take. Gerry found her in the kitchen's walk-in cooler. "Lass, I thought I'd find you in here. Have you had enough party?"

She ran to his embrace and cuddled under his chin. "I have. I feel like I've been on a Tilt-a-Whirl. Can we go home?"

Gerry sighed and drew in the scent of her weariness. "We can sneak out the back and hop a golf cart home." As they snuck out the back door, he squeezed her hand. "I'm feeling the pull of the freezer, myself."

"Just the freezer?" Isla quirked an eyebrow as her thoughts drifted in another direction.

As the couple closed the door on the outside world, Gerry turned and took both Isla's hands. "I love how I feel in your arms when we submit to each other."

Isla ran a gentle fingertip down his nose. "Being pinned to the mattress beneath you? Well, well, well, what can I say?"

The delicious burn of passion steadily rose, and reality slipped from their grasp, as the conflagration overtook them. On their path to the king-sized bed, there was a riot of sensual laughter muffled by kisses. Then lusty sighs began as their bodies hit the sheets.

Isla stretched underneath Gerry and bowed her back, pressing her breasts in his face. "After all my exposure to downstairs…"

"Downstairs? Ah, you mean the Gaoler?"

"Yes, I do! I want to show you what a hungry girl I am. I want to sink round your cock and take you deep into me." With a sinfully seductive tone, she added, "I want to ride you like the stallion you are."

Gerry rose to his knees. "Ah, I thought the room felt hotter."

Playfully, he scooped Isla into his lap and wrapped both arms around her. Her tongue darted over the shell of his ear and a cool inhalation sent a shiver up his spine.

With another playful wrestling match, Isla wrapped her legs around his waist and poised herself over his stiff cock. "So, are you still seeking the freezer or some of this?" It didn't take rocking on him to jumpstart their next dance.

With vamp speed, he took her. Isla rejoiced in every stroke of his thick cock caressing her g-spot deep inside. She swooned as her clit pulsed with delightfully electric shocks. So close to breaking, teetering on the verge, Isla rolled Gerry on his back.

"I see what you're doing here." He playfully caught her breasts and rose to kiss each pert nipple. It was his brand of slow, delicious, deliberate torture that consumed them.

When their bodies affirmed their ecstasy, and her heavenly grasp on his hard flesh became an iron grip, their fangs dropped long.

His opalescent eyes met hers and with preternatural grace, they bit. She leaned into his bite and caught his wrist. What started as a kiss ended with them rolling and giggling at their latest experience as vampire lovers.

"Isla, my dear, what happens when two people meet and get off on the wrong foot?" Gerry winked at her as he stroked her hair out of her eyes.

"Ah, I think they get under each other's skin until," Isla's fingertip stroked down his sixpack and tickled his thatch of pubic hair, "they find out that they're perfect for each other."

Gerry playfully bit her bottom lip. "Exactly." He caught her in an embrace and pulled her up to the wealth of pillows along the headboard. "Then claim me, Isla, and with every twilight and every step, your whispered words will be emblazoned upon my heart, for eternity. Our love will be immortal." He held her left hand and kissed her ring finger.

Isla's lashes blinked as she looked from her finger to his amorous gaze and then his sultry lips. "Is this some kind of vampire proposal?" Her smile spread across her face.

Gerry kissed up her throat, across her jaw, and to her lips. "It is, in fact. Death may, indeed, be final; yet being undead, the love we'll share is a legacy."

Epilogue

Rick Hiatt sat poolside in his residence at Erne Castle with a stack of newspapers. Rachmaninoff's Piano Concerto No. 2 in C minor softly filled the indoor patio. The architects perfectly captured the look of a conservatory with skylights and palms in a vampire-safe design. Player rested in his favorite place, on a rug at Rick's feet.

Anna floated, eyes closed, both hands lazily trailing in the warm salt water as they heard Matt and Cat Brenner close up their side of the shared home.

Casually Matt and Cat took a lounge chair across from Rick. Cat buried a smile as Matt raised a brow, his elbows on his thighs as he leaned toward his business partner and friend. "Before we leave for Los Angeles, I just wanted to say, you pulled a rabbit out of your hat finding the letters patent. How much did that artifice cost us?"

Rick snapped the newspaper in half and half again. "Artifice?" His grin spread wide. "Nay, nay, I say." His hands folded over the paper as his brow waggled. His smile expressed pure Hiatt satisfaction.

Matt shot him a suspicious glance. "What? I thought it was something you crafted to get Adam started in the business, you know, romancing the Cathcarts."

Rick pointed to Cat. "When did my perennial Boy Scout become a 'doubting Thomas'? Is he like this in sunny California?"

Cat grinned and shook her head. "Him, a 'doubting Thomas'? Not quite, more of a 'curious George.' Where did you get those papers?"

"Have no fear, they were right where they needed to be. Safe with monks who had a healthy respect for ... the undead. Where else do you think I 'found' all the Cathcart collectibles? Suffice it to say, although I wasn't in the country when Henry did his good deed, I knew his haunts."

After a moment of silent consideration, Matt and Cat stood, both shaking their heads at Rick's reality. "It's always good to have a five-hundred-year-old friend."

Anna ascended the steps of the pool and dried off. "I tend to agree." She strolled over to stand behind her mate and he rose to help her into a terry robe.

Rick and Anna walked alongside Matt and Cat toward the front door, where the resort's limo waited. After the two couples exchanged hugs and handshakes, Rick opened the leaded-glass front door. "So, what's up next, is this a 'see you later?'"

Cat slid into the limo with a wave as Matt stood with his hands on his hips at the limo's back door. "I don't know." His gaze swept back over the Erne Castle resort and his expression turned wistful. "It just gets better and better. Let's leave it up to serendipity."

Rick stole a kiss from Anna and shrugged. "Serendipity. It's full of possibilities, isn't it?"

Matt's crooked smile spread as he sat down and swung his long legs into the sleek, black vehicle. "For us, yeah."

The End

Where to follow Amber Anthony

AllAuthor
BookBub
BookSprout
GoodReads
The Romance Reviews
Twitter @WriteAmberA
Facebook.com/WriteAmber

Also by Amber Anthony

Appetite for Blood, The Prequel to The Blood Trilogy
Blood Rising, Book One
Blood Emerald, Book Two
Blood Dragon, Book Three
Blood Fugue, Tales from the Gaoler
Arise, My Darling
Roman's Revenge
Roman's Rules
Roman's Return
Becoming Gabriel

Audiobooks
Appetite for Blood
Blood Rising
Blood Emerald

Do you enjoy tea with your reading?

We have blended teas for each book and a few of our characters. They are grouped by Key Word: Amber Anthony, Romance Writer by Patrice Bader

www.adagio.com

We have blended teas to compliment all our romance novels. When you purchase these, 5% is donated to various charities listed on that tea's page.

Other Books by Amber Anthony

Appetite for Blood, Prequel to The Blood Trilogy

A revolution is roaring into the 1920s! Vampires, who previously killed to feed, now thrill to feed.

The revolution is led by a four-hundred-year-old vampire, Rick Hiatt, and his newly turned ward, Matt Brenner. This is not the first time Rick has encountered the brutal treachery of the Moreau family of vampires, but he and Matt seek to make it the last.

Los Angelinos mortal and immortal are under attack by the entitled, remorseless Moreaus. Dragon-shifter Adam Lachlan and seductresses Venus and Luna, team up with Rick and Matt to put an end to the siege. Brute strength won't take these hellions down, but they might be hoodwinked into exposing themselves.

Read about the origins of the fast friendship between Matt, Rick, and Adam, and see how their BDSM empire grew from humble beginnings to an international conglomerate.

Blood Rising
The Blood Trilogy Book One

Drop-dead gorgeous alive, Matt Brenner has never lacked for feminine attention. Undead, he's even more potent. Immortality would be stellar if only he accepted his life as a vampire. Matt and fellow vamp Richard Hiatt created a BDSM empire catering to Vampire/Doms and willing donor/subs who trade sexual ecstasy for blood. The clubs have made Matt's existence manageable, if uninspired. Inspiration comes in the form of Catherine Temple.

Matt has made it a rule not to get emotionally involved with human women, and he sticks to it. Cat is the woman who can entice him to break all the rules. When Matt is introduced to a controversial drug that allows him a human lifetime with Cat, it's too exquisite to resist.

Powerful elements of the vampire nation are against it, and though Matt tries to protect Cat, love must be stronger than death.

Blood Emerald
The Blood Trilogy Book Two

SDV (Single Dom Vampire) unknowingly ISO compassionate, sincere, spontaneous SMW (Single Mortal Woman). Extra points for patience, brains, and beauty. Handsome, powerful, Rick Hiatt has managed romance and sex within the roles of Dom/sub relationships for five hundred years. What if there is something more? What if the delicious Anna Curley, shielded from the world of dark sex games, can show him?

Rick returns to the helm of his international BDSM Empire after confronting a disaster within his vampire Family. His nemesis, Veronique Moreau, could destroy the fragile veil between the Vamp/Mortal worlds, leaving vampires exposed. He meets Anna, a guileless young woman with enough savvy to see trouble coming in the form of a vampire hunter.

Their worlds collide. Swept into the dangers of preternatural conflict, Rick and Anna experience exquisite passion, and heart-stopping peril. Is love enough? They could lose their lives as well as their hearts.

Blood Fugue
Tales from the Gaoler, Book One

Fugue: [fyoog]

noun

Psychiatry. A period during which a person suffers from loss of memory and often begins a new life.

You think your memory stinks?

Meet Harry VanAlt. An apex predator with fading memories of mortal life. Along with his memories, his exalted vampiric powers have faded to vampire-lite. Great taste, less exciting.

Along comes Dr. Lizbet Mitchell, a police profiler who has not yet opened the right door on her future. Thirty-four and questioning, when Harry rescues her from a rogue vampire, she invites him into her button downed life.

Her fascination meets his reticence as flashes and images from some other life intrude on his own.

A 16th-century ceremony reveals Harry's memories and unlocks his powers.

When Lizbet challenges Harry they take steps toward a new and powerful immortality. Henry has two flesh and blood details to reconcile.

Harry closes the door on 1951 and settles a score.

#MetaphysicalRomance
Arise, My Darling

Strangely gifted Jacob King finds Cricket Nielson in his meditations between worlds.

Delightful Cricket is a woman trapped first by injury and then her husband's villainy.

Captivated by her buoyant spirit, intrigued by their elusive meetings, Jake uses his psychic talents to locate this imprisoned beauty.

Their meetings on the astral plane reveal they have loved each other for eons. This newly reignited love calls Jake to draw on every spiritual resource at his disposal. He convinces sympathetic law enforcement professionals to hear him out as he discovers a series of murders and knows Cricket is next.

Will the forces of the universe unite Jake and Cricket before the insidious serial killer strikes again?

#ContemporaryActionRomance
Roman's Revenge
Roman's Adventures, Book One

Jax Roman is the image of courage, nobility, and strength. A clever mind and agile body propelled Roman to the head of his SEAL class.

Handsome and disarming, Jax is in charge of his world, vertical and horizontal. Now, at the pinnacle of his game, he leads his own team until...the Lobos Cartel, the worst Jax has ever fought, sets out to eliminate him.

Lovely and compassionate, Dr. Kameo Alana meets Jax in his most desperate hour. Her family has borne the cartel's punishment.

Without Kameo, Jax would not be free to topple the depraved cartel.

Kameo is more than a balm for his pain. Together they sizzle white-hot.

Jax's mission for a 'happily ever after' with Kameo is an exercise in 'taking no prisoners', SEAL style.

#SeasonedContemporaryRomance
Roman's Rules
Roman's Adventures, Book Two

A complicated situation...

Kirk Roman knows he is the reason his relationship with Jordan Perry has never gotten to first base. His insecurity has been an ongoing barrier between them — until the day a sultry woman with her eye on him makes him re-evaluate his feelings for Jordan.

Jordan Perry is a fighter — and she is a survivor. She thought being widowed at thirty-seven was the worst that could happen until her diagnosis seven years ago. Clean, cleared, but scarred from her battle with breast cancer, Jordan silently dreams of the one man who has kept her going — Kirk Roman.

Kirk's inner battle with his desire to date Jordan isn't only about his insecurities. Jordan is a friend and an employee — two things he doesn't want to jeopardize. What he doesn't expect is the arrival of his estranged adult son and his wife.

The complications escalate when the sultry woman after him has a murderous past. Will all this kill his chance of finally telling Jordan how he really feels about her?

Will Roman's old rules work in this new situation?

#NewAdultContemporaryRomance
Roman's Return
Roman's Adventures, Book Three

Conner

A young cowboy with his boots in the Texas dirt and his heart set on flying fighter jets, until love makes a course correction on a flight to meet his unknown father.

Skyler

An artist gifted beyond her years stands up for herself and wins a place at a prestigious art institute. A stalker shadows her path and drives her back to the last place she was happy.

Their Fate

Each had dreams tailoring their perfect futures. Will their long-held dreams nurture their love? Or will the tolls of achieving their ambitions drive them apart?

#NewAdultContemporaryRomance
Becoming Gabriel

Meet Gabriel Lee, if he were a young billionaire, his last few years would have earned him celebrity status. But he's a mechanic in Baltimore's inner city. Past regrets haunt him. Can he ever win in a rigged system?

Opposites attract when Grace Lerner trades abusive privilege for freedom. Suddenly homeless, she meets Gabriel and in their unlikely bond, they find soulmates come from the darndest places.

When Gabriel's ghosts endanger their joy, criminals cause a painful separation. Will their devotion deliver their happily ever after?

www.ingramcontent.com/pod-product-compliance
Lightning Source LLC
Chambersburg PA
CBHW050243110726
47898CB00007B/2258